CAN'T
FIGHT
THIS
FEELING

CAN'T FIGHT THIS FEELING

MIRANDA LIASSON

Published by Miranda Liasson, LLC
P.O. Box 13707
Fairlawn, OH 44334
www.mirandaliasson.com

ISBN-13: 978-0-9986346-1-6

Cover design by Su Kopil, EarthyCharms.com
Formatted by Author E.M.S.
Author Photo © 2013 Scott Meivogel

Published in the United States of America

For Thomas,

who can grow a great beard, just like Drew.

CHAPTER 1

"I want to sleep with you," Maggie McShae said into her cell phone. "I'm ready to take the plunge." Her words echoed in the high-ceilinged vestibule of Mirror Lake Congregational Church, where her bereavement group was meeting at this very moment in the basement.

The bereavement group, that is, from which she'd gone AWOL, possibly forever. It was not the group she led as part of her practice as a psychologist either, but the one she'd attended since her husband's death over three years ago.

"Did I just hear you right?" Greg Pollard, a fireman on the Mirror Lake squad, asked from the other end of the phone.

"Yes, you heard me right. I'm ready. It's time." There, she'd done it. Finally taken a step forward. Greg was a nice guy, and they'd had three fun dates. He was good-looking and polite, and she wanted him to know she was ready to move to the next level. Being a psychologist, even she could congratulate herself on the progress.

What would Corey think? She could see him sitting in heaven,

1

in his favorite easy chair, laughing his ass off at her awkwardness. Or maybe he'd be scowling instead. He'd been gone three and a half years, but going on a date still felt like she was cheating on him. She squeezed her eyes shut to block out those thoughts. She was doing so well. *Keep going, Maggie,* she thought, trying to cheer herself on inside her head.

"Um, Maggie, I'm at work. Can you give me a sec?"

"Oh, sure. No problem, Greg."

The sound of male laughter echoed around her in the high-ceilinged space, bouncing off the big glass windows that faced Main Street of Mirror Lake, Connecticut. As Maggie slowly turned around, she saw someone sitting on one of the three wide white marble steps that ran the length of the vestibule.

Oh, firetruck. It was her best friend Bella's obnoxious brother-in-law, and he'd just heard everything. Well, she wasn't going to let him sit there and gloat. "Oh hi, Ted Kaczynski," she said, waving. "What made you join civilization today?"

The man smoothed out his rather bushy beard and smiled. Even under all that hair (which he'd seemed to grow to hide behind in the past year and a half since coming to Mirror Lake), that smile was beaming out some major wattage. She'd never personally seen him without the Wolverine look, but she'd seen photos in the tabloids, and honestly, she was grateful for the massive sprouting of hair that hid his make-women-swoon sexy looks. Not that they'd ever make *her* swoon, mind you. She was immune to scoundrels.

Above the beard, his eyes crinkled, showing a few lines that in a man like him spelled interest and experience. He smiled, displaying brilliantly white teeth, reminding her he wasn't a country hick hiding out in Mirror Lake but rather a polished gazillionaire businessman. But the hiding part was right.

Actually, they'd met when he'd run in off the street straight into the group therapy session she was leading, looking for sanctuary from the press after his botched wedding. She was afraid he was deranged and called the cops. She smiled a little thinking of that day when a gorgeous AWOL guy in a tux burst through her office door. She'd gotten to know him a little since he was the brother of two of her best friends' husbands, but she didn't have a very high opinion of him. In the looks department, he was blessed, but the rest of him left a lot to be desired.

"Don't mind me," he said. "Just keep on with your… um…booty call."

She covered the receiver of her cell and dropped her voice. Because they were in a church, after all. "It's not a booty call. We've had three perfectly wonderful dates, and he wanted to…he wanted to… Why am I telling you this? It's none of your business."

He held up a hand. "Right. Sure you don't need a few pointers?"

From him? The guy who created a national scandal when he dumped his gorgeous socialite bride at the altar—at the *altar*, for God's sake—a year and a half ago in front of a sizable crowd at St. Patrick's Cathedral? Which had been covered by all the major outlets, starting a media firestorm that he'd been lying low from ever since. "Like I'm going to ask you for pointers in matters of the heart. That's a laugh, because you clearly don't have one."

He placed his hands dramatically over his chest. "You slay me, Maggie. You just slay me." He waited for her eye roll before he said, "This doesn't really sound like a matter of the heart. More like a matter of…"

"Oh, hi, Greg," she said, because he was back on the line. "Yes. I was just wondering if you'd like to try…another date."

Put him on speaker, Drew mouthed.

No way, she mouthed back as she turned away a little. She didn't like Andreas Poulos. He'd had the reputation of being a love-'em-and-leave-'em kind of guy even before his high-profile engagement, dating beautiful women from around the world. Then, of course, he'd left poor Anika in tears. He was clearly full of himself, rich and entitled, and he would rather act like a recluse than face his problems. All dishonorable traits in her book. Even the *New York Post* ran the headline: THE HUNK'S A PUNK, after the wedding debacle.

But there was one thing he had that just might come in helpful. Tons of experience with women. Why not use it to her benefit? He'd already heard what was going on. Plus, she hadn't had sex in over three years. These were desperate times, and clearly, she could use a little help here. Despite her better judgment, she pushed the speaker button. "Well, you know, Maggie," Greg said, his voice now echoing in the entranceway, "our last date didn't go so well."

Drew frowned, listening intently.

"Well," she said, "I know I sort of chickened out."

"You flinched when I tried to kiss your neck. That's not a great ego boost, you know."

Drew shook his head sadly. Just when she was about to take Greg off speakerphone, Drew made lifting motions with his arms, which she took to mean she should maybe say something to boost Greg's ego.

"Please don't take that personally," she said. "Griffin really did have a fever, and I had to get home. It's just that, well, I think you're really nice and really handsome, and I promise I'll do anything to make it up to you." Oh dear. She was really screwing this up. She'd already thrown in the kitchen sink, and it was very early in the conversation.

"Anything?" Greg asked, sounding interested.

"Too desperate," Drew whispered. "Tone it down."

"Well, not just *anything*," Maggie said, "but I mean, why don't we try another date? I know we can make it work this time."

"Okay, I won't take it personally. I like you, Maggie. I really

4

do. You're a very sexy woman." She shot a see-I-told-you-so look at Drew.

"How about I come to your place Friday?" Greg asked.

Maggie hesitated as a grenade of worry went off in her brain. "Well, um, I mean, it couldn't be at my house, because of Griffin, you know, and it couldn't be overnight, and I would have to make sure I could get a sitter and all…and I wouldn't want you to meet Griffin right away…"

Drew was making slashing motions with his fingers along his neck, which she took to mean *Abort the mission.*

Oh God, her mouth was running, as it always did when she was nervous. She bit the inside of her cheek and tried to remind herself that Greg was the one who'd been interested. Very interested, until she'd acted like he had the plague the other night, which had been a stupid, stupid move. It was really kind of amazing that an eligible man under the age of forty without serious psychological issues or a wife he'd failed to mention had actually been interested in *her*, Maggie McShae, who had an almost five-year-old son and a rather serious case of OCD. That flared when she was stressed.

Calm down, she told herself. All she had to do was let the poor man talk.

Which he did. "I just don't think you're really ready yet. Why don't you give me a call when you are?"

"But—" Oh, why couldn't she have just shut up? She should have just arranged the booty call instead of giving the guy a hundred-page dissertation on everything wrong with her. No wonder he was jumping ship.

"Look!" She was practically pleading. "I'm saying yes to sex. No-strings-attached, no-commitment sex! What kind of man are you to say no to that?"

"You're…you just seem like you've got a lot of…baggage. I'm really not looking for anything…heavy right now, you know?"

"Me? Baggage? No. I'm all in. I'm ready!" She winced. Was she allowed to say that in a church vestibule? Maybe it was okay if this wasn't her denomination.

"I don't think you're all in, Maggie. Or you wouldn't have brought up your deceased husband's name the other night when I was trying to…you know."

"Right." Well, she wasn't going to beg. She had some pride left.

She sat down on the marble steps. God, she couldn't even *force* herself to have a fling. She was pathetic. She'd blown it, done everything wrong. No one was going to date a woman with a preschooler. Especially a woman with…issues. But hey, those traits made her quirky, right? Wasn't quirky the equivalent of endearing?

No. It was the equivalent of *too much trouble*.

"I'll see you around, okay?" Greg said in a kind voice. "You're a nice woman, Maggie. I enjoyed going out with you."

"Thanks, Greg." That was how it was in Mirror Lake. You didn't hang up on people or go through pains to hide from them. There was no hiding, because one never knew when one would meet again, probably across the bananas in the produce aisle. Plus he really was a nice guy.

Drew was eyeballing her from his place on the stairs, where he was sitting with his long legs stretched out. "That went well, I'd say."

"I just don't have it in me to trade barbs with you today," she said.

"Oh, too bad. I was really gearing up for that." He rummaged around in his bag, pulled out a tinfoil-wrapped oblong bundle, and began unwrapping it. It was a meatball sandwich, carried out from Santoro's Italian Restaurant, according to the white bag he'd just pulled it from. It smelled saucy and meaty, and it was loaded with a ton of melted cheese. Maggie's stomach rumbled audibly despite herself, reminding her that she'd skipped lunch to attend her bereavement support group. She must have looked pathetic, because her companion dug out a plastic knife, cut his sub in half, and pushed the wrapper toward her. "Here. Might make you feel better."

She looked at him in surprise. Unabomber was actually doing a kind deed. Not his usual modus, which was to verbally spar until the cows came home. "Thank you, but…I'm not hungry." She was, but she didn't want to be indebted. She didn't want to be on his you-owe-me list for anything. She looked near his feet. "That wouldn't happen to be a Diet Coke by any chance, would it?"

He smiled. When he did, those crinkles showed up again, and his deep dark coffee-brown eyes sparkled. Oh yes, it was so easy to see why most of the women in America salivated over his exploits.

"It is Diet Coke," he said softly, handing it over. Something about how he said it made her shiver. Shiver! Oh, she was sex crazed. That just confirmed it. Because he would be the last man on earth she'd sleep with for too many reasons to count.

"Thank you," she said, forgoing the straw and taking long gulps. Then she let out a long exhale. Wiped her mouth with the back of her hand. Perspective was returning. She suddenly remembered they were standing in a church vestibule. She knew why she was here, but why was *he*?

She frowned. "I'd never take you for a churchgoing man."

He laughed again. God, he was annoying.

"And that's funny, why?"

"You don't know anything about me, Maggie McShae. I'd say that comment was a bit judgmental."

She knew enough. He was a playboy, too handsome for his own skin, and he was too aware of his kissed-by-the-gods looks and his ability to lure women into his sex-appeal web. Which was another reason she wasn't about to fall victim to his pheromones or whatever he—emitted. From his studly body. Which she was not noticing, mind you, not at all.

Three and a half years, Maggie, her inner voice whispered. *That's a long time.*

She shook the annoying voice out of her head. She also knew Drew Poulos was a Spikonos brother, younger brother to Roman, who was her partner Bella's husband. Roman was helping him hide out. She wouldn't have been so merciful.

"So what's the problem?" he asked, casually biting into his sandwich. "I mean, most people don't think that much about, um, dating." He seemed to be holding back a laugh. "Maybe I can help."

She snorted. "I doubt that very much." What did he know about pain and loss? Or about being mother and father both to a sweet, amazing, but rambunctious little boy? Or about nights so long and lonely, they seemed to go on for weeks. No, she was not going to allow Mr. Playboy to weigh in on her problems.

"Not my business, but if you want simple sex, I'd leave the other stuff out of it. Might scare a guy away."

Well, of course, children and dead husbands and baggage scared guys away! "All the good ones are already taken by the age of thirty anyway," she grumbled.

"If you just want sex, go for it. Leave your kid and your other problems out of it."

"Right." She picked up his Coke again and took another hit. "Here's the thing. I don't really just want sex. I mean I do, but secretly I want the other stuff that goes along with it—the tingling in your arms and legs, the weakness in your knees, the hot, the cold, the sweating, and the feeling like that person *gets* you like no one else you've ever met."

His face went a little blank, like he had no clue just what the hell she was talking about. "You want the whole package, eh? In other words, you buy into the myth."

"What myth?"

"The falling-in-love myth. A fantasy, by the way."

"Wow, who crushed your soul?" She studied him as he sat there scowling a little. He seemed very jaded for so young a man. "I mean, I've had all that already. I know it's not a fantasy, it's just rare. I don't expect it again. So just sex would be fine." It would make her feel better and take her mind off her other problems. Except she was incapable of dissociating herself from those problems. And that was preventing her from getting laid.

"I'm tired of listening to my bereavement group. All they do is talk about the past. I want to move forward. The best way for me to do that is to have a fling. So I'm going to go find me a fling to have." It was time to move on and get a life. She knew that, dammit, yet it was so, so hard. But listening to the ladies in her group today... They were so trapped in the past. Just like her. Not living their lives in the present, and she didn't want to be stuck like that. She wanted to move on. If only she could.

She had no idea why she was telling him this. Maybe because she didn't care what he thought of her. Or because she'd just verbalized what she'd been thinking all along.

He gazed at her for a long moment, and she wasn't sure if he was pitying her or if he felt genuinely sorry for her. She felt her face go red. She should've kept her mouth shut.

"Well, best of luck." He crumpled up his wrapper. She handed him back his Coke, but he held up a hand. "Keep it. I insist." He had nice hands. Long fingered. Capable. Tanned too. Since he'd been in Mirror Lake, he'd been helping his brother on various construction projects for his apple brandy distillery. He wore the manual labor look well.

Just then, a woman in a sleek gray suit paused outside the entrance to the church and cupped her hands around her eyes to see through a window. Maggie would have thought nothing of it, a businesswoman on her lunch hour, but Drew immediately dodged behind a nearby marble pillar. "That woman's a reporter," he said. "She caught sight of me when I was coming out of Santoro's. Please don't tell her I'm here." His eyes held a pleading look. They were also big and brown and warm looking. Dark but with some honey-colored flecks, but who was noticing? And right now those eyes were looking around wildly for a place to hide.

"There's a closet right near the entrance to the choir loft," Maggie said, pointing. Drew wasted no time darting over there.

Suddenly, one of the massive wooden front doors opened. A warm breeze blew through the vestibule of the church, bringing in the cleansing scent of sweet May air. Maggie picked up the Coke and pretended to study her phone.

"Oh, excuse me," the woman said. "I'm Lainey Stevens from the *National Register*. You might recognize me from TV."

"I don't really watch much TV, but hello." Maggie flashed her most welcoming smile.

"I'm looking for a guy with a beard. Tall, well-built."

"Was it a big, bushy beard?" Maggie asked. "Was he a little disturbed looking? Sort of a wild look in his eyes?"

"Yes! That's him. Drew Poulos, the billionaire. We have reason to believe he's hiding out in Mirror Lake and we want to interview him."

"There was someone like that in here, but we sent him downtown to the homeless shelter."

She finally left, after Maggie gave her directions to the shelter. Maggie waited until she was a good block away before opening the closet door. The smells of paper and old wood wafted out. Drew's broad-shouldered form was hunkered down in the dark among the prayer books and song sheets.

"You can come on out now," Maggie said.

He looked up at her, squinting in the sudden light. Yup, nice brown eyes. Quite lovely. He had an intense gaze that felt like he was looking through her instead of at her. Good thing it was time to get her butt back to work and her thoughts away from potentially nice-looking but obnoxious men.

"Disturbed and wild-eyed, huh?" he asked.

She shrugged. "Just calling it like I see it."

There went that laugh again. Sort of easy. Kind of deep, with something indefinably pleasant that had the effect of breaking the tension.

She held out a hand to help him out. "I promise I won't mention this as long as you don't tell anyone about my—phone conversation." He took hold of her hand, but he didn't make a move to get up. Or let go. And Lordie, that hand was big and warm and just plain…nice. He just sat there, looking up at her, his eyes twinkling, flashing a grin that was a little secretive, a little conspiratorial. "You've got yourself a deal, Maggie McShae."

A door opened, and a gaggle of women's voices and laughter drifted into the vestibule. Her bereavement group. Maggie quickly averted her eyes and withdrew her hand. Wiped it on her leg. Because darned if it wasn't tingling.

CHAPTER 2

"So glad you could join us," Samantha Spikonos said, kissing Drew on the cheek. He'd just walked onto the rooftop bar in downtown Hartford, where his family was gathering for his brother Lukas's birthday. "Family" being the two biological brothers he'd been reunited with, their wives, and their surrogate mother, a nice Greek lady who showered them with love...and food.

"Well, it's nice to take a break from getting the wine bar up and running," Drew said, looking around the trendy patio, which held a sizeable crowd on the pleasant Friday evening. People were gathered in little groups around a stone outdoor fireplace, the whole space bordered by strings of white bulbs, the city lights twinkling in the distance. Marble Greek and Roman statues stared out pupil-lessly from the corners, where they stood among potted trees and plants. The effect was supposed to be upscale, modern, and trendy, but the statues were a little creepy if you asked him.

"I wonder if Maggie's here yet," Sam, Lukas's wife, said, not at all subtly. "She loves karaoke."

Drew took a sip of his beer while watching his brothers Lukas and Roman flip through the song selections on a little stage set up near the dance floor. Lukas was lean but built, with longish black hair, tattoos and an earring, while Roman was tall, with the same big brown eyes but close-cropped, traditionally cut hair. Weird to see Lukas, a world-class rock star, doing karaoke, when it was likely that some of his own songs were in the selection queue. "Haven't seen her," Drew said.

Okay, maybe he *had* glanced around a time or two for Maggie's pretty blonde head, her big smile, but that was only natural, right? It wasn't a crime to notice a beautiful woman, and that was really all this was with her—an infatuation, an attraction. She was way too complicated to be anything but, and God knew, he wasn't looking for anything serious. Despite all her fling talk, she could be the poster child for a woman looking for a man who wanted 2.5 kids, a dog, and a house with a white picket fence and a big lawn to cut and trim. And that was *not* him. Except for the dog.

Drew wiped away those thoughts and focused on being here for Lukas. This was the first time all three brothers had been together for a birthday since he was six, before they'd all been split up for good and sent to different foster homes.

Lukas and his brother Roman had reunited when Roman had inherited his foster parents' apple orchards last year, and then Drew had sort of skidded headfirst into their lives on the day he went on the lam from his high-society wedding to Anika Brewer, daughter of real estate mogul Richard Brewer.

He'd fled to Mirror Lake, to the one place where he thought no one would judge him…and where he could hide out for a while—both from the press and from his adoptive, well-to-do family in Greenwich.

His brothers had taken him in, no questions asked. Not one of them had questioned why he wasn't off in New York somewhere using his Harvard MBA in some fancy-schmancy business. Or why he'd fled a wedding that had made the covers of all the grocery store tabloids. They'd given him time to find himself. He'd worked the apple farm and learned every aspect of their brandy-making business from the fields on in.

And it had been good. Really good. He'd recently made the decision to stay and put his MBA to use running the financial side of the business.

He felt different now, as prepared as he'd ever be to go back home and face his family. God knew he'd need the strength, because his father wasn't happy he was working in a start-up apple brandy business instead of the family business, AcroPoulos Yogurt, one of the top three Greek yogurt companies in the world.

He had a bigger problem too. His brothers knew vaguely about Anika, that the marriage had been arranged as a business deal by his father. But they knew nothing about Sondra Bower, the woman who'd chosen his adoptive brother, Xander, over him, and who was about to marry Xander in just two weeks.

It was time to go home to celebrate his brother's wedding and face *her* again. *Ugh.* He needed another beer. Or three.

"I mean, I love Maggie," Sam continued, bringing up her name again and stymieing his plans to forget about her. "She's one of my best friends. I hope you two can at least come to tolerate one another."

Drew leveled her his best boardroom let's-cut-the-bullshit look. "Look, you don't have to be so obvious. Thanks a lot, but I'm not interested." And neither was Maggie. She couldn't stand him, preferring to believe what most of America did, that he was a commitmentphobe who'd walked away from the opportunity of a lifetime—being CEO of his father's company. Who'd played the field with beautiful women all around the world in typical Poulos style—at least, that was his father's style—and ultimately abandoned his lovely, innocent fiancée at the altar.

None of it was really true. Well, except for the commitmentphobe part. He couldn't see himself settling down…ever.

He'd dated his share of beautiful women in the years after Sondra dumped him—but none of them had meant anything. He liked to keep things loose and fun—rarely did he ask for a third date. No sleepovers. And he never broke his rules.

Sam sighed. "It's just that Maggie's awesome. I'd really like to see her go out on a date with someone who's handsome, her age, not a stalker, that kind of thing."

"Handsome?" He smiled his best smile. The one that could have graced the cover of *GQ*, if he'd been into that stuff. But Drew preferred to keep a low profile. "I'll take the compliment."

Sam seemed to examine him carefully. "Well, I think you might be without the Brillo pad on your face, but I'm really not judging, okay?"

Drew raised a brow and fingered his beard, which he'd grown during this time of exile from his old corporate life. "Maggie has a stalker?" Not that he cared. But he was curious.

"She doesn't have a stalker, but she has had a batch of awful dates. Anyway, Maggie used to be a hoot before her husband died. If she had a little fun and let loose once in a while, I know her real personality would shine right through."

Drew knew Maggie was a nice woman, raising her son alone after her husband's death, and she'd had it tough. He also knew she was a little on the loony side. She was a compulsive worrier, overprotective of her son to the nth degree, and should probably purchase stock in hand sanitizer companies for how often she used it. All the more reason for him to stay away from a nice woman who was struggling and who had a kid and who might as well have the words *Relationship Material* tattooed all over her pretty little forehead.

Even if she was easy to look at—blonde with blue eyes big enough to take a swim in. Cindy Lou Who eyes, sweet and vulnerable.

Yeah. He definitely wasn't into sweet *or* vulnerable. Or any woman who could be described with complicated emotion words.

Where he could possibly get into trouble with her would be that he did find her to be rather—hot. And, contrary to the tabloids in the grocery store, it had been a while since *you know*. Since he'd gotten some. Almost a year and a half since the failed engagement and no one since.

So when he finally did jump back on the wagon, it was going to be for a raucous romp in the hay. Some fun, a good time. And not with anyone sweet *or* vulnerable. He would never put himself in a position to be hurt again. And he didn't want to worry about hurting someone else.

"You know, hon," Sam said, patting him on the back. "Maggie would be the perfect date for you to take to Xander's wedding."

Ah, the wedding. Drew bit back a sigh and signaled the bartender for another beer. He'd avoided thinking about finding a date just like he'd avoided his father, his Greenwich family, and his old life in general.

But showing up for the wedding was going to be bad enough; showing up *alone* would be plain stupid. He'd dated Sondra for four years. Everyone had expected them to marry. The last thing he wanted was to be an object of pity.

"Thanks, but I'm still working on that."

All he needed was a date. A piece of arm candy to look pretty while enduring a long weekend with the great disaster that was his family. Maggie was far too complicated a woman for that job. Frankly, he couldn't think of a worse choice. She was neurotic as hell and irritating to no end. And unlike scores of other women, she didn't even like him.

"Maybe you wouldn't have so much trouble getting a date if you'd shave," his brother Roman said, who'd walked over to the fireplace area near the bar where they were gathered. He smoothed a hand down his own face.

Lukas, who'd followed Roman, patted Drew's stomach, which was rock hard now, by the way. He'd worked hard to shape up after his initial time here, where the stress from his ruined wedding had made him eat through his feelings a bit. "At least he's stopped the stress eating," Lukas said with a smile meant to get a rise out of him.

"Leave Drew alone, boys," Alethea Panagakos, the nice Greek lady who was the brothers' unofficial adoptive mother, said. "In my opinion, Drew, you're too skinny now. Why don't you have a piece of karithopita?"

"Is that the cake with the walnuts?" Roman asked, giving a nod to the big white cake in the center of the nearby table.

"Anything that ends in -*opita*'s fine with me," Drew said with a grin.

Lukas sat down next to Drew and patted him on the back. "You look restless, bro. Waiting for Maggie to show, by any chance?"

"Nope. Of course not." *Shit*. A little too vehement there.

"Leave him alone, Roman," Roman's wife, Bella, said. "He's been through a lot."

Not really. Oh, he made some big mistakes, yes. Getting engaged to Anika Brewer was on the top of that list. But between the two women he'd been engaged to, Anika's impact ranked low. She might have almost gutted his wallet, but Sondra had gutted his heart. Surviving his brother's wedding with a smile on his face would be the hardest thing he'd ever done. But he would do it for one reason—his love for his brother was greater than a woman coming between them. Period.

"Yes, sweetie," a familiar voice said from behind him, breaking him out of his thoughts. "Make sure you eat your peas for MeMe and PaPa, okay? And MeMe said she'd read you and Mr. Bunny a story tonight before bed. Let me talk to her, okay?"

Maggie McShae. Here at last. Now his night was made. He

couldn't stop the slow smile that spread across his face. There was just so much ammo to use to annoy her. It was becoming an addictive pastime.

"Mom," she said into her phone, "No Disney movies. None of those characters have parents, and I don't want Griffin to get exposed to bad ideas about death. And tell Dad no cowboy movies. Too violent and you know the way they portray the Indians… And the organic cookies are in that bag with his books. Okay, love you too."

Drew resisted rolling his eyes, but barely. There was no way in hell he'd ever go out on a date with this woman. Even if she didn't have a kid.

In his book, kids were a huge liability, and he never dated women who had them. He understood from his own past, from the pain of being separated from his brothers, how devastating it was to have a kid become attached to somebody, only to have that person ripped away afterward. He'd never do that to an innocent child. Not that he had to worry about that. As she glanced up and saw him, Dr. Anal here looked about as thrilled to see him as he did her.

Maggie slipped her phone in her purse and shrugged off her wrap. As she did, Drew startled in surprise. She wore a strappy black number that actually showed a little cleavage—wow, *nice* cleavage—and stopped mid-thigh. Gold hoops dangled from her ears, and her hair was down. Who knew that she even owned a little black dress? She looked a lot different from the usually uptight, professionally dressed woman he'd seen by day. Suddenly he felt something that, in the wake of all his feelings about his brother's upcoming wedding, he hadn't for a long time. *Horny.*

And that startled him more than the sight of her in that dress.

As she stood near the bar, Drew closed the gap between them and lowered his voice. "So did your fireman douse the fire?" He couldn't help teasing her. It was just so much fun.

She shot him an icy glare.

"Just following up," he said, holding his hands up in defense.

"It's unfortunate you had to overhear that conversation. And it's none of your business. That's *private*."

"That means no, doesn't it?" He stifled a chuckle by taking a sip of his beer.

He could tell by the way a frown creased her pretty brow that his guess was correct. "I was just wondering if my coaching helped."

She snorted. "Thanks for trying to help. And for the Coke. But I don't need a dating coach, thanks very much." She leaned over him a little to talk to the bartender, and as she did, a fresh, flowery woman smell wafted over him. Her arm grazed his, soft yet muscular. She was average height, more slender than curvy. And he realized with horror that he was attracted to her. A lot.

"All right, you two," Sam said as she passed by. "Let's pretend we get along for Lukas's sake, okay?"

"Sorry, Sam," Maggie said.

"We'll behave," Drew said, casting a wary glance in her direction. He was surprised to find her smiling. So maybe she wasn't so uptight she didn't have a sense of humor. A very small one. "Let's start over," he said. It was his brother's birthday. He could make an effort. "Can I get you a drink?"

"Sure. I'll have a gimlet." She turned to the bartender. "About a quarter more soda than lime juice, and have you got Tanqueray? Just a splash of lime juice. And a lime on the rim, please."

"She'll have that shaken, not stirred," Drew added.

She skewered him with another look.

"Hey, Maggie. How are ya?" the bartender asked, seemingly unfazed by her complicated request.

"Great, Ned." She looked around the rooftop. A balding, middle-aged man in a tux stood in the corner, playing the violin soulfully. "It's pretty up here," she said.

"Prettier since you walked in," Ned the bartender said with a wink, and for some reason, Drew wanted to punch him. Which scared him. He wasn't a violent guy, and he should be just fine with bartenders flirting with pretty women he didn't care about.

She waved her hand dismissively. "Oh, you. How're things?" She turned briefly to Drew. "Ned's moonlighting tonight, aren't you, Neddy? He's worked at my parents' bar for years. Ned, this is Lukas's brother, Drew. Or do you like to be introduced as Andreas?"

"Drew's fine," he said, reaching over Maggie to shake the bartender's hand and trying to toss him a sincere smile. There went that fragrance again. He had no idea how to describe it, flowery, fruity, just…delicious. It made him want to swoop her silky hair off her lovely long neck and plant a kiss there.

Whoa, where did that come from? He backed up so he wouldn't catch the scent anymore.

"So, I hear you're working on the hospital benefit again this year?" he found himself saying. Immediately, he wished he could take his words back. He should've known better than to mention the cancer benefit put on in honor of her deceased husband every year.

Her quick intake of breath was audible. But her facial expression didn't change, and she remained smiley, chatty. "I'm thrilled they asked me to chair it again. I'm glad they still want to honor Corey—that's my husband. I mean, my ex-husband. I mean—" She stumbled on her words and dropped her gaze to her drink.

"He was a great guy, your Corey," Ned said with a wink.

"Thanks," Maggie replied quietly. "Thanks a lot, Ned."

The bartender's eyes went soft as he looked at Maggie. Uh-oh. "Look, Maggie," he said, "if you ever want to grab a coffee or something—"

Drew got up and grabbed her arm. "I'm sorry to interrupt, but I need to tell you something."

"Now?" she asked, her blue eyes growing wide.

He steered her away from the bar. "Sorry, Ned," Maggie called over her shoulder. "Talk to you later, 'kay?"

They halted near a statue of a Greek guy with a laurel wreath on his head, holding what appeared to be a bocce ball. "That was a little rude," she said.

Drew supposed it was. "You didn't want to go out with him anyway."

A flush of outrage rose up her face. She put her hands on her hips. "I'm sorry, but since when have you become my dating coach?"

"You were giving him a look."

"A look."

"Yeah. The kind a woman gives a guy who's really nice, but she doesn't really want to have anything to do with him romantically."

"Drew," she said, leveling her gaze on him.

"Yes?"

She lifted a finger near her eyes and pointed back and forth between herself and him. "This is the same look, minus the guy-who's-nice part."

"Ha-ha, very funny."

"So you can mind your own business, okay? Just because you overheard my conversation with Greg the other day doesn't mean I want your advice about my love life."

For a moment, he got lost in those gorgeous blue eyes of hers, sucked right in and mesmerized as if he were some sixteen-year-old with a crush instead of a grown man.

"It's not the same look," he said quietly.

"What?" Judging by her wide-eyed expression, he'd thrown her off guard.

"You know. The way you're looking at me. It's not the same."

"You're right." She yanked her elbow out of his grasp. "It's a hundred times more pissed off."

"I was going to say maybe it's because I'm a red-blooded hunk of male, and you haven't had one of those for a while."

This time, she blushed fiercely, down to her roots, and he couldn't help smiling. Not that he was pleased he got her all flustered, but she was just so…pretty. Blushing or not.

"What did you want to tell me?" she asked.

"Oh." What had they even been talking about? "I'll be doing the financials for it," Drew said matter-of-factly. "The benefit. That woman asked me…"

"What woman?"

"Um, the one who's in charge of all the charities in town, what's her name, Mrs…"

"Donaldson. Are you telling me you're the *treasurer*?"

"Well, I do have an MBA from Harvard Business." He let that sink in. But somehow she didn't look that impressed. "What happened was, initially I said no but then Ben Rushford asked me." Dr. Ben was the hometown son who now ran the ER. Everyone knew him, everyone loved him, and no one ever said no to him. Except maybe his wife, Meg, whom he adored.

Maggie looked at him a little strangely. "Somehow I didn't peg you as being a sucker for charity."

"Again, maybe you pegged me wrong." He'd never felt a need to justify himself to anyone, and he usually didn't care too much about what people thought. He didn't know why he had a sudden urge to make her think he was a nice guy when it was clear she assumed the worst about him. The tabloids had done a great job painting him the villain, and he'd taken it all on the chin. It was the price he'd had to pay for leaving Anika at the altar. Contrary to what everyone believed, and no matter what he thought of Anika personally, he didn't revel in the embarrassment that had caused her.

Deep in thought, he hadn't noticed two women seated at a table nearby, talking in heated tones.

"What do you mean, you've seen his violin tattoo?" a woman with very dark curly hair asked, suddenly standing and putting her hands on her hips. She wore a leopard-print, low-cut blouse, a black skirt, and heels.

"The oboe too," the other woman, a redhead who could have been on a Throwback Thursday photo for big 80s hair, answered knowingly.

"But the oboe's on his—"

"I know where it is, Erika."

"You *knew* I was dating him. How could you?"

The redhead shrugged. "I knew you two had dated a while ago, in the past."

Leopard print snorted. "Yeah. If you call *a while ago* last Friday."

The other woman's mouth dropped open. "We've both been sleeping with him at the same time?"

"Oh, excuse me," Maggie interjected, just before the dark-haired woman stalked off. "Does anyone have a phone I can borrow?" Was she insane, asking these two angry women? She was going to get herself clobbered. Drew pulled out his own phone.

"We're a little busy now," Redhead said.

"It's just—I left my phone in the bathroom and someone walked off with it, and I just need to make sure my four-year-old's okay."

The fighting paused as both women automatically dug into their purses.

"Forgive me for butting in, but I'm a therapist," Maggie said. What the hell was she doing? Drew edged a little closer. Maggie barely weighed as much as the redhead's Gucci purse, which was the size of a very large watermelon. "It sounds to me like you've both been friends for a long time, is that right?"

The women looked at each other. "Since third grade," Redhead said a little flatly.

"Having such a long friendship like that, it doesn't seem like you two would ever hurt each other on purpose."

"She knew I was dating him," Leopard said, "and she went out with him anyway."

"That's because he told me that was finished. I didn't want to hurt you."

"But still, you went out with him."

She shrugged. "I loved him. I was desperate. And I believed him."

"Sounds to me," Maggie said, "like Mr. Violin's been lying to both of you."

"She's right, Bree."

"I never would've done it if I thought you were still seeing him. I'm sorry, Erika. You believe me, don't you?"

"I never want to lose your friendship."

"The oboe tattoo wasn't even that hot."

As the two women hugged, the violin player left his perch and began walking over. Once he saw both of the women, he turned on his heels.

"You come back here," Bree yelled out.

"Let's get him," Erika said.

Maggie stood on tiptoe as they zigzagged through the crowd. "I think she just grabbed him by the jacket."

"And he shrugged out of it." Drew smiled down at her. "I think your job here is done."

The two women rushed toward the elevator, trailing after Violin Guy. "Maybe I should stick around and mediate—"

"How about mediating this way?" He tugged her in the opposite direction. "I don't think there's going to be any more violin music. And I just saw Roman give the DJ the mix of songs we picked out for tonight." He nodded toward the dance floor, where both his brothers were heading.

"Well, all right."

"Nice job." He wasn't being sarcastic.

Her gaze flickered over him, like she wasn't sure of his sincerity, so he said, "I mean it. You saved a lifelong friendship."

"That's the thing. Most feuds are caused by misunderstandings. Stopping an argument is like pulling a weed. You have to get it before it seeds and gets beyond the point of no return."

That made him think of his family in Greenwich. His brother's wedding was certain to be four hideous days of grudges, hurt feelings, and people avoiding each other. Since his parents' divorce a few years ago, that's how it was. His brother and sister sided with their mother. He'd tried to remain neutral, but since his wedding fiasco, his dad was barely speaking to him. Fun times. "Bet you see a lot of families beyond the point of no return."

She shrugged. "I'm an optimist. It's usually possible to get beyond the hurt feelings if you can get people to actually talk about them. Make them see there's something more important at stake—like the well-being of their children, for example. Or a lifelong friendship, years of good times and memories."

As far as Drew's parents were concerned, none of that seemed to be a priority. Their feelings of hatred toward one another ran too deep, and they'd been flinging shit at each other for years. "You sound like you work with a lot of dysfunctional families."

"Family therapy is a large part of my practice, yes."

Interesting, but he barely heard her. His mind was busy working on a seed that had just bloomed into a full-blown idea. A crazy, wild idea.

No, it was too crazy.

It would be wrong to expose her to the nightmare that was his family. Fantasizing that anyone without superpowers could heal the rifts that existed between his family members was insane.

It was going to take all he had just to get himself through the wedding weekend. It wasn't his job to try to fix unfixable, irreparable things. But having her there would maybe focus his family on *their* faults instead of *his*.

Plus maybe Maggie could help mend some fences and work some of that magic she'd just demonstrated. His sister Christina was in college. One day, perhaps in the not-too-distant future, she'd marry—and wouldn't it be nice if the family was at least talking to one another by then?

Bella spotted them from across the bar. "Hey, you two, come on," she said as the DJ began playing music.

"Do you like to dance?" Maggie asked.

The expression on her face surprised him. Sort of like a kid with a broken leg watching from the sidelines who was out for the season. Funny. She struck him as the type who fretted a lot, who would maybe be too stressed to really let loose on the dance floor.

He could beg off. Say he wasn't really into it. But she looked so…hopeful. Like she was dying to dance. How long had it been since she had?

Oh, what the hell. "I love to dance," he said.

"Great, let's go," Maggie said. She grabbed him by the hand and tugged him along, stopping for a moment to remove her shoes and place them on her seat. Her eagerness floored him.

Drew followed her out, caught up for just a moment in the fact that a pretty woman was leading him to a dance floor surrounded by white twinkly lights and a black velvet canopy of stars. Long time since that had happened.

Maggie closed her eyes for a minute and felt the beat, which was cool and weird at the same time. Then she opened her eyes and full-out smiled, and God, that smile nearly knocked him on his ass. He didn't have much time to think about it, though, only smile himself and try to keep up with her.

A few times, he spun her about, and once he even dipped her—and he had to admit, she was good. She had an instinctive, fluid way of moving that surprised the hell out of him, like everything else about her tonight.

The breeze carried the scent of new leaves and the promise of a warm summer, and blew little wisps of her hair about her face. He got lost in the music, in dancing with her small hands inside his big, rough ones. His brothers were at his side, the brothers he thought were lost forever but who had somehow become a unit. After a while, Roman went and dragged Mrs. P out there too. Then she began Greek dancing, and then everyone was dancing and spinning and laughing…

In the space of a heartbeat, the music changed from fast to slow, and everyone paired off. He raised a brow at Maggie and offered a hand. Their eyes locked for a moment, and he felt an intense rush of something hot and electric zing through him. He saw her cheeks flood with color even in the dim light. Something had shifted between them, and it wasn't just the tempo of the music.

He held out his hands in invitation for her to slow dance with him.

Maggie lowered her gaze and stepped back. "Oh, thanks, Drew, but I—I've got to check on Griff. That was really fun, though, thanks again!"

With an overexuberant smile and a turn on her heels, she was gone.

It took him a second to recover, to grab Mrs. P's arm before she left the floor and draw her in for a dance. But while he smiled and made polite conversation, his mind was elsewhere.

For a few minutes, he'd forgotten his cares and concerns. He'd forgotten the sick, churning feeling in his stomach he'd been living with ever since he'd learned his brother was about to marry the only woman he'd ever loved. He watched Maggie exit the dance floor in her bare feet. She stopped and grabbed her sandals, coat, and purse off a chair and left the rooftop.

And damn if he didn't wish it would've lasted just a little longer.

CHAPTER 3

"Griffin honey, don't look backwards when you're climbing up the slide, okay?" Maggie watched her smiling son climb the slide's bright red ladder in the park across from her rented duplex, his sneakered feet clanging noisily on the metal as he scurried up, blond hair catching the morning sun's rays. Maggie loved her son's boundless enthusiasm, his endless energy, and his rush to do just about anything. But she could do without his daredevilishness. She'd already lost the love of her life to a rare, random thing—cancer, at age thirty!—and she'd be damned if she was going to let a serendipitous episode of fate do the same to her son.

"Maggie, Maggie, Maggie," her friend Alyssa said as she watched her own little boy, shaking her head sadly. Half her attention was on her cell phone. She didn't seem to care that her son was doing all kinds of ridiculous stunts bound to land him in the ER. And she was a pediatrician of all things!

"What is it?" Maggie asked, watching Griffin hang upside down from a monkey bar and gritting her teeth so as not to run over there and become his human net. She understood that sometimes her fear led her to be overbearing and overprotective. She fought it as best she could.

"You need to call Greg back," Alyssa said, tucking her long dark hair behind her ear. "Do *not* lose this opportunity. He's gorgeous, single, and not looking for anything too deep. He'd be the perfect guy to get back on the bandwagon with." She pocketed her phone and pulled her beeper off her waist. "I envy you in a way. I mean, I don't want to sound crass or anything, but sometimes I miss…I don't know…the chase. The idea of a hot guy wanting you. I mean, lighten up. This is just what you need, some fun in your life."

Maggie took one eyeball off Griffin, whose hair was now wildly vertical from hanging upside down, to glance at Alyssa. She was gorgeous, well put together, smart, and a good friend. Not to mention a woman who helped kids and their parents all day. But Maggie wondered if she had any idea what those words did to her.

Alyssa and Corey had done their pediatric training together in Hartford, and both she and her husband, Keith, had been great friends of theirs since day one of residency. Plus, her son, Owen, was exactly Griffin's age. But life had moved on for her…because now she had a beautiful baby daughter too.

Maybe that was why Maggie had a difficult time being around her too much. It wasn't that the memories of their friendship were painful—the dinners, hiking and biking, even a weekend trip or two where they'd gone camping and once a trip to a quiet, remote island in Maine for a long weekend—no, not at all. Rather, being with Alyssa and Keith was more like watching a movie of what her life would've been like *if*. If her husband hadn't died. If tragedy hadn't struck. So it was hard to have patience with the "I miss hot guys" comment.

Maggie didn't miss hot guys. She missed *Corey*, her husband, her lover, her friend, Griffin's father. Her soul mate, for God's sake. The sex had always been great, but the years of sickness had made those memories dim, had replaced the happy ones with heartbreaking ones of her sick, debilitated husband she would rather not remember.

She couldn't imagine missing *the chase*. Maybe because she and Corey had been high school sweethearts, and she'd never really experienced much of a chase. Maybe Alyssa was just having a bad day, failing, for whatever reason, to appreciate her husband. Maggie knew as well as anyone that marriage had its ups and downs. But being wistful over hot guys wanting you seemed an extravagance when Alyssa had *everything*, and how could she possibly wish for something else?

So no, at the moment, Maggie had no sense of humor as far as this dating thing went. She looked on reentering the dating pool with the enthusiasm of plucking chin hairs. And she tended more and more to have a built-in grouchiness with Alyssa. Maybe because she was *too* happy, because she had it all, because Maggie had been *just like that* but was now being forced to start from square one with her life.

Maggie scolded herself harshly. She had to remember that tragedy had changed her. Made her hypersensitive to just about everything—even the little everyday annoyances of married life seemed precious to her now. And maybe she *was* being a little sanctimonious about it.

"I just worry about you. It's been three and a half years. It's time to take a leap. Do something different. A fling would be invigorating."

"Right." Maggie's parents had been married for thirty-five years, and she'd been raised on a steady diet—from the womb through all her years under Sister Mary Catherine's tutelage at St. Stanislaus Grade School, and then at Our Lady of the Lake High School—that good Catholic girls did *not* have "flings."

But that was before life had handed her this particular bitter-tasting fruit. Maybe it was time to be less black-and-white and look a little bit into the gray.

She didn't want to be swept off her feet. She didn't want to fall in love again that deeply, that completely. Because look where that had gotten her! Years of feeling like she'd been run over by a semi but was somehow left alive and writhing on the pavement.

But she wanted to feel alive again. She wanted to enjoy happy little things again without feeling a slash of pain afterward—like looking at the brilliant blue of the lake on a warm spring day without remembering every time Corey and she had done just that, never realizing that those days would be so numbered. Or listening to Griffin say something amazing and far beyond his years, indicating how brilliant he was, and not being able to share that with his father. And she wanted more children. If she wanted a real family for Griffin, she had to get working on it. And stop expecting what she couldn't have. Corey was gone. And it appeared she had a lot of life to live without him.

"Promise me you won't rule it out, seeing Greg again."

Alyssa looked so concerned, Maggie almost laughed. "All right, all right. I'll take it under consideration."

"Great." Alyssa looked pleased. "You know, they put up the new lettering on the cancer center."

Maggie blushed a little. "I know, the hospital sent me a letter." After Corey's death, the town had been so devastated by the loss of their hometown son that they'd renamed the cancer center after him. She, however, had never seen the big bronze plaque they'd erected in the little meditation garden right outside the building, or now, Corey's name in shiny silver lettering on the side of the building. Maggie could not even bring herself to drive down the street. She couldn't imagine herself ever doing so in the future either. It was too real and final a reminder that he was gone for good.

"You should go see it, Maggie. Corey would be so proud."

Maybe he would. He was a humble man, her Corey, and frankly, she wasn't sure what he'd think of having his name on a building. But she knew for sure he would want his mission remembered, to help sick children with cancer. And the center and the annual benefit that she'd initiated and was currently chairing kept that alive for sure.

"I've got to go," Alyssa said. "See you at the library next weekend for story time?"

"It's a date," Maggie said. "Thanks, Alyssa—for worrying about me."

"Hey, no problem. If you need any help with the benefit, just call me." Alyssa gave her a hug and ran off to collect her son.

"Was that Alyssa?" her friend Bella asked, suddenly stopping her stroller in front of Maggie. Maggie took a peek at Bella's eight-month-old daughter Vivienne, who was sleeping soundly with her thumb curled in her mouth.

"Yeah. She was just encouraging me to keep dating Greg Pollard."

"And what do you think about that?"

Maggie shrugged. "I suppose I should."

"Don't sound so thrilled." Together, they began to stroll toward a park bench where Maggie's mother, Maureen, and Helen McShae, Maggie's mother-in-law, sat chatting.

"I have to start somewhere. In fact, I ran into him at the grocery store the other day and we scheduled another date in a few weeks. He's willing to give me another chance. Which is kind of amazing after I wasn't able to…you know. Last time."

"Everything's difficult, right?" Bella patted her on the back. "The first step is often the scariest."

"Right," Maggie said, trying to sound optimistic.

"Look, Alyssa can't tell you what's right for you. You'll know when you're ready."

Maggie smiled at her friend. "You always make me feel better."

"But there's nothing wrong with pushing your comfort level a little," Bella said.

"Except when you nudge me like that," Maggie said.

"The other thing is, how are you doing chairing Corey's event? I worry about you. It's too emotional for you to keep doing that year after year."

Fool that she was, Maggie had offered to be in charge again this year. The first year or two, it had kept her mind occupied, and she'd had a dogged determination to preserve Corey's memory properly—but Bella was right. The whole thing was exhausting, physically and emotionally.

She side-hugged her friend. "I'm fine, and you're right. I think after this year, I'll turn over the reins. Thanks for asking."

"You know, you say that every year," Bella said.

They'd reached the park bench, so greetings and hugs went around. And exclamations about the adorable baby.

"Helen's coming with me to the St. Stanislaus cookie bakeoff," Maureen said, winking in what she must have thought was a sly fashion but looked awfully obvious.

"Oh, fun," Maggie said, feigning enthusiasm. The two women could not have been more different. Maureen MacNamara at one time looked like her idol Maureen O'Hara, with fiery red hair and nice boobs. Even though her hair had faded a bit over the years, her personality had not. Helen, petite with a short blonde bob, was much quieter, and even more subdued after her recent divorce from Corey's father.

"Your mother wants me to meet some unattached Catholic bakers," Helen said with a shrug.

"If that doesn't work, you could always go with Mrs. Panagakos and meet some Greek ones," Maggie said.

"Look," Maureen said, "all I'm saying is that the men who

34

volunteer for the church are usually nice guys. I'll introduce you around, Helen. And if we find no one there, I've got a dozen other places to check."

Helen exchanged a knowing look with Maggie. Both of them knew what it was like to be swept away by Maggie's mother's enthusiasm. Even though her mom and dad had recently retired from running MacNamara's, the local pub that her brother, Scott, now ran, her mother had thrown herself into various volunteer causes. And apparently Helen was now one of them.

"How's *your* dating life going, honey?" Helen asked Maggie. "I heard you went out with Henry Pollard's son."

"Greg? Yeah, we've had a few dates. It was…fun," Maggie hedged.

"So are you going out with him again?" Helen asked.

"Yeah," Maggie said, hesitating. She left out the part that Greg was sort of expecting her to sleep with him. And she wasn't quite sure how she felt about that.

"My daughter's being picky," Maureen said.

"Mom, that was my first date in three and a half years. Give me a break." For God's sake. Her *mother*.

"I just want you to have an open mind," Maureen said. "It's time to get going again." That was her ma, never one to encourage a pity party. Plus she wanted more grandkids.

"Look, maybe this Greg guy just isn't the right one," Helen said. "Either you've got that spark or you don't."

"Thank you, Helen," Maggie said, patting her arm. She gave her mom an I-won-this-round look.

"I can take Griffin Friday night for you, by the way," Helen said.

"But dear, I just called you about that this morning," Maureen said.

"Oh, thank you both," Maggie said quickly. "How lucky am I—two grandmas fighting over my kid. But I'm planning on staying in this Friday." They were constantly jockeying over who would get to watch Griffin. She *should* feel lucky, but the competition seemed a little unhealthy. So did the fact that she often felt she had to intervene between them like she did between Griffin and his preschool friends.

Bella reached into the stroller and picked up her eight-month-old and held the grinning, drooling baby out at arm's length. "Here's a consolation prize—whoever doesn't get Griffin could have Vivienne for the night." Bella chattered a greeting to her sweet little girl, whose entire face lit up at the sight of her mother.

"Oh, she is a sweetie," Maureen said, cooing at the baby.

"And I'm sure you'll be saying that when she wakes up at three a.m.," Maggie said, kissing Vivienne on her head of thick dark curls.

"Hey, whose side are you on?" Bella asked.

Maggie didn't have to answer, because Griffin called, "Watch me, Mom!" from the top of the slide.

Maggie waved and smiled back, biting back the impulse to shout out *be careful!* Most days she felt her main goal was to get Griffin through the perils of childhood—the ear infections, the fevers, the endless concerns about accidents—and get him to adulthood in one piece. Sometimes she felt like she was navigating a video game where one false step could cause an explosion or other disaster.

"Oh, I forgot my purse," her mom said. "I'm going to run home and get it. Helen, I'll meet you at the church, if that works."

Griffin tore off to the swings. Maggie said bye to her mom, left Bella and Helen talking, and walked over not far behind him. A father was there, pushing his son, who looked to be around the same age as Griffin, while a mom shot pictures. Suddenly, a sense of absolute aloneness knifed her, and with it a familiar anger.

As a therapist, she understood all about anger and grief. But for the millionth time, she wondered why Corey and her? They'd been a golden couple, perfect together from day one, and frankly, it had never occurred to her—not even one time—that they wouldn't be together forever. Corey's grandparents were hale and hearty in their mid-eighties, and he even had a hundred-year-old great-grandmother who still played bingo at assisted living every Monday night. How on earth could he have gotten so sick and died so young?

His death destroyed the only plan she'd ever had for her life. They were supposed to have a brood of kids, buy the kind of quaint and quirky house that would make a home for the ages, and grow old together. She was not supposed to be in shock for years or still have to fight just to make it through each day. Nor have days when her gut clenched so tightly, she couldn't eat, or times when she would cry so many tears, they could name a significantly sized body of water after her.

No, she would never even begin to know how to fall in love with anyone else.

Strangely, that made her think of last night. Tugging Drew onto the dance floor had been unexpected and fun. For a few minutes, all she'd done was dance and forget every worry and problem, every stress and strain. When was the last time *that* had happened?

Plus she'd been so…aware of him. Maybe it was those big, broad shoulders and powerful arms, ones she could too easily imagine wrapping around her, surrounding her with strength and heat. He'd sort of been a train wreck when he'd first arrived in Mirror Lake, but he'd clearly beefed up his fitness regimen and gotten his act and his body together. And what an amazing body it was.

He'd smelled so good too, like some kind of woodsy, spicy mixture of something masculine and delicious. And that was why, at the end, when he'd asked her to slow dance, she'd panicked. For the first time since Corey's death, she'd noticed a man. *Really noticed*, as in knees getting wobbly, stomach pancake-flipping, tingling-in-special-places type of noticing.

Then she'd bolted. She honestly couldn't say how much of her freak-out was due to the all-out, full-body attraction she felt for this completely inappropriate man versus the fact that he was *not Corey*. Wouldn't Corey be upset, looking down on her from wherever he was? Saying something like, *Hey, Mags, what are you doing? Why is that guy in my place?* No wonder every single nerve ending in her body had signaled that *this was wrong!*

Just then, her phone rang. It was her mother, who must've just gotten home.

Another problem with her parents being retired: constant and easy phone contact. She answered with one hand while swinging Griffin with the other.

"I think I'm going to divorce your father," her mom said casually.

"Hi, Mom," Maggie said, rolling her eyes. "Haven't seen you in a while."

"Did you hear what I said? I can't live with that man anymore."

The man next to Maggie had started a business call, and she couldn't hear her mom, so she backed up a few steps. "What's wrong?"

"I didn't want to say anything in front of Helen, but your father hates retirement. He's bored to tears. He keeps poking around in my business, and he's home all the time. I'm about to lose it." There was a hammering noise in the background. Maggie was afraid to ask what it was.

"Mom, why don't you come over for dinner tonight? We'll watch a movie, and it'll get you out of the house for a while."

"What? I can't hear you. Too much noise. Your father's replacing all the screens in the screened porch. They don't even need it."

Maggie stepped back from the swing a little more and repeated the offer.

"I have my own life," her mom said. "My girlfriends, my clubs, my charity work. I can't be available for him every time he wants to fool around."

"Okay, Mom!"

Maggie looked up. In the few seconds she'd glanced away, Griffin had taken it upon himself to stand up on the swing. He'd been piston-pumping his knees and feet, hanging on to the chains with his little arms, laughing and pushing himself as the swing climbed higher and higher.

What she saw next happened like a slow-motion video. One minute, Griffin was swinging, going higher and higher. She opened her mouth to tell him to slow down, hold on tight, but it was too late. She dropped her phone and rushed forward just as he launched himself from the swing at the top of the swing's height. Her legs felt like they were stuck in pudding. Panic clogged her throat, and she couldn't even scream. Her little boy sailed through the air, against a background of bright blue spring sky, arms and legs flailing, plummeting to what was surely his death.

A jogger who was passing by ran in front of the swings just in time to catch him like a football. The impact of the catch jolted the guy a little as he caught Griffin's body like a wide receiver stretched out for a great catch. They both buckled together to the ground and rolled.

Adrenaline coursed through Maggie's limbs. She dropped down at her son's side. "Griffin, Griffin, oh my God, are you all right?"

The little boy pushed against the hard muscle of the man who cushioned his fall, the man who'd risked his own safety for her kid's.

"Mommy, did you see?" Griffin was excited, smiling. "I was flying through the air, and look who caught me! Thanks, Drew!"

Her brain finally computed the face of the man sprawled on the playground dirt under her little boy. And he was grinning too!

"Griffin! This is not funny," she said, fight-or-flight hormones full speed ahead. "That was very, very dangerous and you gave Mommy a huge scare!" She'd thought Drew would be irritated at being on the ground, getting dirty and likely scraped up, having to step up and save her kid, whatever, but he looked...amused.

Griffin disentangled himself, but Maggie caught him before he could tear off to another playground thrill.

She bent down to his level. "Look, Griffin, what you did was dangerous. You could have broken your bones, and you were very lucky Mr. Drew was there to catch you. Please don't ever do that again."

Griffin's eyes grew bigger than usual, and he looked chagrined at last, which was what she'd wanted, wasn't it? "I'm sorry, Mommy," he said solemnly. "I was just having fun."

Oh God, she was a dream killer. She saw it in her son's eyes. But what else could she do? He could've been lying right now in a tangle of broken bones.

Drew tousled Griffin's hair. "Next time, have fun closer to the ground, okay, buddy?"

Griffin smiled at Drew. "Thanks for catching me." Drew held out his hand for a fist bump, which Griffin reciprocated. Then he turned to his mom. "Can I go down the slide again?"

"As long as you hold on tight. Okay?"

"Okay. Bye, Mom!"

He tore off to the slide. Drew got up and dusted himself off. He wore a simple gray T-shirt that was a little sweaty, and black running shorts. His calves were very toned, and his eyes were very, very brown, and...

"Thank you," she said, standing up herself and brushing herself off. Not because she was dirty but...she needed something to do besides stare at him.

"No problem," Drew said, his mouth turning up in a smile.

"Nice catch," Bella said. Maggie turned to find her and Helen standing behind her.

"Who is that man?" Helen asked loudly enough everyone could hear.

"I'm Drew," he said, extending his hand to Helen, who shook his hand reluctantly.

"Helen's my mother-in-law," Maggie explained.

"I was worried he was some pervert running away with our boy," Helen said to Maggie.

"Oh no, Helen," Maggie said. "Drew isn't a pervert." She bit back a smile. "You aren't, are you?"

Drew smiled back, the kind of smile a gorgeous guy gives a pretty girl, and that made him so hard to hate. And for a second, he wasn't the most irritating man in the world. "It's okay," he said. "I just happened to be in the right place at the right time."

"I'd better go," Helen said. "I can't be late for the bakers."

"I've got to get going too. See you two later," Bella said.

Maggie said goodbye and watched them walk off. "Thank you again for what you did." She paused. "Maybe I—overreacted. Maybe I was a little too tough on Griffin. But I just didn't want—"

Drew smiled. "He's a boy, Maggie. They test limits, you know?"

She nodded. Right-o. Limit testing of a mom whose limits were already maxed out was not a very good idea. But she didn't say that.

"Anyway," he said, "I'm glad we—ran into each other. I have something to ask you. A favor."

A favor? A thread of worry weaved a path through her gut. After he'd just saved Griffin's life, how would she be able to say no? "What is it?" she asked, trying not to sound suspicious.

"Do you mind if we have a seat?" He gestured to a hunter-green bench. Griffin had wandered into a giant sandbox nearby, which she wasn't thrilled about (how many stray cats used that as litter?) but he was happy playing with a couple of other kids.

As she sat, Maggie wished she didn't feel so…distracted. Her nerves felt taut as a high wire, and it had nothing to do with Griffin's recent brush with death.

Then suddenly, something occurred to her. Maybe Drew was going to ask her out! She'd always had a certain sense about when men thought she was attractive and were about to approach her for a date—a rusty one, granted, but still. This would not be a good idea with both Sam and Bella married to his brothers. If things got awkward, everyone would be upset, and it would affect their friendship. No, not a good idea at all.

"I was very impressed with you last night."

She frowned. If this was a pickup line, it was the worst one she'd ever heard.

Could he possibly be talking about her dance moves? That was so inappropriate. Plus, just who did he think he was? *Impressed* with her? Did he think that was some kind of compliment?

It might have been. From the Dark Ages.

"Impressed with me?" she said, trying to keep the indignation out of her voice.

"Your people skills," he said hurriedly. "Your mediation skills."

Oh, okay. So he wasn't going to ask her out after all. Her relief was short-lived, because what *was* he up to? He sounded as if he were about to offer her a job. At the UN, maybe, where mediation skills would come in handy.

He flashed her a grin that would make angels break into the Hallelujah Chorus. "Let me clarify."

God, the man was stunning. She suddenly remembered the tabloid photos over the past few years, how he was New England's resident hunk, his dating exploits reported on conscientiously and often. And then photo after photo with Anika Brewer, often as they vacationed together in exotic locales, her tall, willowy form next to his (often shirtless) brawny one. Up close like this, Maggie could completely see why the world had been so infatuated with his every move.

"I need a date for my brother's wedding," he said a little hastily. "The brother I grew up with. In Greenwich."

This was getting even more bizarre. Maybe he'd spent too much time hiding away from civilization this past year and the lack of social interaction was really starting to show. "And you want me to help you find one?"

"No, I want you to *be* my date."

"Because of my mediation skills." She was so confused! Not what a girl wanted to hear. For her lovely personality, her brilliant mind, okay, even for her great rack, but mediation skills? Ugh.

"In a nutshell, yes. I saw what you did last night, calming those women down."

"You're a nutshell! Let me see if I understand this. You want me to be your date because people in your family need to be calmed down?"

He sighed heavily. Thrust his hands into his shorts pockets. Looked everywhere but at her, until he suddenly made dead-on eye contact. She gasped. Because his gaze was so…intense. And he had gorgeous deep brown eyes with little golden flecks that were absolutely mesmerizing. He cleared his throat, which made her stop obsessing about his looks and pay attention. "My family is completely crazy, and there are certain…tensions that are a bit hard to…overcome…"

"Look, Drew, I really appreciate that you just saved my kid's life and all, but I just don't think—" She broke off just as she saw what her son was up to in the sandbox. "Wait just a sec—" She stood up and cupped her hands around her mouth and yelled, "Griffin! Stop eating sand, please!" Then, after she caught the little bugger red-handed and he guiltily stopped, she sat back down.

"I'll be honest with you. My father is—" He paused, as if

struggling for a word, "—displeased about my called-off wedding. And he's unhappy I didn't go back to work for the family corporation. But I can handle that. A few years ago, my father and mother divorced, and there are—hard feelings, between them and on the part of my siblings. Part of my job going home is to deflect some of those so my brother can have a nice, calm wedding. And if I bring you, you can help me."

Maggie examined him carefully. His gaze was…pleading. He would never admit it, but the big guy seemed…cornered. Could it be that the billionaire businessman was out of options?

"I'm sorry for your family problems," she said. "You're right, weddings are stressful, especially when everyone's essentially forced together for a few days. But that can also be an opportunity for conflict resolution."

"So you'll do it?"

"No! I mean, I couldn't take time off from my practice or from Griffin. Plus I've got a lot of work to do with the big cancer center benefit this year and it's coming up in just five weeks. I'm sorry."

The expression on his face turned dogged. Determined. Downright menacing. She imagined this was his strategy in the boardroom, no doubt, when deals were about to go south and he needed to pull out all the stops to save the day.

Well, she was a professional herself, and she didn't intimidate easily. There was just the teensy problem of his gorgeous wavy hair that resembled Jon Snow's a bit. Now that it needed to be cut, it was curling at the ends—very thick and dark—and she bet her fingers would slide silkily through it like a tropical waterfall.

She tore her gaze off him, located her son in the sandbox like a proper mother should, and scootched away from him a little. There. She was now immune to his charms. She hoped.

"I can sweeten the pot," he said.

She laughed. Which made him carefully raise a brow. "I wouldn't laugh if I were you until I heard the whole deal."

"Sorry, just that I'm starting to feel like I'm in a Godfather movie." She did her best Marlon Brando imitation. "Are you gonna make me an offer I can't refuse?"

This time, *he* laughed. And this time when his gaze lit on her, it threw heat. Maggie was no innocent, even if she had been with Corey forever. She knew what it meant when a man stared at her that way, and man oh man, he was *staring*.

Oh my God, she had to stop…imagining things. Like those soft, full lips on hers, and those big biceps wrapped round her, and his chest hair tickling her breasts…

Maybe he didn't even have chest hair. But judging by the look of that beard, she'd bet the farm on it.

She snapped back to professional mode, and at the same time, he sat up straighter. Scooted back a little. And his face became as placid and unreadable as a yoga instructor's. "I can pay you. Your going rate. Twenty-four seven. And before you object on the grounds of being sanctimonious, your mother already told me about Sidwell Friends School for Griffin."

He was making fun of her, of course, using the name of the famous school the children of presidents attended.

"It's called Mirror Lake Academy and…wait. You met my mother?"

"She was accepting donations for the clothing drive at the church."

Which was more unbelievable? That he'd met her mother or that he'd donated clothing to the church? Maggie groaned. Her mother would be in love with this guy for sure, missing no opportunity to torture her endlessly for details…

Maggie rolled her eyes. "I'm sure she told you she thinks the school is hoity-toity."

A corner of his mouth tilted up. "It's your decision, Maggie. What you want. After this weekend, you'd be able to send your son to preschool at Harvard if that's what you want."

45

"My going rate is $175 an hour."

"I'll give you double that."

She had to forcibly close her mouth so her jaw didn't hit and bounce off the rubberized surface of the playground.

"Tell you what." He paused. "I'll make it four hundred." His gaze dragged up and down her in a way that made her face flame with heat. "Think about it. I'll be in touch."

Then Don Corleone left her sitting on the park bench, wondering what the hell just happened, staring straight ahead at his amazing ass as he stopped at the sandbox to tell Griffin a quick goodbye, then strode confidently away.

CHAPTER 4

Late the next Friday afternoon, Drew walked with his brothers and Mrs. Panagakos into MacNamara's Pub. The place was quiet, the calm before the weekend storm, and held the biting aroma of strong, freshly brewed coffee. A few people sat nursing beers, and a young woman with thick glasses sat by herself reading a book and drinking coffee. The coffee thing was a little odd, but after spending over a year in Mirror Lake, Drew didn't find it so unusual that everyone knew that the best place to get coffee was Mac's. Maggie's brother, Scott, was behind the bar, polishing it with a cloth under the watchful eye of an older, balding man whom Drew knew to be their father.

"How's the wine bar coming, guys?" Scott asked as he took their orders. Drew's brothers each ordered beers. Drew was already on edge about that wedding date, or rather his lack of one, but he ordered coffee anyway, mainly because he could never pass up a good cup.

Everyone in town knew about the wine bar he and his brothers were opening in the middle of downtown, which they would use to showcase Roman's apple brandy and other spirits. "We're beat," Roman said. "We spent the afternoon lugging a two-ton antique mahogany bar across the floor."

"With Tiffany glass inserts. And a marble counter," Lukas added.

"Sounds like a job for a moving company," Scott said.

"Brothers are cheaper," Drew said. "Besides, the opening's a month from tomorrow. Lots to do."

They all took a seat in a booth near the front, ordering the house cheese dip and chips to go with the beers. Drew was always kind of amazed the MacNamaras didn't resent the addition of the wine bar. But then, the wine bar was primarily for the tourists who frequented the lake and the quaint downtown, and MacNamara's had always catered to town folk.

"You missed a spot," the older man said, looking over Scott's shoulder. Then he addressed the Spikonos brothers. "Nice to see you boys again. And you too, Alethea."

"I thought you retired, Mac," Lukas said.

"I thought so too," Scott said wryly.

Mr. MacNamara was already headed to the kitchen. "Retire, schmire," he said, waving a hand in dismissal.

"That means he'd rather hang out here and torture me all day," Scott said, leaning his tall frame on the bar and massaging his temples.

"Sounds like you could use a drink," Drew said. He liked Scott. He was a hard worker, a good listener, plus he made a hell of a pot of coffee.

"Some Tylenol might be better," Scott said, holding up the coffeepot he'd grabbed from the counter. "Hey, Carol Ann," he called out to the solitary young woman seated at the back of the bar. She had short black hair and black horn-rimmed glasses. On hearing her name, the woman startled, shut her book, and looked up, blushing. "You need a refill on that coffee, sweetie?"

She smiled and did a finger wave. "I'm good for now. Thanks, Scotty," she answered in a quiet voice. Even in the dim light, Drew could see her face was flaming.

Someone loudly scraped back a chair. A pretty woman with stylish blonde hair and bright red lipstick walked up to the bar.

"Who is that woman?" Drew asked Mrs. P, who was sitting next to him.

"His ex-girlfriend, Marcia," she said in a low voice. "They dated for five years."

"Please do *not* tell me you're flirting with Carol Ann," the woman said, possibly louder than she intended. Drew wondered if the woman in the back could hear, but her nose was buried back in her book.

"I asked her if she wanted a refill on her drink." Scott said quietly. "How is that flirting?"

"You know very well that it is. Not to mention you're also robbing the cradle. She's barely twenty-one. I mean, she's drinking coffee, for God's sake."

"Marcia, please go home," Scott said.

"I just wish you'd come to your senses," Marcia said, leaning across the bar in a way that exposed her considerable cleavage. "Why don't you come over after work? I'll make you dinner."

Scott sighed. "Marcia, we broke up. I'm sorry, but I'm not getting back together with you."

"You always did before," she said. Then she waggled her eyebrows suggestively. "Plus it's Friday night."

Everyone at the table seemed to be listening to Scott's drama play out until Lukas took it upon himself to talk. "Speaking of Friday night, I'm playing at Reflections later." He motioned to Drew, who was sitting across from him. "Want to come and hear some music? Might take some of the tension off."

"What tension?" Drew asked, who was fiddling with his coffee cup while his brothers dug into the cheese dip. There was no tension. Only his need to get a date for that damn wedding.

"Things must be bad if *you're* not eating," Roman said.

"Man, I hate it when you guys make fun of me," Drew said, smiling to be a good sport. He'd tamed his stress eating a long time ago.

"I take it Maggie wasn't interested in being your wedding date?" Roman asked.

"How did you know about that?" He paused. "Never mind. I keep forgetting how information flows around here." Straight from one best friend to the other.

"Why do you need Maggie to come home with you anyway?" Roman asked. "I can probably set you up with another one of Bella's single friends."

"He thinks Maggie can use her psychology skills to calm things down in his family," Lukas said. "Especially since his father is still upset about his big wedding fiasco."

"Bella thinks it would be good for Maggie to get out of town," Roman said. "She hasn't had a break in a long time."

"She probably doesn't get out much," Mrs. P said. "She'd probably enjoy someone making her feel special. Not like just a mom all the time. But what do I know? I was never a mom."

"You're like our mom now," Lukas said. "And make sure you tell everyone who's your favorite." He cast Mrs. P a big rock-star wink. Even Drew admitted it was irresistible. Except these days, Lukas focused all his charm on his wife, Samantha.

"Lukas, you are teacher's pet, aren't you?" Roman shook his head.

"I spent so many years being teacher's nightmare, I have to capitalize on my newfound popularity, don't I, Mrs P?" he teased, referring to his time in high school where he was sort of an edgy outcast.

Mrs. P patted Lukas's cheek. "You're a dear. And so are you two. And to think, you all have a baby brother out there somewhere. I pray every day that he can be reunited with you three as soon as possible."

"My PI has sent our brother Jared letters," Lukas said. "He chooses not to respond." Drew knew he lived about an hour away, in Jersey, and he'd grown up in the Connelly family, owners of a national sports apparel company.

Roman sighed. "Maybe we should just be grateful that we've found each other and we all get along so well."

"No," Mrs. P said without hesitation. "He's your brother. Blood is thicker than water. You must find him."

"Okay, maybe I don't want to be your favorite, Mrs. P," Lukas said. "Too much work." She looked crestfallen, so he leaned over and kissed her on the cheek. "I'm teasing. Between you and my wife, I'd be in big trouble if I stopped working on this."

"That's what I wanted to hear." Content for the moment, she turned back to Drew. "Now, Andreas, maybe your Maggie just needs a little more convincing."

Drew leaned back in his chair. "She's not *my Maggie*. I offered her double her salary for the whole weekend."

Lukas snorted in his beer. "You offered to pay her to come with you?"

"Classy," Roman said. "Bet she jumped all over that."

"Look, this really is a simple business proposition. I do *not* want to date Maggie."

"Oh, I think you just might, brother," Lukas said, slapping him on the back.

"What makes you say that?" Roman asked.

"Because whenever she's around, you act like you're in tenth grade," Lukas said. "You stare at her all googly-eyed when she's not looking. You pretend you don't notice her when you're really listening to every word she says. Admit it. You have a crush on her."

"Do not."

"Do so."

51

"Boys…" Mrs. P scolded.

"It doesn't matter anyway," Drew said. "She said no."

"Giving up after one try. I'm so disappointed in you," Lukas said. "What happened to turning on the old Spikonos charm?"

"Maggie's a nice woman," Drew said. "She deserves a man who's serious about a relationship, and that's not me. End of story." He wasn't going to mislead her about his interest just to get her to go with him.

He supposed he could just tell her about his father's disappointment in him for not marrying Anika and not joining the company. No need to tell her how his girlfriend of four years dumped him for his own brother.

Right. Any sensible person would *never* get involved with this mess if he did that. Plus telling her would turn him into an object of pity, and he would rather die than be that.

Drew was a businessman to his core. He knew how to play to people's strengths. Maggie was a compassionate woman, down to *her* core, no matter how much she disliked him. He had a feeling her sense of kindness wouldn't allow her to leave him in the lurch.

In fact, he was suddenly counting on it.

He drained the rest of his coffee. "You know, maybe I'm in the mood for some music tonight after all."

Let them rib him all they wanted. He could take it. It didn't matter, as long as he got that date.

"Put some lipstick on, for God's sake," Maureen MacNamara said, standing with her hands on her hips in the middle of Maggie's living room as Maggie descended the stairs of her half of the old Victorian house she rented. "And change your shirt. It's only nine o'clock, and you look like you're ready to climb into bed." Maggie's mother then settled into the couch, tucking the remote next to her, preparing for an evening watching lewd housewives somewhere in America. After Griffin went to bed, Maggie hoped.

"Griffin, MeMe's here," Maggie said, calling up to her son, who'd had his bath and was now in her room watching the end of *Mulan*.

Maggie was grateful her mom came running over at a moment's notice, but now she'd have to endure her commentary to get out the door. And knowing her mom, she wasn't about to let her go unscathed. Maggie gave her soft gray T-shirt a tug. "This is *not* a pj shirt, Mom."

"Well, it looks like one. Put a blouse on."

"People don't wear *blouses* anymore."

Her mother's brow did the arch of I-am-right, you-are-wrong-and-don't-you-dare-cross-me. "They do if they want to attract a man."

"Mom, I'm just going down to the lake to listen to Lukas sing a set." Because Sam had texted her like, fifty times. Finally, she'd figured, why not? Her mom loved spending time with Griffin and it was almost bedtime anyway and…maybe it would do her good. She'd promised to stretch herself out of her dating comfort zone. And she was *not* thinking about the possibility of Drew being there. Not at all.

"Is that cute guy going to be there? The one who saved Griffin. I can't believe I missed that."

"I don't know, Mom. Sam didn't say."

"Oh, that man is so handsome. And I think he's got a soft spot for you. Bella told me she always catches him staring over at you when you're not looking. Have you ever noticed that, dear?"

Maggie glanced back from where she was rifling through her closet. "How can I notice if I'm not looking?"

"Don't be cheeky, young lady. And you should really clean out that closet. You know we have hoarders on both sides. Hoarding is a form of OCD, did you know that?"

Maggie held her tongue. The closet wasn't *that* bad. And she might have other obsessions and compulsions, but hoarding was *not* one of them.

"Anyway," Maureen continued, "he donated a bunch of very expensive dress shirts and pants to the church the other day. And he was telling me about his brothers."

"Lukas and Roman?"

"They grew up very poor. The parents were alcoholics, you know. They got split up young. He said he thinks he accumulated too many clothes because part of him feels afraid of being poor again. So he was trying to get rid of the extras. Besides, he's been doing all that farm labor, and he says he doesn't need the fancy clothes anymore—have you seen his muscles? What a hunk. His old business shirts probably don't even fit him anymore."

Trust me, she knew about the hunky muscles. Not from personal experience but—well, who could fail to notice them? "Mom, he's a despised hunk. He left Anika Brewer at the altar. He left his family's business. I mean, he has issues."

"Relationships are complicated, dear. Don't judge."

Maggie couldn't believe it. Her mother had been charmed by Drew Poulos. One of the countless.

"Well, I couldn't help but notice his big beautiful brown eyes. When he saved Griffin, was he looking at you like he was interested?"

Maggie sighed. Only her mother, single-minded and relentless, would bring this up. Sometimes Maggie thought she had a good idea exactly where her OCD came from. "If he was, it would've been pervy. I was fairly hysterical at the time."

"Well, Bella told me she thinks he's sweet on you. Ah, her little Vivienne is so adorable. A pity neither of my children are giving me more grandchildren. There's your brother, breaking up with Marcia Hurst after five years—five years! Her mother isn't even speaking to me."

"Mom, I thought you didn't like Marcia all that much."

"I didn't especially care for how clingy she was or how she always seemed to insist she and Scott go out to eat even after those long shifts he does, but I do like her mother. And you know how I hate it when someone's angry with me. As if it's my fault they broke up! She even told me she's afraid Marcia won't have any more prospects because she's almost thirty. I mean, really, what am I supposed to do about that? It's not like I raised you kids to carry on with someone for years and then dump them, you know?"

"Mom, I don't think Marcia was the right one for Scott. I'm glad he had the courage to…break up with her." She was going to say something meaner, like *extricate himself from that dreadful woman and her awful family,* but she held her tongue.

Maureen nodded solemnly, then rummaged through her purse, probably for the hard candy she always kept there and would hand out to Griffin in fistfuls as soon as Maggie walked out the door. "Anyway. Maybe you didn't see how Andreas was looking at you because you've only dated one man your entire life."

"I can't help it that I met the love of my life when I was seventeen."

Her mother sighed and assessed her daughter, her features softening. "Yes, you did, didn't you? And he was a wonderful man. Forgive me, dear, for pushing. It's just that you may not think this, but I don't believe that the best part of your life is over."

Maggie shrugged. "Look, I'm going out, aren't I?" She waved her hand over the light cardigan she'd just draped over her couch as proof. "I'll even go change my shirt, okay?"

Her mother clapped her hands. "I've always been so proud of you that you've never let your anxiety stop you from doing things. Don't let it do that now, when maybe he's a little different from what you're used to. Give the man a chance, okay?"

Maggie couldn't help but see the contrast. An international jetsetter, heir to a yogurt empire, a face recognizable to everyone who read *People* magazine. Versus her husband, her hometown honey whom she'd met at their local high school. "Mom, Drew Poulos is not interested in me that way. He needs a date for his brother's wedding. He wants to pay me to go, to psychologize his family. Apparently, some of them aren't speaking to each other. I have no desire to get involved with a hotshot playboy—"

Her mother snapped her purse shut and looked up, her eyes widening. "He wants to *pay you* to go with him?"

"It's just business to him," Maggie said hurriedly, lest her mom jump to some crazy conclusion. She headed to the stairs to go find another shirt.

"You should go."

Maggie turned back to face her mom. "What did you say?"

"It's just a long weekend, right? Your father and I will watch Griffin."

"No! Absolutely not." But the words sounded weak and watery.

"You've never shied away from a challenge. This family sounds like they could use your help. Plus, you've been struggling so much with the bills. No matter what happens, look at all the money you'll walk away with! Besides, what is there to be afraid of? He's made it clear what he wants."

"Mom, I don't know—"

"Why don't you go put on your black V-neck shirt? The one that shows a little cleavage." Her mother literally nudged her up the stairs. "And don't worry about me and Griffin. Now hurry up. You'll miss everything."

Maggie was relieved when Griffin came barreling down the stairs to greet her mother and give her another mission to focus on. She went up to her bedroom and changed her shirt and even reached for a little necklace from her jewelry box on the old fireplace mantel. It sat next to an eight-by-ten of Corey and her on their wedding day, her absolute favorite photo of the two of them, running out of the church laughing, a cascade of iridescent bubbles surrounding them.

As she put on the necklace, her gaze skimmed over a little white-shelled turtle next to her jewelry box. She ran her finger over its mother-of-pearl exterior, feeling the smooth shell surface and the ridges of the different pieces. Corey had bought it for her during a weekend trip to the beach. He'd seen her looking at it in a gift shop, and he'd surprised her with it. To remember our trip, he'd said. They'd spent every minute of that trip that they weren't at the beach in bed, stuck together like magnets. They'd come back tanned, rested, and so in love.

That was what the turtle was. A little piece of him. Of them.

She used to keep earrings in it, but on the day of his funeral, she'd taken the urn with his ashes and tipped a bit into the little box and snapped the shell closed. It was a comfort to her, touching it as she started her day, as she worried about Griffin, and at night when she faced climbing into her cold bed alone.

What would he say about her trying to move on now? When it was clear to both of them he wasn't going to make it, he'd talked about it, with his usual wry humor. *I don't want you moving on without me,* he'd said. *I'm a selfish bastard, but the idea of you with another man makes me crazy.* Then he'd laugh, and kiss her, as if it were sort of a joke between them. But he'd never given her his blessing. And she wasn't quite sure she really had it.

Nor was she now. Sighing, she put two fingers up to her mouth, placed a kiss on them, and touched the turtle. Then, determined, she set out for the door.

CHAPTER 5

Drew drummed his fingers on the fashionably distressed wood table before him and glanced around Mirror Lake's finest restaurant, Reflections. He was sitting on the deck that stretched directly over the lake, enjoying the breeze and the warm spring evening as his brother Lukas finished crooning some very catchy love song that everyone around him seemed to know.

The setting couldn't have been more perfect: the stars looked painted on a black velvet canvas of sky, the spring breeze was fragrant with flowers and the typical but not unpleasant lake smell he'd gotten used to during the past year and a half. Couples sat together listening to the music as candles flickered softly on the tables. All in all, this was just the type of romantic evening he did his best to avoid.

"That is the sappiest song I've ever heard in my life," Drew said when Lukas walked over during a break. Lukas often did impromptu sets here when he was home; tourists were initially shocked but then delighted in having a free private concert compliments of one of the world's most popular pop artists.

"That song is number one on the charts," Lukas said, gulping down Drew's water. "Don't you ever hear your own feelings reflected in a song? Doesn't music remind you of a woman or a special time in your life? What it feels like to be in love?"

"Yada, yada, yada," Drew said, holding up his drink. When he was younger, love songs might've made him act like a goof. But he knew better now.

"You sound like someone who's struck out at the game of love. And my guess is the pitcher was *not* Anika."

Drew laughed. "Something like that."

"Want to talk about it?" Lukas asked, draining the water.

"Absolutely not."

He and Sondra had shared romantic evenings just like this, holding hands, listening to good music, going home afterward and making love, falling asleep tangled up in each other's arms. He'd been naïve enough to believe those times would never end.

No wonder why he was getting the creepy-crawlies sitting here. He could barely stand to sit amid all this happiness. The couples relaxing together. Bella and Roman, enjoying a date night out, Sam sitting in the front row, watching Lukas sing with stars in her eyes. Drew felt like a cynical old man, jaded before his time. And he could not wait to cut out of here.

But he was on a mission. The misery of sitting here would be worth it if he achieved his goal. Sam said she'd done her best to get Maggie to show up, and she hopefully would at any minute.

He just had to keep it professional. Not that Maggie wasn't easy to look at and even easier to fantasize about, but getting involved with her was an entanglement he couldn't risk. Sam and Bella would never forgive him if he hurt their best friend, and like falling dominoes, that would affect his relationship with Lukas and Roman too.

But dammit, he *needed* her as his date. She was smart and savvy, and he felt like she'd be someone he could trust to say the right things around his family. If only he could get her to say yes.

He was so busy thinking and half listening to the music that he startled a little when someone scraped back one of the chairs at his table.

And suddenly there she was, standing across from him wearing ankle jeans and a black V-neck sleeveless blouse, her hair tied back in a ponytail. Not a provocative outfit by any means, but suddenly he found himself knocked off his usual game, stumbling to his feet, greeting her. She looked young, not old enough to have a kid or a thousand worries.

Worse, for him anyway, she looked…amazing. Her scrubbed, nearly makeup-free look demonstrated clearly that she was a natural beauty, with a perfect oval face and full, sweet lips. The breeze from the lake was blowing little wisps of her hair around in a way that made him want to reach over and tuck her hair behind her ear. An inappropriate gesture, to be sure. But he clenched his fists to avoid making a fool of himself.

"Hi," he said awkwardly, helping her with her chair. *Business,* he reminded himself. *Strictly business.*

"Wow," she said, sitting down. She stared at him, mouth open. He knew that some women found him good-looking, but what on earth was she…

His hand flew to his chin. "Oh. I shaved."

"You certainly did." She flashed him a wry smile as she sat there assessing him, her elbows propped on the table, her index finger drawing imaginary circles around his face. "You have cheekbones." She leaned ever closer. "And dimples! *Two* of them."

He felt himself blush—and he never blushed. What was *wrong* with him?

She laughed. "I thought you didn't care what anybody thought about that beard."

He didn't. He was used to the double takes and the sidelong glances and even outright flirtatious come-hither looks. But

Maggie's perusal of him was unsettling in a way he preferred not to think about.

"Yeah, well, I'm still old enough to care what my mother thinks. And if I go back home to Greenwich looking like that, she may not let me in the house." Besides, he needed one family member on his side, and it sure wasn't going to be his father.

"Well, I must admit," she said, "you do look—different."

"More civilized?" He stroked his chin. His natural charm was kicking in. Maybe it was okay to turn it on just a bit.

The disconcerted look she suddenly shot him said *oh no, not at all,* even as she calmly said, "Of course." But their gazes tangled and held for a long instant until she finally flicked her attention to her phone.

Somehow that pleased him that she seemed just a little…flustered. He discounted for the hundredth time the possibility of getting involved with her. Reminded himself of her son and her neuroses and then sat a little farther back in his chair. As if that small distance would make him immune to her.

Too late, a little voice inside his head scolded.

No, it was not, he argued with the voice. It was just his current state of abstinence making him act a little irrationally. He had to get it together and keep his distance, even if they had this…*thing* going on.

Something caught his eye. Her purse, a small shoulder bag, sat on the table, a daisy threaded through the zipper handle. A memory suddenly flitted though his mind. *His botched wedding.* In a panic, he'd run outside the church into a little garden and sat down, trying to breathe some air into his lungs, which suddenly seemed encased in iron. There were clusters of daisies all around, bunches and bunches of them. He found himself surrounded by their simple, pure whiteness. The flowers had struck him in an odd way—made him suddenly realize that he'd lost track of every simple, good thing in life.

Suddenly, he was up and leaving the garden, the church, Anika, and all his friends and family. Those damn daisies had made him run.

Maggie noticed him staring at the wilty flower. She cleared her throat, pulling him out of his fog. "My son," she explained. "He knows I love daisies, and he did that. Anyway," she said, looking around nervously. "Where's Sam?"

He forced his gaze from the flower, but looking at her wasn't any less disconcerting. "She went to sit up front. And Bella and Roman are over there in the corner." He saw a tiny crease of worry appear between her pretty brows as she realized they'd be alone for a while. "I'm afraid you're stuck with me. Want some wine?"

"Sure, I'd love some."

He scanned the wine menu. "What's your favorite?"

"Oh, I'm not fussy." She started to laugh.

He frowned. "Did I just say something funny?"

Maggie leaned over the table toward him. When she did, the scent of sweet-smelling woman hit him full force. "When your family owns the local watering hole, it's all about the beer," she said. "I don't know very much about wine. When Corey died, my best friends showed up with a giant jug of it. I couldn't for the life of me tell you the bouquet, the body, the finish, or whatever, but it was just the right thing." She fidgeted her fingers on the table. "I probably shouldn't have said that. When I get nervous, my mouth runs. Sorry."

"In the social circles I grew up in, it was kind of a necessity to know how to order wine. Frankly, I'm more of a beer guy too."

The waiter appeared, a young guy in his mid-twenties. Drew glanced at Maggie. "So what will it be?"

"I'm up for trying something different," she said with a shrug.

He turned to the waiter. "What are your dessert specials?"

"Chocolate cake, tiramisu, and a mean strawberry cheesecake."

He looked over at her. Raised a brow in question.

"Oh, really, Drew," Maggie protested. "That's not nec—"

He set aside the wine list. "Come on. I'll pick the wine if you pick the dessert."

"Fine," she relented. "I'm a cheesecake girl all the way."

"All right, then." He grinned, oddly pleased. "We'll have a bottle of your Riesling with the strawberry cheesecake."

"It must be a special occasion," the waiter said.

"Oh, we're not a couple," Maggie said as Drew snapped the menu shut and handed it to the waiter, who nodded and took off. "How expensive was that?" she asked, back to protest mode. "Really, you didn't have to…"

Now it was his turn to lean toward her. "There's no reason for us to be enemies."

"If you think I'm going to get drunk and high on sugar and say yes about your wedding, you're absolutely wrong," she said, a smile tugging at her lips.

"I intend to get you to say yes *before* you get drunk."

"There will be no drunk. I'm sorry, Drew. I just don't think I could be of much help to you. So maybe you'd better cancel the bottle."

"I never cancel good wine." The waiter returned, opened the bottle, and poured some for Drew to taste. "Nice," he said. Then he poured some for Maggie, and she took a sip.

Out of the corner of his eye, Drew could see his brothers standing together, looking at him and poking each other in the ribs. Roman pointed to Maggie and gave a big thumbs-up sign and Lukas gave him a high five. They were both grinning.

Idiots.

"Wow. This is amazing." Maggie smiled the smile of someone who is sort of thrilled—and who probably needed to get out more. Still, it was one hell of a smile, and it warmed him to the core. Or maybe that was the expensive wine. As for what she'd just said—no, again—he tried to disguise his disappointment. Or desperation. He racked his brain—what could he do to sweeten the pot? "If it's the money…"

She set down her glass. "Please don't think I'm playing coy for more money. I'm just not the best woman for the job. The whole idea of happy people celebrating at a wedding—I don't want to be a Debbie Downer or anything, but sometimes weddings are a little tough for me."

"Believe me, the only happy people at this wedding will be the ones who've been drinking." He held up his glass in salute to her and sipped.

She laughed. It was a little snorty.

"Can I ask you a question?" he asked.

She shot him a wary look. "Sure? I mean, I think so."

"Are you afraid I'm going to make a move on you?"

Surprisingly, she looked him dead in the eyes, pausing carefully before she answered. "Maybe. But if you are, I'd have to say I'm not interested."

He pretended relief, but an odd sense of disappointment rifled through him.

"It's nothing personal," she said. "Just that you'd be the worst person to get involved with. After we broke up, imagine how awkward it would be for the rest of our lives—all those birthday parties, picnics, family events…"

"Yet you're wanting to have a fling with the fireman."

"The fireman isn't my good friend's brother-in-law."

"Forget that. Are you saying the fireman is better fling material than I am?"

She frowned. "In what way?"

He paused. She was right, of course. About everything. He'd thought the same thing—that anything between them was too complicated for all those same reasons and more. Still, he couldn't resist riling her up. "Hotness scale."

She sat back and rolled her eyes. "I can't believe this. You're asking me to rate your hotness compared to Greg? He was Mr. July on the charity calendar."

Drew tsked and rubbed his chin. "And here I shaved my beard, only to be insulted."

"Surely you must know you're an attractive man. That has nothing—"

He stared right at those swimming-pool-blue eyes of hers and cut to the chase. "I think you don't want to come away with me for the weekend because you're afraid something might happen between us." There, he'd said it. The truth. Or maybe he was just voicing what *he* was afraid of.

She snorted for real this time and flicked her wrist. "Oh pu-lease."

"Some women wouldn't be so immune to my charms."

"You mean to tell me you've been using your charms on me all along, and I haven't even known it?"

"Trust me, if I were doing that, you'd know it."

"Well, why haven't you been?"

He should have. But for some reason, he'd stupidly chosen to play it honest with her. Well, as honest as he could go without revealing what a nightmare this wedding really was.

"Because I don't believe in love or soul mates, and you clearly do, no matter what you say about wanting a fling. So that's the real reason you have nothing to worry about. And actually, I was about to resort to charm next."

"Save the charm for someone it will work on. And don't even pretend to know what I want as far as men go. And about your family—you're thinking I can fix something that's impossible to fix."

He fidgeted a little. It was clear she was not going to say yes. In a last-ditch effort, he was going to have to pull out all the stops. That meant drilling down deep and scraping the bone. And it was going to be painful. He took a big breath and jumped in. "My father wanted to groom me for the CEO position of his company over my brother, who's his biological son."

He had her full attention now. "Why?"

"Because he felt I had more talent. That was the problem, *is* the problem between my brother and me. I got better grades. I had more friends. I did better at sports. This was the icing on the cake."

"You obviously didn't take the job. What happened?"

What happened was that he'd left his family's company for his MBA, and while he was gone, Sondra had fallen in love with his brother. So when his father had suggested marrying Anika, he'd been too heartbroken to care. "My father was upset that I left the company, and to smooth things over, I did agree to marry Anika. The engagement with her was a business merger, right for all kinds of practical reasons. But at the very last second, I couldn't go through with it."

"Why?" she asked softly.

She was looking at him with compassion, which he hated. It was too close to pity. Something about her made him want to tell her the truth. How after Sondra left him for his brother, he didn't think he had any heart left to care about who he married. But he couldn't bare that much of his soul.

"Oh, don't think it had anything to do with romantic love. I know that disappoints you, but I can tell you up front I don't believe romantic love lasts. Anika and I simply weren't...well suited, and I finally realized that before I married her. Unfortunately, my timing was a bit off."

Suddenly, his loss seemed petty compared to hers. He hadn't married Sondra or had a child with her, and no one had died. His girlfriend had simply fallen in love with another man, who happened to be his brother. Life dealt one tough blows, but nothing about his life's disappointments seemed to be on the same scale as hers.

"The point is, my father is still pissed as hell at me. And he's displeased I'm working for Roman's brandy business and not with him. I want to make things right."

"How does your brother feel about this?"

How *did* Xander feel? Frankly, Drew had been so consumed pretending everything was all right in front of his brother that they'd never really discussed it. "My brother wants to run the company. It's been his dream. So you see, I had to step aside. It's better for everyone this way."

"Except what you did took you away from your brother and your father. You've exiled yourself."

Translation: he'd run away. What else could he have done? The situation had been intolerable. Watching his own brother with Sondra… "My presence was an interference."

"Have you talked with your father and brother since you left the wedding?"

"I went home for the holidays, but my father was in France with his girlfriend." Drew had been there Christmas morning, when Sondra opened a gift under the tree…a four-carat diamond.

Maggie blew out a breath. "Okay, then. I think I need more wine." She smiled and held out her glass.

He liked her style. She was quick and perceptive, but not pushy. It made him want to spill his guts even more, but that would scare her away for sure. So Drew poured more wine.

"I haven't even told you about my parents' ugly divorce and the fact that my mother and sister don't even want my father showing up at the wedding with his latest girlfriend." She looked a little worried, so he threw in some humor. "So you see, I'm going to be way too busy. There'll be absolutely no time to contemplate having a fling with you. Even if you *did* think I was cuter than the fireman."

She laughed. Gave him a little bit of the stink eye. "Okay, fine. I'll do it."

Yes. Mental fist pump time.

"I just hope I don't let you down as far as fixing your family."

"Honey, Sigmund Freud couldn't fix my family. But thanks." He sat back in his chair for the first time that night. "I just need someone who will pretend to be my girlfriend and who can maybe help calm things down a bit."

Maggie reached her hand across the table. "Let's shake on it," she said.

"Shake on it?" He had to take her hand, because it would've been impolite if he hadn't. But he didn't want to. Because it felt soft, like maybe how the rest of her would feel. Smooth. Warm. Yes, she did indeed have pretty hands.

"Drew?"

"What is it?"

"I said shake, not hold hands." She was smiling a little.

He pulled his hand away hurriedly. Cleared his throat. "Oh, well. I was just practicing."

One fine brow shot up. "Practicing?"

"Yeah. I mean, when we go to my house, we'll have to convince everyone we're dating."

"Isn't it enough I'm going as your date?"

"No one will trust you with any of the family secrets if they think you're just some woman I brought with me. We have to convince them we're…close."

"Yeah, sorry, but I'm just not into…"

He rushed to talk before she changed her mind. "Look, I've already told you that you don't have anything to worry about. And you've essentially told me the same. So we're good, right?" Even as he said the words, a strange stirring fluttered in his belly.

Liar, liar, the voice inside his head chanted.

The waiter set down a thick slab of creamy cheesecake topped with strawberries and drizzled with chocolate sauce.

"Okay, then. No worries?" He held up his glass.

"All right, then. No worries." She touched her glass to his, then took a sip.

He congratulated himself for his brilliant plan, and for getting her totally on board, even though he did have to spill his guts all over the table. Well, most of them, anyway.

She was the perfect person to bring home. Friendly and chipper, she'd totally win their hearts. More importantly, she'd distract them while he focused on surviving the wedding. Plus, she was a trained psychologist who maybe could work a little magic with his dysfunctional family, and then *voilà*, the weekend would be over and done.

He looked at her, her fork poised above the cheesecake, savoring the bite she'd just taken. Like she'd never tasted anything quite so delicious. She looked like no one had bought her wine and dessert for a long time, and he suddenly wanted to order up something else just so he could see that expression on her face again. Maggie Light. A different version, where her cloak of sorrow lifted and she seemed…different. Happier.

He'd been so intrigued by her that he hadn't noticed that Lukas had stopped singing, the lights had dimmed down, and the restaurant staff was starting to vacuum inside the building and sweep the deck. Suddenly the churning in his stomach was back, stronger than ever. For all the reasons Maggie was exactly the right person to bring along, there were a couple more that made her the wrongest person in the world.

He would just have to keep his attraction for her at bay. And no one needed to know about Sondra. There was no help for that anyway.

What could possibly go wrong?

CHAPTER 6

By the time Maggie opened the passenger door of her car in front of the Poulos family's palatial Greenwich estate the next Thursday afternoon, she was ready for a cigarette, even though she didn't smoke. But she was contemplating starting. Drew had been…not impolite but basically mute the whole way to Greenwich from Mirror Lake. Conversations she tried her best to sustain went the way of an overdone soufflé. Jokes died, quips flopped. She'd done her best to pull him out of his funk, but no luck there.

And this whole long-weekend thing was making her very, very nervous. Even calculating that she'd just made $418.75 on this drive didn't cheer her up. Finally, she turned to him as he stared up at the sprawling turreted gray brick mansion in front of them, which looked like something out of Regency England rather than Blue Blood Connecticut.

"Drew! Lighten up," she said, thunking him on the arm to force him out of his stupor. "This is a wedding, not a funeral."

His response was a glare followed by more silence.

She took a minute to assess him. His fingers were knuckled so tightly around the steering wheel that they were turning white. She didn't think it had anything to do with him driving her car. He'd wanted to take his BMW, but she'd asked if they could take her Honda Accord instead. It was just a little assurance that if things went south, she could have a way out. He hadn't seemed embarrassed and didn't even act like the animal crackers Griffin had shoved far down between the seat seams were an unusual occurrence.

But now she couldn't help feeling there was definitely something wrong. "I can't help but feel there's something you're not telling me," she said.

"It's just been a while since I've been home."

Was he that concerned about meeting his father again? Over the years, she'd developed a good feel for when clients were hiding something, and Drew had all the signs. The inability to sit still or meet her gaze. The peculiar way he was acting.

And something else too. It had always disturbed her that he was fairly dispassionate whenever he mentioned Anika. He certainly didn't seem upset about their breakup. She feared something completely different was troubling him, and she wanted to know what it was before she got out of the car and stepped into it ankle-deep.

"Drew, I wish you'd confide in me, if for the only reason that I might be able to help out. You know I would never tell—"

"I'm fine," he said, flashing her a smile that didn't meet his eyes.

Just then a tall, willowy young woman with long dark hair ran up to the car. "You're home!" she said, opening Drew's door and launching herself at him as soon as he had a chance to step out.

Maggie got out of the car and walked around in time to see Drew whoop and lift her and swing her around. It was the most exuberant Maggie had ever seen him. When he finally let her down, he gave her ponytail a tug and said, "Maggie, this is Christina, my baby sister. Chrissy's premed at Vassar. She's got a 4.0. But she doesn't like to brag. That's why I get to do it for her."

Christina rolled her eyes at her brother's antics and hugged Maggie warmly.

"Everyone's by the pool," Christina said. "We've been waiting for you. Come on."

Christina linked arms with her brother. Maggie was about to ask if they should bring their luggage when a short-cut little black-and-tan Yorkie dog shot out of the house and bounded down the driveway, followed by a thin older man in a black suit. "Get over here, you mutt," he said in a British aristocratic accent. "So sorry, sir. Genevieve usually has better manners…"

"Genny!" Drew said as he bent down and the dog tackled him with kisses. "Oh, I've missed you. There's my good girl."

The dog was clearly bonkers about him. It was now lying on the cement, belly up, reveling in the tummy rubs Drew was bestowing on it while its tiny tail was doing quarter time against the pavement. Drew talked incessantly to the dog in a voice unlike anything she'd ever heard come out of a grown man's mouth. "You are the sweetest girl! Yes, you are! Daddy missed you!"

Wow. Was this the cool, nerves-of-steel man who barely batted an eyelash over anything? He was usually so cautious and reserved about his feelings that this behavior was oddly reassuring. It showed her he was capable of loving…his sister and, apparently, a little dog.

Maybe she didn't want to know that. It made him even more appealing. Another reason this weekend was a very bad lapse of judgment. This side of Drew was…charismatic. Spellbinding. Fun. And it raised so many questions in her mind about who he really was—and it was not the Ted Kaczynski type she'd originally thought.

"Pardon me, madam," the black-suited man said, "I'm happy to collect your things, as well as move your vehicle to the family's private lot."

Drew stood up and dusted off his shorts. He was grinning widely. "That would be excellent, Arthur." Drew patted the man on the back. "Great to see you," he said. "This is my friend, Maggie. Maggie, Arty."

Maggie felt like she'd just walked onto the set of *Downton Abbey*. She offered the man her hand, but he simply nodded, forcing her to make an awkward gesture halfway between a bow and a knee bend because she had absolutely no clue what the proper etiquette was about greeting a butler.

Drew thanked him and tugged her away by the arm. "Was that a…curtsey?" he asked close to her ear.

Her face bloomed with heat. Oh God, she was doing the wrong thing already, and she hadn't even met his parents yet.

Somehow, in the middle of her internal freak-out, Drew reached out and took her hand, which actually made her nerves worse but better too, if that made any sense. Even though he *was* just doing it for show.

The dog sniffed her feet delicately, like it was sniffing gourmet sausages. She bent down to pet it, but it growled and trotted away to follow closely at Drew's heels.

Christina laughed. "Genny's always been very possessive of Drew."

Yes, she completely saw that.

"Give Arty your keys," Drew said. "He'll take care of your car."

Maggie made sure to smile as she turned them over, trying not to look like she was surrendering her only means of escape. So the dog was a little weird. At least his sister seemed normal. So Maggie smiled politely and followed Drew. Mostly because he was tugging on her hand and she had no choice.

"Is that the family dog? It seems really attached to you," Maggie said as the thing scampered along at Drew's ankles.

"Yeah. I've really missed her."

"I've never seen you so enthused about anything. Not even food."

"On to meet the rest of the family," he said, his mouth lifting up in a smile. At least the dog seemed to put him in a better mood. She'd have to remember that if things got traumatizing. Bring on the dog.

"Did you...grow up here?" she asked, trying to look around without her tongue lolling about.

"Yep. I was adopted when I was six," he said. "Frankly, I don't remember much before then, but from what I've heard from Roman and Lukas, that's probably a good thing."

Drew followed Arthur into the massive entry that spanned the length of the house and opened to a great room with a glass wall of windows. The view outside was bucolic, all rolling hills and trees, and appeared to be right in line with the illusion that they were somewhere in the middle of rural England.

Maggie half expected a bunch of aristocrats to gallop by on horseback with polo sticks. Massive antique tapestries hung from the walls, depicting knights and, yes, there it was, a foxhunting scene on one of them. A far cry from her parents' simple mid-century home in the burbs. They loved sitting on the little deck her dad had built a few years back that looked out over a few spindly maples and Mr. Shamansky's bright red shed. In fact, their entire backyard could fit right into this massive foyer.

Out they went through heavy, ancient-looking double doors that opened onto an immaculately groomed stone patio that seemed to span the entire back of the house. After a few steps down and around English-style gardens full of blooming flowers and topiaries and shaped miniature hedges, they arrived at a large infinity-edge swimming pool.

A tall, elegant-looking woman in a skirt and high heels stood near a table on the poolside patio, wearing a headset and talking on the phone. "I don't care what the board says, dammit, I'm in charge. And I'm not letting our new yogurt blends go to market with pictures of cows on the containers. Cows are *not* sexy marketing. Unless you're Chick-Fil-A."

His mother was, of course, talking about the family company, AcroPoulos Yogurt, Dannon's main competitor. She remembered Drew mentioning that his mother was the head of marketing.

"Something's come up." Drew's mother said into her phone. She ended the call and stepped forward to hug her son.

"Mother," Drew said, hugging his mother and kissing her on the cheek. His mom reciprocated with a side hug, which was a little weak, if you asked Maggie, the kind you give when you don't want to get your makeup or hairdo messed up. That was the first warning sign.

The second was that Drew hadn't called his mother *Mom*. The only time she or Scott had ever called their parents "Mother" or "Father" was as irritable teenagers: nothing like a cold hard stare and a well-articulated *Mother* to express just how uncool her mom was. But, to be fair, her own parents were teddy bears. They hugged indiscriminately and often. It was impossible not to be affectionate back.

"Maggie, my mother, Cecilia."

Drew flashed Maggie a triple-wattage smile, effectively making her forget all about his mother. Oh, he was a handsome devil, with those gypsy-dark eyes and those dimples! She practically swooned. Being on the receiving end of that smile—man oh man, it was something. Like stepping out of a plane in January in Key West when you've just touched down from Minnesota. And right now, a heat wave was sweeping through her. Pretending to date him probably wasn't the best idea if it was going to mess with her head *or* her body. And it didn't help that he still wasn't letting go of her hand.

Finally, she got hold of the sense to tug it away and shake his mother's.

"Drew tells me you're a psychologist," Cecilia said. "Where did you do your training?"

"University of Connecticut." Maggie felt like she was on a damn job interview.

"Not an Ivy," Cecilia said to her son with a regretful sigh, while perusing her with the hawkeyed gaze of a military sergeant. "But it'll do."

Well, guess I didn't get that job, boss. Maggie had just decided to switch tactics and tell Mrs. Poulos how beautiful her home—er, mansion? estate?—was when the clatter of high heels on cement sounded behind them. A man a little shorter and stouter than Drew approached, on his arm a beautiful woman with white-blonde hair, big gold earrings, and a flowing, multicolored maxi dress. Maggie, in her simple navy sundress and flat sandals, felt like Shirley Temple standing next to a woman ready for an elegant evening out on the yacht with Bond.

"Hey, bro," the man said, slapping Drew on the back. Drew's brother had the look of someone who lifted a lot of weights. In fact, he playfully squeezed Drew's biceps and then did a curl or two to show off his own. That struck Maggie as a little odd, but not quite as odd as the tiny spouting whales all over his pristine white pants, which made him look more like a retired businessman headed for the golf course than a young man in his prime.

Drew hugged him, then turned to Maggie with introductions. "This is my older brother Xander and his fiancée…Sondra." He hesitated just a little bit before saying her name. Oh, it wasn't really even noticeable. But still, for some reason that little pause put Maggie on guard.

That and the expression in his eyes. Soft, wistful…painful. It lasted only a moment, but Maggie *noticed* it. And it chilled her to the bone.

"Hi there," Sondra said, extending her hand politely to Maggie. Even with her legs hidden by her dress, Maggie sensed they were tanned, lean, and long. Sondra was...beautiful.

It was crazy, she knew, but something just seemed off. Drew's posture had suddenly become a bit too straight. And Sondra's smile a little too wide. It was as if a sudden awkwardness infused the air. Probably just Maggie's usual nerves doing what they did, buzzing and making her more anxious than usual.

Sondra turned to Drew. "You look fantastic," she said, her eyes round and doe-eyed. "I've been so worried about you."

"No need to be worried, Sondra. I'm fine," Drew said tersely. "Great, actually. Couldn't be better."

Just then, the little dog marched up to Sondra and began growling, barking, and jumping up and down—Armageddon barking.

"Genny! Down, girl!" Drew said sternly. But the dog continued to have a complete doggie freak-out.

Finally, Sondra, who was half hiding behind Xander, said, "Can this dog please get put in the house, Cecilia?"

"Of course, dear," Cecilia said. Xander ended up picking up the dog and handing the furry bundle over to Christina, who carted her off, still growling and raising a ruckus.

"That's why your father told you never to get a rescue dog," Sondra said to Drew, but she looked at Maggie as she straightened her dress. "With that kind of background, you just don't know what you've got."

Sometimes Maggie over-read things, especially when she was nervous, but Sondra couldn't possibly be insinuating that Maggie had a questionable background? She might not have gone to Harvard or Yale, but she was 100 percent Irish! So there. And did Sondra even realize she'd unknowingly just insulted Drew too?

"Drew, I'm so glad you've found someone," Sondra said, kissing Drew on the cheek. "Now my wedding day can be complete, knowing you're happy." She turned to her fiancé. "Isn't that right, Xander?"

In response, Xander reached over and planted a possessive kiss on Sondra's lips. "Anything that makes you happy makes me happy too, sweetheart."

Aw, that was sweet. There was so much happiness going around, Maggie didn't know what to do. But Drew's face had paled, and he was scowling a little. Actually, he was kind of trying to smile, but the scowl was winning.

Suddenly, Drew wrapped an arm around Maggie's shoulders. Which threw her a little. Because he was big. And strong. And he smelled nice. And being held by him felt really—good.

Maggie really had to take care of this lack-of-man problem because, geez, one simple touch set her entire body to humming. Which, while embarrassing, wasn't really surprising, because, well, you know, *three years*. And a half.

Unfortunately, Drew didn't stop with just holding her close. "I'm really lucky to have found Maggie," he said, staring intently into her eyes. The next thing Maggie knew, he'd reached over and placed his mouth over hers.

It wasn't just a kiss. Or a peck. No, he'd gone straight for the kill, slowly, languorously placing his beautiful full lips over hers. Her traitorous body instantly turned to butter as his hands circled her waist and he pulled her flush against him.

And oh, the man could kiss! He was not in a rush, nor did he have an ounce of shame in front of his entire family as he slid his lips over hers, finally nipping gently at her lower lip. Releasing her slowly.

She expected to see his same, usual calm and cool demeanor. With a hint of sarcasm, of mischief. Or at least a wink to remind her of the game.

Trouble was, all her thoughts had flown. She had to focus on not going to ground in an amorphous heap. Or gazing stupidly into his eyes like she was some smitten fool. Because that kiss…that kiss had done things to her. Terrible, awful, incredible things. Like sending an electric current zipping through her body, awakening parts unknown.

Drew stared at her strangely. For once, the mask of careless confidence he wore so well was gone, and in its place was confusion. Maybe even a faint tinge of horror. *Just like her.*

Xander came up to them then and started talking with Drew. It gave Maggie a chance to step away for a second to pretend to admire the botanical-center-quality gardens while she struggled to get it together. Vaguely, she could hear Sondra discussing honeymoon destinations—they'd considered Bora Bora, she said, Indonesia, South Africa…

Cecilia, unfortunately, found her as she was attempting to gather her wits. "Drew *has* made you aware of his…past history with the bride, hasn't he, dear?"

"Of course, yes," she said, not having a clue what Cecilia was talking about. Frankly, she didn't have a clue about much of anything at the moment. "We have no secrets."

"We almost made it to Galapagos that one time, remember?" Sondra said, lightly fingering Drew's shirt, looking at him with her big doe eyes.

Maggie bit back the words that suddenly bubbled to her lips: *Hands. Off.*

Galapa—what? Maggie's stomach did a nosedive. Because the truth suddenly dawned. She glanced at Drew. His gaze was downcast…and his cheeks held color. Color! Yes, and for a guy with Greek heritage and permanent five-o'clock shadow, that was one hell of a blush. Worse, he was subtly shifting his weight from one foot to another. Maggie knew about body language. She observed it in her clients every day. And shiftiness was not a good thing, no sirree.

That could mean only one thing: she really was in it ankle-deep. And Oh. My. God. He'd slept with Sondra. Hopefully *before* she became his brother's fiancée, but who knew? She didn't know this man at all, not really.

Behavior like that violated the code of brothers, didn't it?

Drew's apprehension suddenly became explainable. His silence. The odd way he looked at Sondra. Even the way Xander seemed to hover over his fiancée. It all became as crystal clear as the lake back home on a thoroughly sunny day.

My God, Drew was still in love with her! That explained everything—his moodiness, his discomfort, his need to have Maggie here as a cover…

Maggie sucked in a sharp breath. He'd gotten her here, all right…by omitting one hell of a whopper of truth. The most important truth of all…that he'd been in love with his brother's fiancée. And maybe he still was.

Other unpleasant feelings stirred too. She'd thought they'd had some measure of trust between them, but clearly, she was wrong.

"Um, excuse me, Drew," Maggie said, tapping him on the shoulder, "but can we talk for a sec…over there?" She tilted her head to a garden path just off the patio, out of earshot of the others.

He shot her a look…of concern or guilt, she wasn't sure, but whatever it was, she knew one thing: ankle-deep was an underestimation. She'd have to change that body part to her neck. And then she'd have to wring his.

CHAPTER 7

Maggie crossed her arms. Did her best to shake off the residual fog created by his kiss. They were standing somewhere in the maze of the English garden, Drew across from her, hands in his pockets. With the backdrop of the infinity pool stretching behind him, he looked like a *GQ* model posing on a palatial estate. She forced herself not to dwell on his distracting good looks that made her think more of kissing him than having it out with him. "You led me here under false pretenses."

He shot her a look. A one-brow-raised, don't-go-there look.

Oh, she was going there, all right.

"You said your *family* was messed up."

"They are messed up," he said, as if she was comprehending at grade school level.

She threw up her hands. "You implied that the messed-up part didn't include *you*."

He stabbed her with a look. She could practically see his neck hairs bristling.

"Just tell me the truth, Drew. Was it a one-time thing, or more?"

"Was it a—" His brows knit down into a deep, dark frown—dammit, how could he even look hot frowning?—but then he smiled. No, more than smiled—he laughed. The laugh increased until he was holding his stomach and his eyes actually started watering. Tiny little lines were forming around his eyes that were so appealing, she almost forgot how pissed off she was.

She was not going to fall for those little crinkles or anything about him. His brother's girlfriend, really! "What's so funny?" she asked, hands on hips.

"My God, you actually think I tried to steal my brother's girlfriend."

"I'm trying not to judge here, all right?" But he did leave poor Anika at the altar, didn't he? Who knew what else the man was capable of?

He stepped forward until he was inches from her face. And oh, those deep brown eyes were even more startling and gorgeous when he was angry. They seemed incapable of such deception, but what did she really know about men? Corey hadn't possessed a dishonest bone in his body.

Drew tapped her bluntly on the sternum. His brows dipped farther into a big, angry V.

"Try four years. We dated all through college."

Her mouth dropped open. "Wait. You actually had a relationship for four years?"

One glance told her everything he'd been hiding. For once, there were no saucy retorts, no teasing quips. His eyes said everything he couldn't say. He'd loved Sondra. And maybe he still did.

But if Sondra had been Drew's long-time girlfriend, how on earth did she end up with Xander?

Oh God. Maggie didn't really want to know.

There was much more going on under his easygoing sarcasm, and for the first time, she saw it all clearly.

He sighed—softly, almost inaudibly—the sigh of a man who'd gotten his heart broken. But by his own brother? She couldn't even imagine.

"After college, I started working in my father's company, but I left to get my MBA, and she fell in love with Xander."

"After you two broke up?" Maggie asked.

"No, actually. He was the reason she dumped me."

"Oh," Maggie said, her anger deflating as suddenly as a popped balloon. "I'm so sorry." She was sorry, for his heartbreak. But it was hard to muster enough steam to truly be upset. Yet what did she know of Sondra, except for first impressions? She supposed it was the fact that Maggie prided herself on being a good judge of character, something that helped her every day in her job. Based on the not so subtle glances and the inappropriate touching, she would place Sondra in the *not good enough* category as far as Drew was concerned. Not to mention she'd dumped him for his own brother.

Still, Maggie spoke the language of loss. And it seemed from the way Drew was acting that this one was so painful, he couldn't even bring himself to discuss it. If that was the case, she could probably forgive him for not telling her until now. "And I'm sorry I misjudged you."

He narrowed his gaze and looked like he was about to say something, but he stopped and seemed to reconsider before speaking again. "I should've told you everything. I don't want you to think I brought you here to take advantage of you. It was more—this thing with Sondra isn't the issue here. It's about my family getting through this wedding. And to be honest, you seemed like the perfect person to get them to stop worrying about me. You're intelligent and pretty. It was a no-brainer."

Maggie sucked in a breath of air. Pretty! He'd called her pretty. Her heart jumped, despite her not wanting that *at all*. She tried to focus on how sad she felt for him. She also believed what he'd just said, that he didn't want this weekend to be about him. Since she knew he'd spent the past year and a half in Mirror Lake by himself, he seemed the type to shoulder things on his own.

"Now that you know everything," he said, "we can move forward with the weekend. If you're willing, that is."

That's it? She had a million questions! Wasn't he upset at all with his brother? And Sondra? How could he still look at Sondra with that sad-puppy expression when he thought no one was looking, after the crappy thing she'd done? Didn't he want to punch someone, punch the universe for dealing him this awful hand?

He began to walk back to the patio. But then she tugged at his shirt until he stopped in the middle of the manicured path. "Wait a minute. Your brother and your ex-girlfriend get together, and you just…namaste it? You're okay with it?"

He shrugged, but he didn't make eye contact. "It's no one's fault. It just happened."

Judging by the way a tiny muscle in his jaw was vibrating, and the fact that his fists were clenched lockjaw tight, he certainly didn't look okay.

His gaze flicked up. "So will you help me?"

Up until this moment, she'd never seen anything except his glossy, smiley, devil-may-care surface. She'd never seen him *vulnerable*. And she'd never, ever thought of him as someone who was hurting.

Now she saw him simply as a heartbroken man who loved his brother enough to do the right thing.

A pox on Sondra and his brother and anyone else who would cause such havoc in his life and in his family.

One thing was perfectly clear. Sondra did not deserve him. He needed to stop wasting his time over her, that was for sure.

Part of her realized this was getting too personal. She wasn't sure where this possessive urge came from, that made her know down to her core that she'd do everything in her power to help him through this heinous weekend. "Yes, I'll help you," she said with a little smile.

He smiled back. In his eyes, she saw relief, and that stirred something deep within her.

"Thanks, Maggie," he said, and reached over and kissed her on the forehead.

A simple forehead kiss, little more than a peck, really, as he held her briefly by the shoulders. Yet it seared clear through her, all the way down to her toes, in much the same way as his earlier, much more passionate kiss on the patio.

For the first time, she'd caught a glimpse of the man Drew Poulos really was. And she was beginning to like him way too much.

As Drew sat with Maggie and his family around the fire pit after dinner, he felt like he was living his very own, specially-made-for-him brand of hell. Maggie was right. He *was* pissed. Maybe he should stop pushing down all his bad feelings and deal with them in some way, but he had no idea how. He wished he were back in Mirror Lake, hanging out, having a beer with his brothers, where life was simpler and the expectations on him would not be so high. Running away from his problems had been so much easier.

"So we're going to Santorini for our honeymoon," Sondra said. "It's going to be so romantic." She curled into Xander and nuzzled his neck. Drew tried not to look, but the image of Sondra looking adoringly into his brother's eyes stuck even after he turned his gaze elsewhere. He could always read his older brother like a book, and it was clear Xander was over the moon in love with Sondra.

Xander had protected him tooth and nail when they were

boys, when Drew was the scrawny, undernourished adopted kid, and he knew that however this effed-up situation had developed, Xander would never intentionally hurt him. Sondra, on the other hand, kept eyeing him when she thought he wasn't looking, and it was making him uncomfortable.

She probably had more things to say to him like she had when they'd broken up. She'd accused him of not being able to express his feelings. Not sharing enough. But at least he hadn't cheated on her while they were apart like she had with his brother.

When he'd fallen in love with her, they'd been kids, away at college for the first time. Her father had just declared bankruptcy of his bath products company, and her family was still reeling from that. Drew supposed they'd forged a kinship—an outsider status both of them shared, her from being suddenly ostracized from Greenwich society and him from never quite fitting into the role his father expected him to play in his empire.

He'd never been the most open or expressive person. He kept things inside. Avoided conflict. That was part of the reason why he'd eaten through his feelings after his wedding debacle last year.

Maybe swallowing his feelings had been the way he'd survived being separated from his biological brothers so long ago. But he wasn't a psychologist, what did he know?

Looking at Maggie didn't help his discomfort. Her eyes were filled with the one thing he could not take: pity. It was bad enough he'd been forced to tell her the truth, thanks to his mother, who'd thrown him under the bus.

"Oh, I'd love to see the Greek isles," Maggie said, moving a little closer to Drew until their thighs were touching. Her leg was very smooth against his, and he felt a jolt of attraction from the contact. Frankly, he was grateful for the distraction.

It proved he wasn't dead yet, that he could still feel something other than anger through this whole debacle. Although feeling it for Maggie was not a good idea. "We've got a little romantic trip planned too, don't we, sweetheart?" she said, running her fingers lightly up his thigh. His mother's brows shot up.

Drew gave Maggie a sideways glance. Tried to sit up straighter, but she clung like a barnacle to his side. What was she up to? And was she going to get him back for that kiss, which he'd meant to be a simple distraction, an impulse, but had blossomed into something else entirely? He'd chalked it up to living like a hermit for the past year and a half. Lack of sex was catching up to him in a bad way. He vowed from now on to keep their pretend displays of affection to the bare minimum.

"He's so modest," Maggie said, waving her hand. "I'll tell you. We're going to drive the California coast, Highway One. All the way from San Diego to San Francisco."

"You'll have to stay at the Hotel Del," Christina said. "Marilyn Monroe stayed there."

"We've already got a suite booked." Maggie cast him an adoring look and hooked her arm through his. Then just to seal the deal, she leaned in very close and nuzzled his ear. Actually, she did more than that. She licked it.

His eyes widened in genuine alarm, and he jumped a little in his seat.

Holy shit, she'd licked his *ear*. And, God help him, he'd *liked* it.

His mother sat forward in her chair, incredulous. Sondra coughed. Christina hid a grin behind her drink. Only Xander seemed oblivious.

Maggie went on, her tone perfectly serious. "Drew knew my birthday was coming, and I've never been to California. What a great guy, huh?" She beamed a big smile at him. He smiled back but wondered if she could read eyes. Because his were saying that he wanted to toss her over his shoulder and throw her into the damn pool.

She wasn't dissuaded. She ran her hand over his cheek. That hand was soft too, and it felt amazing to be touched like that. And there was that tantalizing smell again, something clean and fresh and light—lemony. It suited her. "I knew from the moment I saw his amazing beard that we were meant to be."

Sondra laughed. "Beard? Drew, you've never had a beard in all the years I've known you."

"Well, he was exploring his wild side, weren't you, honey? And you all have heard what they say about Greek guys, right?"

"No, I haven't at all," Cecilia said.

"That the amount of hair they have correlates with the size of their…"

Oh God, please, no, she was not going there. "Okay, um, Maggie dear," Drew said quickly, pulling her hand off his face and kissing it, anything to get her to stop touching him. "Thanks for sharing, but no one wants to know about our—relationship."

His mother's usually placid face blanched. Christina outright giggled. Sondra looked shocked. He really was going to toss Maggie in the pool.

"Well, I certainly do," Christina said enthusiastically. "Drew, how did you know Maggie was the one? You two look so in love."

He wasn't quite sure how Christina would get that impression, except that she was a hopeless romantic and very young. Without thinking, he said, "She broke up a bar brawl."

Xander looked Maggie over. "Why, you barely weigh enough to break up a couple of toddlers fighting,"

Sondra shot him a dirty look. "She definitely weighs enough."

"I didn't physically break them up," Maggie said. "I appealed to their common sense."

Maggie was absentmindedly kneading Drew's fingers, and he wished she would stop, because despite all his discomfort, it was turning him on. And making him unable to concentrate on whatever the hell conversation he was trying to make.

"And Maggie," Sondra said. "What first attracted you to Drew?"

Maggie pulled her hand away, which left him with a pins-and-needles sensation that spread up his arm and into his chest. Was this what a heart attack felt like? Because it certainly was uncomfortable.

"I admit it," Maggie said. "It was pure, raw attraction at first sight." She gave him a loving glance.

He felt nervous. Frankly, he was terrified she was going to lick his ear again. Or something worse he could only imagine.

"Well, honey," Maggie said, glancing at her watch, "I'm sure you and your brother and sister have a lot of catching up to do. It's getting late, and I think I'm going to excuse myself."

"I can show you to your room," Christina said.

"That would be nice. Thanks," Maggie said, flashing a charming smile. He had to admit, she was entertaining. Funny. Easy to like. And she definitely played the part well, even if the ear lick was a little out of control. Maybe things were going to be okay after all.

Maggie said her goodbyes. When she turned to Drew to plant a kiss on his cheek, she suddenly turned her head so that her mouth landed directly on his.

The warm softness of her lips on his shocked him for a moment. Got him to thinking *Oh no, not again*. But then she leaned into him, coiling her hand loosely around his neck, and before he knew it, his lips adjusted to hers, to the delicious feel of her, and he was lost.

She went to pull back, end the kiss, but he circled her waist and tugged her closer, smiling against her lips. Then he went back in for another, pressing his lips against hers, opening her mouth with his, and taking charge.

But kisses are funny sometimes, and this one was like a runaway train. Because he forgot about where he was, and the misery of watching his brother's happiness, and even his mother being there, until all that existed was that kiss. He was addicted to the sweet taste of her, the silky brush of her hair as he cupped her cheek, the way her curves melted into him.

Somehow, by the time his mother finally cleared her throat, he found he'd tangled his hand in Maggie's hair and his tongue had just made its way to slide against hers. He barely had enough sense left to break apart.

"Drew, stay here and visit," his mother said from behind him, patting him firmly on the shoulder. "Come with me, Maggie."

"My room. Yes! Of course," Maggie said, standing up fast. A little too fast, because Drew had to reach out and grab her hand to steady her.

"Well, good night, everybody!" she said cheerily as she slowly backed away and followed his mother away from the pool. From her uncertain steps, her overly cheery demeanor, and the way she avoided his gaze, he knew exactly how she felt.

He too was dizzy. Discombobulated. Out of breath. And wondering what the hell had just happened.

CHAPTER 8

"Look," Cecilia said as she kept up a brisk clip across the yard back to the house, forcing Maggie to half jog to keep up, "you're very pretty and are clearly an intelligent young woman, and Drew is quite smitten with you. So I'm going to be honest with you. I hope you're not out to use my son."

Maybe Cecilia thought she was an opportunist? Trying to land herself a billionaire? This woman clearly had no idea what her son looked like before he'd shaved that beard. Plus he'd been a runaway groom. Did she not understand what a flight risk he was?

Maggie looked her in the eye. "We're both professional women, Cecilia, and I can tell you that I most definitely do understand what's going on. I'm here to support Drew. I honestly don't have a secondary agenda." Well, maybe Mirror Lake Academy for Griffin, but honestly, things seemed so much more complicated now.

"Drew used to be so carefree and fun loving, but this thing with Sondra has changed him. He never would have agreed to marry Anika if he hadn't been so hurt by this. It's bad enough our family suffered through the divorce, but it's another thing entirely when the relationship between two of your children is strained to the breaking point. Not that Drew would ever admit that, but he and Xander barely talk anymore. This marriage…I just don't know what it's going to do to my sons."

Drew, fun loving? His stunning, sarcastic wit and easygoing personality overshadowed that characteristic for sure. Except when that obnoxious dog was around.

"Drew knows what he can handle," Maggie said, "and he's committed to doing everything it takes for Xander to have a wonderful wedding." And she'd do whatever was in her power to help him, but she didn't say that out loud.

Cecilia scanned her face, and for just the flash of a second, Maggie saw beneath her hardened veneer to something Maggie knew very well. The worry of a concerned mother. It somehow humanized her.

Then she was on the move again, making it clear their chat had ended. Her pace picked up as she ushered Maggie down yet another long hallway and stopped at an ancient-looking door in a rounded wall.

She opened the door, which was heavy and thick with a pointed arch. "There you go," Cecilia said. "Breakfast is at eight tomorrow. If you need anything, just ring for the staff."

"Thanks," Maggie managed, but Celia was already taking off, putting up a hand in a curt wave as she walked away down the hall.

Maggie pushed open the door the rest of the way and *wow*.

The room before her was round—like a medieval turret. Or rather, it *was* a turret. The walls were stuccoed, with dark beams running across the ceiling. Two crossed swords hung above the heavily carved bed, which was covered in a rich blue tapestry.

For a moment, she stood, her back against the door, taking in the over-the-top décor—which made her feel like she'd suddenly been dropped onto the set for *Game of Thrones*. There was a chandelier with fake candles, a full-size knight in armor, a massive shield hanging above the door, and a sculpture of a dragon breathing fire, which she instantly turned toward the wall—too reminiscent of the conversation she'd just had with Drew's mother.

Across from the bed sat a—well, there was no other way to describe it—a throne, probably a real one—elaborately carved, upholstered in red velvet. Maggie found herself wondering about her hosts. I mean, who decorated like this?

At last her eyes lit on a familiar object—her suitcase, resting between a massive set of arched windows and the bathroom.

Suddenly there was a scraping at the door. Maggie opened it to find Genevieve, pawing desperately to get in.

Maybe the dog wasn't so bad after all. Maybe it sensed, like her own dog, an eighty-pound hairy black mutt named Bear, that she needed a friend. "Well, hello there, Genevieve. So you decided to be friends after all, huh?"

She prepared to offer tons of affection, but the dog trotted right past her, sniffing affectedly, finally flopping down on a red velvet pillow next to the throne.

Wait, this was the dog's room? Maggie walked over to the shelves. Between the medieval flail and the battle axe, which looked like they were borrowed from the Smithsonian, she saw a photo of a handsome boy wearing a graduation gown and cap, sandwiched between his two parents. She picked it up to examine it more carefully. Drew was so young! His face was rounder, but still devastatingly handsome, even with a few visible teenage blemishes, and his hair was cropped in longer layers. He was grinning, his diploma tucked under his arm. Cecilia had a strained smile on her face, as did the man, who, with his meaty, muscular form, resembled Xander in appearance.

There were more pictures. Drew, even younger, with Xander, both boys holding up a giant fish. A more recent photo of Drew kissing Christina on the cheek as she wore a birthday crown and prepared to blow out candles on a cake. Drew and three college buddies holding up beers at some party.

The shelves were littered with trophies—for tennis, for debate team, and a big one that was so tall, it needed a special cutout in the bookcase...for being valedictorian of his high school class. Interesting, but hardly surprising.

She turned back around toward the dog. "He's not here, buddy." The dog turned her head to the side as if to say, *what do you* mean *he's not here?* "You're stuck with me tonight. Sorry."

So they'd given her Drew's old room, which now belonged to the dog. Great. She looked around for Drew's suitcase, wondering if his mother had decided to put them together, but praise Jesus, all she saw was her own.

"Okay, fine," she said, flipping her suitcase over so she could open it. "I don't mind sharing with you if you don't snore."

The dog yawned and laid her head down on the princess bed.

"Okay, whatever. I tried to make friends. And don't think you're coming in my bed tonight either. I only let four-year-olds who have bad dreams do that." Her words went unheeded, because the dog was already asleep.

Conscience clear after attempting to make peace with her roomie, Maggie opened her suitcase. That was when it dawned on her—she was alone, in this room, by herself. An exotic, slightly creepy one, but also one where a certain little four-year-old wouldn't be running in in the middle of the night after having a nightmare or waking her up because he was so excited to start his Saturday—or any day, really—at the butt crack of dawn. Not that she didn't adore her son, but it was kind of wonderful to be somewhere exotic and different without him—just for a couple of days. Because when had this happened to her before? Exactly never.

She blew out a big breath, feeling some of the tension that had accumulated over the past several hours dissipate a little. She'd take the museum-worthy décor, as long as she could be alone for a while.

The more she thought about it, the better it sounded. Several nights without household chores, work, or parental responsibilities... This could be sort of...wonderful. A massive armoire held a flat-screen television but she preferred a book, so she dug her e-reader out and placed it by her pillow. A little alone time would be just what she needed to wind down from this tense day and prepare for tomorrow. And try to forget about what had happened with Drew. The touching. The handholding. The *kiss*.

Oh, that kiss. She reached up and touched her lips, which appeared to be tingling in remembrance. Yep, the man could kiss, she'd give him that. What had started out as an impulsive stunt in front of his family—for Drew's sake, of course—had gotten a bit out of control. His lips had felt so wonderful gliding over hers, his body so big as he'd drawn her closer. There was simply no comparison between this kiss and Greg the Fireman's, not that she'd tell Drew that. But say, was it hot in here? She got up to crank open one of the enormous windows to let in some air.

And took a minute to remind herself that Drew appeared to still be in love with the bride.

And a twinge of guilt settled in as well, reminding her of another reason not to get carried away. Maybe that kiss hadn't been all about Drew. Maybe it was about her stamping him with her own mark of possession. Because the thought that he would want Sondra was...awful. Maybe some medieval part of her had rushed in despite all sense to claim him. A scary thought, because Maggie never would have thought of herself as aggressive but...somehow sense had taken a backseat.

Her heart went out to him despite herself. She'd seen the look on his face when he'd first seen Sondra, and she'd known...she'd *felt* it. She knew what it was like to desperately want someone you couldn't ever have again. In a way, they were very similar...two damaged people, caught up in their own webs of pain, not doing a great job moving forward.

Maggie pulled some things out of her suitcase and headed straight for the shower. The bathroom, like the rest of the house, was state-of-the-art granite counters with elevated glass sinks, an enormous walk-in shower, and a huge spa tub. She put on her favorite cotton nightgown, called her mom to ask how Griffin's day was, checked her email, then finally collapsed on the bed.

The mattress must have been stuffed with memory foam, or clouds, judging by the insane softness, whereas her mattress at home was The Price Is Right Special. She'd just snuggled down and cracked open her e-reader when a knock sounded on the door.

She'd made it halfway to the door when Drew himself walked in...with his duffel bag, a very bad sign. Genevieve went ballistic, jumping and yipping and trying to climb his leg to get to her beloved. Maggie was just about to tell him to take his annoying dog and go to one of the twenty-plus other bedrooms, but something stopped her.

In the lamplight from the bedside lamp, shadows played over his handsome face. His jaw was taut, and he had circles under his eyes. His gaze raked over her nightgown and bare feet, and he quirked a brow. She thought he was going to make a sarcastic comment—her nightgown was white with bright red cherries all over.

She crossed her arms across her chest, but he kept staring at her, and for a second, something else entirely flashed in his eyes...but no. He couldn't have just looked at her *that* way—a lusty, hungry look that sent a shock of heat through her and curled her toes.

His full mouth slid up in a grin. "Only you would own a nightgown covered with cherries."

"Wait till you see the matching slippers."

She walked over to the chair, grabbed her robe, and stepped into her slippers, her cheeks as flaming red as the cherries. Maybe she should add socks, because she suddenly couldn't be covered up enough.

He laughed.

She frowned. "What is it?"

He shook his head and rubbed the back of his neck. "Just that I've never seen a woman...match quite so well. Cherries, cherries...cherries." He pointed to her nightgown, her robe, and her white plush slippers, which had of course two cherries dangling from the tops.

She felt her face flame again. She usually slept in loose boxers and old comfy T-shirts, and she'd made an effort to look nice because she'd had no idea what the sleeping arrangements would be. She thought more in terms of sharing with his sister or another wedding guest—she didn't think she'd be sharing a room with him. Definitely Not. With. Him.

"Look," she said, "I'm sure you didn't come here to comment on my nightwear. What do you want?" Because she needed to get back to her romance novel. Where guys were awesome and sexy, not real and scary and irritating like the one standing in front of her.

It suddenly occurred to her that maybe he'd come to talk. Maybe he'd sought her out. Like he trusted her and he needed someone to listen. That would be fine, as long as he didn't touch her. Because being in the same room with him was setting off fantasies in her head of her dragging him down on that poofy bed and getting all King Arthur and the Holy Grail with him. As long as they left the torture instruments out of it.

The Turret Room, instead of *The Red Room*. That made her chuckle a little to herself.

"Er, Maggie," he said. "Did you know this used to be my room?"

"You know, I did happen to put two and two together on that. What's with the medieval fetish?"

"Actually, I was all about swords for a few years when I was a teenager. But my mother always goes a little overboard."

Yes, she saw that, but she wisely kept her mouth shut.

"She and my father fought a lot. I think this was overcompensating for the unhappiness that caused."

He picked up the photo of him and his brother. Xander had his arm around him, a skinny, adorable boy of around six or seven with no front teeth and a shock of thick dark hair. They were holding fishing poles, and a big fish dangled off the line.

"Your fish?" Maggie asked.

"No," he said. "Xander caught it. But he let me hold it for the picture."

Oh. Well, that was certainly a memory from a different time. She watched something flicker over his face as he set down the photograph. "My brother always looked out for me."

Maggie bit her lip to avoid saying something she'd regret. Like, *he sure wasn't looking out for you when he stole your girlfriend, was he?* But it wasn't her place to judge, only to help Drew through this.

She absently picked another photo. It was one of the entire family at the beach—Drew's mother and father, and the three kids. Drew had his arm around his little sister, who had pigtails. "How old were you here?" she asked.

He took the photo from her and perused it. "Sixteen. This was the last family photo before the divorce."

That would make Christina ten. Sixteen couldn't have been the greatest age for a kid to experience a divorce. But then, what age was? "That had to be difficult," she said.

"Sometimes I feel like it's my fault Sondra left me for my brother."

"What do you mean?"

He shrugged. "Well, I…left."

"Yeah, leaving to get an MBA. What a crime."

He stood there, staring at nothing, really. Lost in some memories she wasn't privy to.

"Oh, Drew." She couldn't think of anything else to say.

"Don't feel sorry for me. It's all right. I would've done it all over again. The relationship with my brother was more important than a job I really didn't care all that much about anyway."

He really didn't hold a grudge against his brother. Pretty amazing, if you asked her.

Drew shrugged and set the photo down, giving her a back-to-business look. "Anyway, Maggie, I—my mother put us both in here for tonight."

She stared at him. Oh God, no, please. Wasn't it enough to have to deal with the bride-was-my-ex-girlfriend-who-I-might-possibly-still-have-feelings-for angle, and the mother who showed her fangs as soon as they were alone, and the brother who stole the girlfriend, and the girlfriend who was beautiful in a Maleficent kind of way? Was mental duress enough to demand alone time? Those few precious minutes she'd just spent alone—well, with the bratty Genevieve—were possibly the only ones she'd had in about a year. Or two.

Maggie spoke up, crossing her arms over her boobs, where she happened to notice his gaze was wandering. "I'm sure in a house this size, you can find another place to sleep. Actually, since this is your—and your dog's—bedroom, I'm happy to move." He could just be the one to stay and listen to his dog snorting and squeaking in her sleep all night.

"I told my mother we…preferred it. She assumes we're…intimate. Especially after that ear lick." His mouth turned up in a smile, and his gaze hovered on her for a few seconds, long enough for her to forget the routine act of breathing.

She held her hands in front of her in a defensive gesture. "Full disclosure. I'm not usually an ear licker. I don't know what got into me."

She kept hearing that word...*intimate*...the way he said it...slow and deep and matter-of-fact, as if he was stating a simple truth like, *you have blue eyes* or *you're pretty*...and it made her imagine, just for a second, his face above hers, staring at her just like that, heat flashing in his eyes.

She shook her head to try to clear it, but the image was so vivid, she felt a tingle down to her bones. Oh Lord, she had to find a way to get one of them out of here fast.

"Look," he said. "I'm not really thrilled about the arrangement, but I didn't have a choice. You can take the bed. I'll just take a blanket and sleep on the floor."

Protests bubbled up to Maggie's lips, but he looked so...stressed and miserable. He looked like he didn't want to share his room with her any more than she did. Besides, he was so tired that something like sex would probably be the very last thing on his mind.

His gaze drifted to the bed and then to her.

Oh God, he was a healthy red-blooded male, and he was *definitely* thinking about sex.

As was she. She started to tell him he really had to leave, this was not going to work, when he pulled the fluffy comforter and a pillow off the bed and tossed them onto the carpet. The dog promptly walked into the middle of the comforter, circled three times, and plopped down.

"No worries, okay?" Drew gave her a little smile and a wink and headed to the bathroom.

Great. She was sharing this medieval torture chamber with a big solid hunk of male who made every hormone in her body stand up and sing the "Star-Spangled Banner." And a lovelorn dog who was gaga about him.

Her night of relaxation had just flown right out the window.

CHAPTER 9

A shower didn't help Drew's pounding headache. Or douse his hormones, which appeared to be in overdrive, thanks to the woman now occupying his childhood bedroom. He re-entered the room with boxers on. Maybe he should've added sweats, but frankly, he usually slept naked. He just wanted to zone out and go to sleep. Hell of a day.

He flopped onto the floor on top of the comforter and plumped up the pillow. "Look, Maggie. I'm sorry I got you into this." He forced himself to make eye contact and to maintain a neutral expression. To prove to himself it wasn't really her he was attracted to, just the fact that it had been a while for him.

But looking up at her was a mistake, because, she looked like the sweetest thing he'd seen all day. Her ridiculous little nightgown with the cherries should have made him laugh, but instead it made him want to lose himself in her soapy fresh scent, plant kisses on the soft skin between her breasts, and lift up the gown and explore everything that was underneath. And somehow stop his pain with an entirely different diversion.

Yeah, yeah, he knew. That would be using her. He had to keep his distance, but how the hell was he ever going to do that when they were trapped in the same bedroom?

She reached up and turned out the light. All was quiet except for the sound of his little dog burrowing in at his side. For a minute, he wondered if Maggie had fallen asleep. "Drew," she said a little later, "I want you to know that I can help you through this. There are ways…"

"I didn't bring you here to psychologize me," he said, then instantly regretted his snappy tone. "Look, it's not your fault you walked into this mess. I appreciate what you're trying to do, but—"

"Can I ask you something?"

God, she was going to psychologize him anyway. "What?" he forced himself to say.

"What's your goal?"

"Excuse me?"

"What I mean is, it might be too much to say, *I need to get over Sondra right now and enjoy this weekend,* or, *I need to stop being angry at my brother* or I *need my sister and brother to talk to their father* or whatever.*"

"I'm not angry at my brother. I understand things just…happened."

"I think you *are* angry. Maybe it's okay to be angry."

"You don't understand. I *can't* be angry with my brother."

"It's not good to hold all that in."

"What choice do I have?" Shit, he sounded defensive *and* angry. "My family's not like your family. We don't say everything that's on our minds. We're repressed and noncommunicative, okay? And you know what else? It doesn't make a damn bit of difference if I show my anger or not. What's done is done."

"All right, then," Maggie said softly.

He waited for her to say more, but she didn't. "That's it? You're not going to tell me something to do to make it better?"

God, he wanted somebody to make it better. He knew he was being an asshole, but he couldn't seem to help it.

"I think you said it exactly right. Focus on your brother."

Hell, he was trying to. He'd tried to get his brother alone earlier, but he seemed stuck like cement to Sondra's side. Maybe Drew would feel a little less bitter if he could have a talk with him, but he wouldn't even know where to begin. *Hey, buddy, you know that woman I dated for four years? The one you stole? The one who's going to be your wife? How the fuck could you do that to me?* And how was he so blind he never even saw it coming?

And was this whole thing some colossal payback on his brother's part for all the things that Drew had done better? No, he couldn't imagine his brother doing this out of spite. Xander wasn't like that.

But how could he reconcile the brother who'd protected him all those years with the one who'd stolen away his woman?

Funny, but maybe it was a good sign he was angrier with Xander than Sondra. Seeing her didn't twist the knife quite so deeply as it used to. Frankly, she was very different from the Sondra he'd known. And to be honest, right now he wasn't thinking about her at all.

He just couldn't stop thinking about that kiss.

The bedding rustled, like Maggie was turning over. He lay on his back on the hard floor, thinking about how good it had felt to pull her against him, how soft her skin was, how she'd kissed him right back, full of ardor, full of *life*. He hadn't felt like this about a simple kiss in ages.

It had been one hell of a kiss, and if he read her right, she'd felt it too.

"I'm sorry…for being irritated just now," he said. "Think I'm just…tired."

"You're allowed to be," she said. "Good night, Drew. Sleep well."

Sure thing. With her a few feet away, he wasn't likely to sleep a wink.

"Wake up, princess." A deep, rumbly voice penetrated Maggie's consciousness, accompanied by a nudge in her arm that roused her from sleep. She propped open one eye to see a big bare-chested male full of muscle, a white towel wrapped around his lean waist, standing next to her bed, staring down at her. The delicious smells of shaving cream and soap permeated the air.

If she was dreaming, this was definitely a dream she'd like to have every night.

Dream man spoke again. "No dawdling. Wake up already."

The accompanying poke in the arm assured her this *wasn't* a dream. She bolted upright, brushing the rat's nest of hair from her face, straightening her nightgown, rubbing the sleep out of her eyes. There was not a chance of being even remotely presentable. When she stopped adjusting herself, she found he was staring at her.

"Rough night?" he asked, his sinfully beautiful mouth turning up into a smile.

Rough didn't even begin to describe it. She'd tossed and turned for what seemed like the entire night, then finally fell asleep as the sky was lightening up from black to gray. "I slept like a baby," she said, smiling a sweet smile. "How about you?"

"The floor was fantastic," he said. "My spine is totally aligned now."

"Maybe the idea of a comfortable bed will be an incentive for you to get your own room tonight?" she asked, unable to disguise the hope in her voice.

"We'll see," he said noncommittally. "Anyway, I'm waking you up for a reason."

"Which is?" And oh, those gorgeous pecs, his sexy wet hair, and that towel slung low around his hips, turned her thoughts to one fine reason that was warming up her insides faster than her favorite fleece-lined socks.

"It's time for the annual family tennis competition."

Maggie's stomach clenched. The most competitive her family ever got was fighting for the remote—HGTV vs. some kind of sports. The boys usually won, and her mom and she went off shopping, problem solved. As far as her girlfriends were concerned, their idea of a competition, when she was single, anyway, was seeing which one of them could finish up Friday night Zumba, shower, and be the first in the car to head to MacNamara's for drinks.

"I'm happy to cheerlead for you all." She pictured Cecilia standing on the court with a clipboard, critiquing moves, suggesting better ones. She had no idea how seriously the family would take this, but judging by the USTA-grade tennis court she'd noticed in the backyard, all the Poulos kids had probably had lessons since birth.

Drew tossed something white at her that dropped onto the bed in three pieces. "My mom dropped this by in case you didn't bring tennis wear."

Maggie lifted the pieces of clothing. A tennis skirt. A sleeveless top. A sports bra. Okay, great. The outfit smacked of country club. Her tennis experience growing up consisted of lessons in the park, wearing cutoff shorts and worn-down running shoes. She forced a smile. "Drew, I'm really not very competitive. Plus, I bet everyone in your family's great at tennis."

"That's pretty accurate, actually. You play?"

"A little," she said. She'd been on the high school team, if that counted. Played third singles against other tiny schools. Okay, so maybe that didn't count.

Drew rummaged around his duffel bag and grabbed a few

items of clothing. Then he glanced up—and caught her staring at his towel. Well, she couldn't help it if he had beads of water on his back. She was just fantasizing about pulling off his towel and using it to wipe them away when the corner of his mouth lifted ever so slightly. "I'm going to change and go down to breakfast. Sound like a plan?"

"Sure," she said a little too cheerily as she sat on the bed, fiddling with the tennis clothes.

He turned the corner into the bathroom, the towel hitting the tiled floor. A flash of muscular calf flitted by. She swallowed hard, wondering if what was under that towel was just as fantastic as the rest of him. She'd bet her breakfast that it was.

A second later, he poked his head around the doorway. "You okay with it? The tennis, I mean."

She swallowed hard. "Sure, I-I'm game for anything." No, she wasn't. Not tennis, and not thinking about him being naked. Which he was. Very, very naked, and grinning from ear to ear.

"It's not about winning," Drew said a few minutes later, emerging from the bathroom fully dressed and walking to the door, Genevieve scurrying briskly behind him. "It's about how you play the game."

In this family, they seemed like they were very concerned about both. And that was exactly what she was afraid of.

Drew didn't really care that every muscle in his back ached, thanks to his night on the floor. Or that Genevieve had insisted on snuggling up to him all night, or that he'd awakened to doggie breath in his face and dog hair in his mouth.

More troubling was the fact that he couldn't shut off these constant...thoughts...of Maggie. All night long, he'd imagined getting off that rock-hard floor and climbing into bed next to her, tugging her close until their bodies were flush. Kissing her and helping her off with the cherries or whatever the fruit of the night was and having his way with that sweet little body of hers.

Right. She was supposed to be his family psychologist—he was *paying* her, for God's sake—and all he could think of was ripping her clothes off and doing her. Doing her so well, she'd collapse in a boneless heap on his bed with a smile *he* put there.

He took a big breath of morning air to clear his head and ran his hands through his hair. It was just the stress of being here and the temptation to use sex to blow off some of that steam. He made a mental note to take a run after tennis. A long one.

He made his way to the court, where he could see his brother and Sondra warming up. A strange pang hit him as she took a ball from Xander. It was still weird to see them together, laughing and joking around. Sondra was dressed in a bright green tennis skirt, a sleeveless top, and a visor, looking picture-perfect as always, in full makeup too.

He remembered a time when she hadn't known Nike from Fila. The girl he'd known so long ago wouldn't have thought twice about showing up anywhere without makeup. From what he'd seen since he arrived, maybe that was no longer the case.

Xander looked ready for the US Open in white shorts and a navy-and-white tennis shirt, making Drew feel seriously underdressed in his athletic shorts and T-shirt. His brother called to him as he approached. "Get out here so I can whup your butt."

"Be right there," he said. He wasn't sure when everything with his brother seemed to turn into a competition, from clothes to sports to business.

On the sidelines, Maggie was sitting with Christina, looking at her phone and laughing. His mother was sitting courtside, drinking coffee and poring over spreadsheets.

Drew walked over to the net, stopping to fill up a cone of ice-cold water from the watercooler that was installed there. "It's

Xander and me versus you and Maggie," Sondra said, coming up behind him and squeezing his shoulder. "Ooh, I see you haven't stopped working out, have you?" She slapped him playfully on the arm.

Drew looked at Sondra carefully. She seemed oblivious to the fact that Xander was right there too, getting a drink himself. And she seemed to miss the expression of hurt that settled on Xander's face like a shadow.

Tactfully, he stepped back and punched his brother's arm. "My muscles are nothing like this guy's. What do you bench-press now, two hundred fifty?"

"Ten more than you can, just to piss you off."

Drew laughed but remembered a time when joking around with his brother was a whole hell of a lot easier.

From the patio, his sister laughed. "What's so funny?" Drew asked, glad to walk over to where Christina and Maggie sat.

"I was just showing Maggie some pictures from my birthday," Christina said.

Maggie handed Christina back her phone and walked with Drew onto the court. "That was a good look on you. A black-and-silver sombrero with dangling pom-poms."

Drew felt his face redden.

"And I *really* loved the photo of all the teenage girls holding you horizontally with the sombrero on. I was torn, though."

"About what?" he asked, his eyes narrowing.

"Who was enjoying it more, them or you."

"Ha-ha." So he'd taken his sister out on her birthday at college when she couldn't make it back home to celebrate. They'd gone with her gaggle of girlfriends to a local Mexican place, where they'd danced and had fun. He wasn't ashamed to be silly in front of Christina, who tended to take life seriously and worry a lot.

"I think it was really nice of you. Your sister adores you."

"The feeling's mutual," he said.

She picked up a tennis ball off the court and started toward the service line.

"Hey, wait a minute," he said, trying not to watch her fine ass in the cute little tennis skirt as she jogged away. "Aren't we going to talk strategy?"

Her big blue eyes were the exact color of the sky overhead. "Okay. What's the plan?"

"Um, let's see. Sondra has a weak backhand. Xander is good at everything but he tends to flub his overheads." He looked over at his brother, who was holding his racquet, rolling his right arm in big Ferris wheel circles, doing calf muscle stretches and jogging frantically in place.

Maggie's eyes got a little big. "Drew, I have to tell you something."

"Sure. What is it?"

"No matter what you say, it seems like winning is really important to you. To your family. I—um—just want you to know I'm an average player at best. I hope I don't disappoint."

He smiled, because she had tiny worry lines on her forehead that he suddenly wanted to rub his thumb over until they disappeared. And she looked *really cute* in that tennis outfit.

No! Focus, man. Not on her fantastic legs. Or her nice rack.

"Winning's not important to me," he lied. He'd love to whup Xander's butt, as it would likely be the only satisfaction he'd have this long, horrible weekend. But it was only a game, right? And he didn't want Maggie to stress.

"C'mon, you two, let's get going," Xander called in his eager-for-blood voice.

Drew looked Maggie in the eye with mock seriousness. "Just do your best, okay, Venus?"

She put out her fist for him to bump. "Got it, Andre."

During the warm-up, Sondra danced from one foot to another, switching her racquet ambitiously from hand to hand. She looked powerful and somewhat terrifying, and between Xander and her, he wasn't sure if Maggie would be intimidated.

But turned out Drew didn't have to worry about that. From the get-go, Maggie landed a great shot right in the middle between Sondra and Xander.

"Your ball!" Sondra called at the last minute. They both swiped at it and missed, causing Sondra to curse and Drew's mother to look up from her work.

In fact, Sondra and Xander were both doing a lot of cursing. And bickering. He didn't remember Sondra having such a potty mouth. But then, he seemed to remember her as being very…different. Sweeter, nicer. Back in the day when she'd been known as Sandy, not Sondra.

When Maggie suddenly drilled a shot down the alley, Drew looked back in amazement. Maggie gave him a wink. It appeared his partner could play tennis. Plus she looked really hot. His day was looking up a little.

Games passed, mostly with Sondra and Xander secretively strategizing with intense whispers and hand signals he didn't understand. Maggie and he managed to get ahead 5-4 with Drew serving.

Maggie was at the net, her racquet ready. He couldn't help but notice her pretty legs, and of course her adorable ass that was swaying back and forth in front of him in that little tennis skirt…

"Heads up!" Maggie yelled, suddenly turning around.

Too late. Something green and fuzzy smacked him right in the forehead.

"Oh my God, I'm so sorry," Sondra said, her hands covering her mouth in horror as he rubbed his head. "Are you all right? I thought you saw that. You must've not been paying attention."

Of course he hadn't been paying attention. He'd been staring at Maggie's ass. To make up for it, he took up the ball and threw all he had into it, acing his brother.

"Xan, come on. You can do better than that!" Sondra stood on the court, hands on hips.

"That was a hell of a serve, bro," Xander said, shooting Sondra the stink eye.

Maggie retrieved a ball and ran it back to Drew. As she put it into his hand, she smiled. A full, radiant smile that about knocked his socks off. "We can win this," she said.

"All righty, then," he said, holding on to her hand a second longer than necessary. "Let's do it."

Sondra hit a winner past Maggie at the net, barely missing her head, except Maggie ducked at the last second. "Nice shot," Maggie called politely. Drew was starting to wonder if Sondra was taking aim at both of them.

When it was at last their advantage, Sondra pulled out all the stops and took off her shirt, exposing a lime-green sports bra and her toned abs. But Drew barely noticed. He was too busy deciding if he'd try to ace his brother again. It would be satisfying, and it would make them win. But Xander was the groom, it was his wedding weekend, and maybe Drew shouldn't do that. Maggie, however, turned and marched back to him at the service line.

"Okay, this is war. Drew, look at me."

She looked so…serious. Strands of her hair hung to her forehead in damp tendrils. Even her ponytail was wet with sweat, and a killer instinct gleamed in her eyes. She grabbed him by the arms and shook.

"Do not choke. Do not go easy on them. Now is not the time to be a gentleman. Put the ball where it needs to go. Do it, Drew. We are one point away from a total win."

He laughed. Because he'd never seen this side of her. She was a fountain bursting with competitive energy. She spun back around. "No laughing. We need total concentration here!"

"Okay, Doc," he said, winking. She rolled her eyes and looked like she was personally going to come after him if he screwed up, which made him laugh even more.

"Drew, they're using cheap distraction techniques. You have to leave all your personal feelings off the court. It's us against them, okay?"

He realized that she must've thought he was preoccupied by Sondra's abs on display. But it wasn't Sondra who was distracting him at all. It was Maggie.

He let it rip. The ball sailed over the net, bounced into the corner of the service court, and whizzed far past Xander, who stood there looking like he was preparing to get yelled at.

"Oh my God," Sondra said, tossing her racquet to the court and folding her arms in a huff in front of Xander. "This is…unbelievable. You suck!"

"We won!" Maggie tossed her racquet up in the air and ran up to Drew, fist pumping and high-fiving. Suddenly she was in his arms, soft and curvy and, okay, a little sweaty, but he didn't mind at all, and he was twirling her around like they'd just won Wimbledon, whooping their heads off.

"I think this win deserves another ear lick," he whispered.

"Okay, that's a little gross," she said, looking up at him.

"Not if done properly," he said.

Her eyes widened. Color streamed into her already-overheated face. For a long second, they stared at each other.

His heart was beating wildly, and it had nothing to do with exertion. He had the crazy impulse to scoop her up and carry her back to their room and strip them both out of their sweaty clothes for the rest of the hot, lazy afternoon.

He tried to pull back to friendly. "So you don't care about competition, eh?" he said, tugging on her tennis visor.

"Okay, so I'm a little competitive," she said, shrugging. "So shoot me." She was grinning widely, and it made him grin too.

In the background, he heard Sondra and Xander passionately

discussing their loss. Everything—the wedding, the worries, his family—suddenly faded into a dim background buzz as he became aware only of the sweaty, victorious, beautiful woman in his arms.

Aw, the hell with it, a voice in his head said. He focused on her full, pretty lips, which parted in a little gasp as she realized what he was about to do.

And then he did it. Kissed her. Her lips were soft and her cheeks were flushed and sun warmed, the taste of her sweet and a little salty. She kissed him back with equal enthusiasm, and he let himself get lost, for the first time in a long time, in the uncomplicated fun of kissing a pretty woman.

Maggie gave a little sigh, and he'd just pulled her closer so he could really kiss her when a familiar voice boomed out loud and clear.

"Well, look who finally came home." The unmistakable baritone of his father, spring-loaded with a twinge of the prodigal-son-returns sarcasm.

As they broke apart, Drew tried to telegraph a silent apology to Maggie, but it was too late. "Hello, Andreas," Maxim Poulos said, slapping him on the back. "I see you've brought a guest."

CHAPTER 10

"You've always had a penchant for beautiful women," Mr. Poulos said to his son while Maggie tried not to cringe under his drilling gaze. "Does this one have a job?"

"Meet *Doctor* McShae, Dad," Drew said, taking hold of her arm. A little thrill went through her that he'd come to her defense. Not that she needed it, but it was nice to have him care how his father addressed her. And being referred to as *this one* just didn't seem right.

"Where did you go to medical school?" Drew's father asked her, flicking his cigar ashes to the court. He was muscle-bound like Xander, with a head of bottle-black hair and a shrewd glare that missed nothing.

"Actually, I'm a psychologist, Mr. Poulos," Maggie said.

"Oh. Not a real doctor, then."

A tiny muscle in Drew's jaw ticked. "Dad…"

Maggie stepped forward and put out a hand, cutting Drew off. "I'm Maggie. Nice to meet you," she said with a big smile. Surprisingly, she didn't even gag on the words.

"You don't usually like them smart," Drew's father said.

She was beginning to see why Drew had avoided his father for the past year and a half.

"Dad, that's enough," Drew said.

"No offense to you, Doctor," Drew's father amended, looking her up and down. Maggie knew well enough what he was thinking. Boobs too small, not curvy enough, and definitely lacking Anika's bone structure or height. Basically, a bad substitute for the famous mogul's model-perfect daughter.

"None taken," she lied, holding her chin up a little and threading her arm through Drew's.

"Maxim, darling," Cecilia said, approaching them on the court. "Considering Drew is the only one of your children who is on speaking terms with you, you'd think you'd be a bit nicer to his girlfriend."

Maxim smiled widely. "Maybe if his mother wouldn't poison him and the others with lies, they'd have a better attitude toward me."

Cecilia snorted. "Maybe all your children would have a better attitude if you were worthy of one."

Under Maggie's hand, Drew's forearm muscles turned rigid. Xander had just walked up, but sensed the tension and hesitated. Next to him was a tall, shapely woman who vaguely resembled Sofía Vergara.

Cecilia turned to the woman. "Valentina, darling. How lovely and—*shapely* you look." Her gaze lingered on Valentina's boobs. "Whoever did those did a splendid job. Perky as ever." Her gaze flicked back to Maxim, who had turned a violent shade of red. "Won't you both join us for some iced tea?"

"Thank you, Cecilia," Valentina said graciously. She even pecked her on the cheek. "I feel so much better since my breast reduction. No back pain, no straps digging into my shoulders."

They all went to sit on the patio. "Val and I are here to

115

celebrate your wedding, Alexander," Maxim said. "A happy family event."

Xander didn't say anything, which made the moment even more awkward. Arthur approached with a silver tray containing a pitcher of iced tea and a plate of cookies.

Maggie took the plate off Arthur's tray. "Fresh from the oven. Why don't we all sit down and have some? It would be a shame to waste them." She practically shoved the plate under Maxim's nose. Even grabbed one and took a bite. "Mmm! Delicious!" She was mostly sincere. Under all the nerves, she was more than happy to eat one. She'd even call it the high point of her day so far, except for seeing Drew half-naked this morning. Oh, and kissing him, of course.

Maggie sat down next to Drew on an outdoor couch that probably cost more than her parents' entire living room set.

"I miss you at the company," Maxim said to Drew.

"But Dad, you have me," Xander protested.

"Of course I have you, Xander, but AcroPoulos Yogurt is a family business." He turned again to Drew. "It's not the same without you. I'd like to ask you to come back where you belong."

That seemed like something nice to say. Maggie hoped Drew would pick up on the concerned-father vibes she was definitely feeling.

Surprisingly, Xander spoke up. "It's not the same without Drew, but we're doing fine without him. His interests are elsewhere."

"You may not want to share a leadership spot with your brother, Xander, but it's Drew's rightful place."

"I appreciate it, Dad," Drew said, "but I'm happy helping get Roman's apple brandy business up and running."

"Bah! You're wasting your time with glorified apple cider. And I don't know why you're refusing any of the family money."

Drew wasn't using any of his family's billions? Maggie sat

there with the cookie plate while that muscle under Drew's eye twitched and color crept up his neck. "Another cookie?" she asked him, smiling hopefully.

"No, thanks," he said. He addressed his father. "Sometimes it doesn't matter how big the business is. Sometimes it's about doing things on your own, not having everything dictated to you by your family."

"Fine. You're clearly still angry about the wedding. If you want to talk about it, we can talk about it. That was done in your best interests, may I remind you. Anika and you both come from similar backgrounds. She would have understood your life."

"She wasn't who I would choose to be my wife."

"And this one is?" He turned to her. "Tell me, Maggie, why did my son choose you?"

Oh my God, if this man referred to her as a pronoun one more time, she was walking back home, she swore it.

"Maxim, you're being rude," Cecilia said.

"I want to know. What is it that Dr. McShae has that is the magic formula for your happiness?"

"You don't have to answer that," Drew said quickly.

"No, no. I want to. Really." Sure she did. About as much as she wanted to visit her gynecologist. She and Drew were from completely different backgrounds. Drew was Ivy League all the way and came from a strata of wealth she could barely fathom. She couldn't imagine not talking to her parents, as annoying as they sometimes were, for more than a week. They were warm, loving, affectionate, hardworking people. And frankly, they both hated yogurt.

"Do you want to know the truth?" She looked over at Drew, whose jaw was tight as a screw. And who looked as if he were standing in line for the confessional.

"I made a mean souflaka. That's it. The way it all began."

Actually, it began that day he burst into the therapy group she was leading. Or maybe it really began a few weeks ago on the church steps, when he'd handed her his Diet Coke. Suddenly, she felt heat creep up her own face.

"Souvlaki," Drew said, a smile creeping to his lips. "She makes a mean souvlaki."

"That too," Maggie said.

"Bah," the elder Poulos said, waving his hand dismissively. "That's just a translation for my son is good in bed."

Would this man never stop?

Drew stood up so quickly, the love seat scraped on the pavers. The playful expression on his face was gone. His hands were balled into fists, his lips drawn into a thin line. "You can insult me, but I'd expect you to treat the woman I bring home better."

Uh-oh. Maggie did not want the tenacious peace of this family to be disrupted because of her, that was for sure. And judging by his crimson color, Drew looked angry enough to burst an aneurysm.

"It's okay," Maggie said quickly, reaching up to touch Drew's hand. "I've got this." She turned to Drew's father. "Seriously, Mr. Poulos, you must know what a terrific son you have. I've watched him get involved in every aspect of the brandy business, not just the financial stuff—from working the orchards to running the stills to managing the marketing and even the launch of the wine bar. He's hardworking and enterprising. And levelheaded and practical."

Suddenly, she was on a roll, and she couldn't seem to stop. "He saved my son from falling off a swing, but then he reminded me boys have to be boys. He's an amazing dancer. He knows how to order a good bottle of wine, and he knows the difference between a tennis match and real life. He loves dogs, and he'd do anything for his brother. And he's a great kisser." She paused. "Oh, I almost forgot the most important one. He makes me laugh—and that means a lot to someone like me, who tends to worry about everything."

She glanced over at Drew, who was staring at her in a strange way. Wishing she'd shut the hell up, no doubt. She could've added, *and when he gets that certain twinkle in his eyes, he's irresistible,* but she decided she'd probably said enough.

Drew's face colored. Maybe because he was so pissed off at his father. Or maybe because Maggie was still staring at him. As she'd mentally ticked off that list, a realization had dawned. He *was* every single one of those things. And gorgeous too. *Oh, crap.*

She wasn't ready to fall for anybody. She was only supposed to be testing the waters with men. She'd wanted something easy and flingy, and she was determined to keep it that way.

When she thought about how she felt about Greg, it was the complete opposite of how she felt about Drew. Both men instilled a healthy sense of fear of getting involved—but with Greg, it was more of a *wrong guy* kind of fear.

She feared Drew for entirely different reasons. He made her…feel things. Powerful things she hadn't felt in a long, long time. Drew also annoyed her far more than Greg ever could. And made her want to shake some sense into him. Like telling him Sondra was an idiot and he could do so much better.

And the way he kissed! That kiss just now on the court had been spontaneous, not staged like the other ones, but they'd all somehow managed to spin out of control. And they'd all been *amazing,* leaving her wanting and desperate for more.

Whatever she felt about Drew, good or bad, she felt…strongly. There wasn't a wishy-washy feeling about him to be found.

No, no. She was not ready for anything real! Just look at this guy's family. It was nothing like her own close-knit one. A man who came from a family like this was bound to be riddled with emotional troubles. There was enough drama here for a Netflix series. Or to keep her practice full for years.

All the more reason to focus on keeping it light.

Drew cleared his throat and gave his father a cutting look. "So you see, Dad, sometimes there's more to a relationship than sex or a juicy business deal." He got up and patted Xander on the shoulder. "Great match. We're going to go shower and get ready for the rehearsal dinner. See you all tonight." Then he took Maggie's hand and led her away.

It couldn't be fast enough.

"Do you—do you want to talk about it?" Maggie asked Drew after they'd walked into his room and she'd closed the door. He hadn't said a thing all the way back from the tennis courts. They'd stopped at the enormous kitchen that looked like a spread from *Architectural Digest* and could have housed ten of her parents' kitchens. He'd handed her a can of sparkling water from the massive fridge and then…dead silence.

He didn't even bother turning around. Instead, he headed to the window, set his can down on the sill, and looked out over the verdant golf-course-grade lawn, the spread-out gardens with fountains and blooming floral works of art that looked more like they belonged in the gardens at Versailles than anyone's home. He gripped his hands around the edge of the sill. Weariness marked the slump of his back, the bow of his head.

"I knew this was going to be hard," he said. "I expected it. I'm sorry you had to witness that."

She walked up behind him and spoke to—his back. His fine, broad, strong-looking back, which was covered in his blue T-shirt and was a little bit sweaty. "Your dad is angry and hurt. I'm sure with time…"

He sighed. "I can't believe you're so willing to excuse him after all he just put you through. My family can't be fixed. All we need to do is survive tonight and tomorrow, then it'll be over. I'm sorry I dragged you here."

Finally, she rested a hand on his back. He flinched a little. Maybe he didn't like her touching him. "No family is perfect," she said, withdrawing her hand. "Every family has their problems. But I feel certain your father loves—"

"Maggie, stop," he said firmly but gently, shrugging out of her reach. "What's done is done. It's years' worth of damage." He turned toward her. "I know it's not in your nature to give up, but sometimes there's no choice."

She'd held her tongue all this time, but now the words spilled out. "Don't talk to me like you think I don't know when to give up, dammit. Families are screwed up, Drew. Do you think yours is the only one? But no one here is talking to each other. No one is telling anyone how they really feel. You all walk on eggshells with each other and then complain no one gets you."

"You act like you think I'm feeling sorry for myself."

"I didn't say that, exactly. But you blame your father for not understanding you. Have you really sat down and told him why you didn't marry Anika? Because he may be sarcastic and have a little edge on him, but did it ever occur to you he's hurt too? You haven't seen him in over a year."

"I emailed him." He must've realized how ridiculous he sounded, because he sighed. "All right. Maybe that wasn't the best way to communicate. But the man tried to marry me off to a woman I didn't love because of a business merger."

"And you agreed to it."

He turned back to the window.

"He came up with the wedding idea after Sondra left me. I agreed to it because I didn't give a damn anymore."

"So what stopped you from marrying her?"

He faced her. "I was at the church, waiting for the ceremony to begin, and I suddenly felt sweaty and a little panicky. So I walked out into this little courtyard and sat down on a bench. There were bunches of daisies blooming everywhere. And I just…noticed them. I kept thinking, such a simple flower. Simple but beautiful. And suddenly it made me sad. Nothing about Anika or my life with her was simple. Then everything snowballed from there. And I just…left. So I guess a tiny part of me did give a damn after all."

Maggie's eyes suddenly filled with tears. She didn't know if it was the daisies, which she'd always been partial to, or that he was finally talking to her, or that she was still shaken by what had happened between them on the court.

She gripped his arm. "I'm sorry Sondra broke your heart and ruined you for all other love. But frankly, I don't understand it."

She gasped a little, shocked at her own words. This wasn't supposed to be personal, and she'd just crossed a line she should not have crossed.

Drew whirled around, his brow arched in surprise. Oh God, she never would have said that to a client. His eyes looked hard as stones. "You of all people should understand what it's like to struggle to move on."

Her face heated. She certainly hadn't done a very good job of that, had she? "This isn't about me," she said weakly.

"My brother stole the woman I loved."

"The woman you loved is a self-indulgent princess." *Shit.* She clapped her hand over her mouth to stop the verbal diarrhea. What was it about him that made her lose all her professional composure? "I'm sorry."

A flush spread over his face. A tiny muscle under his eye twitched. He opened his mouth to speak, but then something strange happened. He smiled. "No, you're not."

"I don't usually allow my personal feelings to get in the way of helping a client."

"I'm not your client, Maggie. And you're right. That was pretty damn unprofessional."

He was right—on both counts. She wasn't sorry. Before she could say so, he poked her in the chest. "You're jealous."

"What?" She folded her arms over her chest. "Of Sondra? I am not!" God, she wanted to wipe that smug expression right off his handsome face.

He laughed. "Yes, you are. You want me, pretty damn bad. And you can't believe I used to be in love with her." He sighed. "Sometimes I can't believe it either. She used to be so…different. I don't know—less fussy. Less makeup. She's…changed."

"Maybe you should talk with her too," Maggie said. "Put it all to rest. That's the number one thing people regret in life—not talking to their family or friends about the past. It's so painful, it's often very difficult to discuss. And so stuff festers for years."

He got in her face. And oh, those big brown intelligent eyes up close, those chiseled cheekbones, so much more defined than her own, which really were such a waste on a man. That pitch-black hair, so thick a woman's fingers could get lost in there.

She tried to back up a step, but he moved forward. "Maybe. Let's start by being honest with each other. Do you want me, Maggie?"

"We're not talking about—that. Back off already." She pushed on his chest a little. A mistake. Because it was hard as boulders and made her knees go weak. "Besides, you just—flinched when I touched you."

"I think we need to do what you said, talk about it. I flinched because I felt what I think you feel too. That there's something going on between us. What are we going to do about it?"

She flipped her hand dismissively. "It's all that touchy-feely stuff we're doing in front of your family. That has to stop."

"This has nothing to do with playacting," he said quietly.

123

"And I think you know that. That kiss on the court… It was real."

"That kiss was…impulsive. Heat of the moment, fueled by our hard-won victory." Joking now was not stopping the shivers that were running up and down her arms. Or the hot and cold coursing through her veins. Somehow, she sensed how it would be between them. Wild. No holds barred. And God help her, she *wanted* that.

She tried to pull some common sense out of her sex-addled brain. It would be a very bad idea on both their parts to forget their troubles with a sweaty round of sex, wouldn't it?

Yet wasn't that what she'd wanted? To get her life going again? To have an opportunity to meet someone she could maybe share her life with and make a family for Griffin, even if she wasn't anywhere near expecting the soul-binding love she'd experienced with Corey.

"I—I'm not in the right place for a relationship," she said.

"And yet you were ready to have a fling with Greg the Fireman."

"That was different." She sensed danger with Drew. The ability to drill down to a place deep inside her that she'd buried for a very long time. And she was terrified to let anyone in that far. "I don't even really know you," she said. For some reason, her voice came out in a whisper.

"You know enough." His gaze was piercing right through her, hot and quick, and all her willpower started circling the drain like Griffin's bathwater in their ancient claw-foot tub.

There were so many things about him she *didn't* know. She had no idea what he'd ever seen in Sondra. Or many details about what had happened between him and Anika. But maybe she didn't care.

"We could keep it casual." He shrugged his elegant shoulders. "A little fling could be good for both of us. Release all that tension."

"Absolutely not." But his words were velvet, conjuring images of his body and hers, his lips roaming over her, his hands...

He was very close now, staring at her lips, moving in for the kill. And her head was humming and her knees were wobbly and her heart was fluttering crazily. He was so close, she could reach out and touch those big shoulders of his. Run her hands down his powerful arms. Circle his sweet neck with her arms. She didn't even care that he was a little sweaty. And dear God, she was so, so sex crazed, she wasn't sure she could control herself. But, like a magnet drawn to the fridge door, she could not turn away.

Finally, he snuffed out the space between them and lowered his mouth to hers.

Oh, his wonderful mouth. His lips were soft and seeking, tentative at first as he took his time learning the feel of hers. He tasted like cookies and tea and his own uniquely intoxicating taste. From the start, these kisses were completely different from the ones they'd done for show in front of his family. Needy, more aggressive, *unleashed*.

Fleetingly, she thought of Corey, how this was *different*, and she felt a dim panic—this man was taller, his shoulders broader, his kiss so different from the familiar, comforting kisses she'd gotten used to over so many years.

At another moment, those thoughts might have bloomed into a full-blown panic—except Drew's hand curled softly around her neck, drawing her closer, at the same time his mouth invaded hers. He dropped a few firm, short kisses and then went in for the kill, sliding his tongue inside and tangling with hers in a relentless, hungry way that made every cell in her body cry out for more.

She whimpered. The whimper of a woman who hadn't been kissed properly in a long, long time. Every wayward thought was driven from her head. She had to restrain herself from clawing his back and pushing him onto the bed. And oh, she kissed him back, standing on tiptoe and planting her lips over his and thrusting her tongue right alongside his, needing everything he could give her.

His hands crept to her ass and pulled her against him. His erection raged against her inner thigh, and she ground into his crotch because she was completely gone now, unable to control herself, ready to beg for it…

A mild scratching sound invaded her consciousness, which she promptly forgot as Drew slid his hands under her shirt, his hands roaming over the sensitive skin of her sides and back, skimming lightly over her bra. Her fingers curled in the fabric of his shirt, gathering it and pulling it upward. He tugged it off, tossing it to the floor.

He did the same to hers. His fingers moved under the edge of her sports bra, finding her nipples and rubbing over them with his thumbs, stroking them gently until they hardened into peaks. A wave of pleasure rose through her so quickly, so intensely, she couldn't stop the full-out moan that escaped her lips. She felt his smile against the sensitive skin of her neck. Heard his comforting "shhh" over the rapid thrum of her heart as he pulled her closer and kissed her again. Sensations crashed through her, exploded like multicolored fireworks. She clutched at him, clung to his back as her knees buckled and she could barely stand.

The clawing sound intensified, accompanied this time by several loud barks that could no longer be ignored.

Oh, that damn lovesick dog.

They broke apart at the same time. Maggie was breathless, her chest heaving like she'd just run a 5K. She grabbed for her shirt and let Drew open the door. The dog trotted right in, rubbing against Drew's leg and begging for attention.

As Maggie came to her senses, she supposed she should be grateful for the stupid animal, who had likely interrupted a disaster from happening. Maggie walked over to her suitcase and began pulling out clothes, but frankly, at this point she couldn't tell a pair of panties from a T-shirt.

Drew stood up from rubbing the dog's belly. She made the mistake of looking at him, his gorgeous bare chest, his slightly rumpled hair. "Get in your bed, Genny," he said in a no-nonsense voice, and the dog obeyed. But he was looking at *her*.

Dully, she thought that she would easily have obeyed him. But she'd had a few seconds to think, and thinking was a real buzz kill.

Drew walked over and stood by her, touching her arm. "Sorry about that. We don't have to let the dog—"

Maggie shook her head. She couldn't find words.

"Don't let the dog stop what was happening between us." His tone sounded pleading.

She put down the clothes and looked at him. God, he was so handsome. Those big brown eyes beseeching her, telling her in no uncertain terms he wanted her. It was thrilling to have a man look at her like that again. To have *him* look at her like that.

"This would be a mistake. You're using me to forget your troubles and I'm—"

"Sex starved?" A little smile curled up his lips.

"Call it what you'd like. The point is, this is not a good idea for too many reasons to count."

"No, it's a great idea for just those reasons. Besides, you're the one who wanted a fling, right?" He opened his arms in a demonstrative gesture. "Here I am, Maggie. Yours for the having. Think about it."

She opened her mouth to protest. Say that she really wasn't a fling type of gal. But the truth was, she wanted him. *Bad.*

He glanced at his phone, which sat atop the dresser. "I'm hitting the shower," he said, pulling some boxers out of his duffel bag and giving the dog a dirty look, which for some reason made *her* smile. "We leave for the rehearsal dinner at seven," he said and closed the bathroom door.

A few seconds later, the shower turned on. Maggie blew out a big breath and collapsed on the bed, trying to gather her senses. And trying to ignore the dog, who was sitting near her feet, staring at her with the intensity of a prison guard.

She did not want a serious relationship, and he was offering her everything she wanted. He was probably good at this and wouldn't come with a list of unrealistic expectations. All she had to do was say yes. And under no circumstances allow herself to get attached.

CHAPTER 11

The rehearsal dinner was held in a chic microbrewery in the warehouse district, but Drew barely noticed the two giant silver brew tanks gleaming against one of the brick walls, or the exposed pipes and cement floor that lent a casual but classy ambience to the place.

He was too busy thinking about Maggie. Kissing her, tasting her, just starting to explore her sweet, soft body. They'd only just begun to scratch the surface. He could barely concentrate on this evening. Her scent was still in his nostrils, her taste still on his tongue. And all he wanted was more.

He felt better than he had in ages. Sondra wasn't the same woman he'd known—the one who'd worked two jobs to get through college, who ate macaroni and cheese and ramen noodles to save money, and who'd never cared in her life whether or not she'd won or lost any kind of game. Seeing the demanding, hard edge to her made him worry for his brother's happiness. He wondered if he should take it up with Xander, at the risk of appearing spiteful or jealous.

But it appeared he had another problem. She was sitting right next to him at the bar, looking over the beer flight menu, wearing a little black dress with straps that crisscrossed her lovely back. Her hair was done up in some complicated twisty way with little wisps curling on her lovely, kissable neck. She had this amazing ability to morph from someone demure and sweet in a mommy nightgown to hot-blonde-I-want-to-do-right-now.

Except he'd wanted to do her even in the mommy nightgown.

But there was more than the sexual attraction going on. She was smart and sharp witted and fun to be around.

And she'd felt so soft in his arms, and he liked the way she kissed and those little noises she made—and he knew, dammit—knew right down to his marrow—that he could make up for all her sex starvedness. He wouldn't mind helping her with that a bit. Not at all.

But watching her as she intently studied the menu, he felt his heart twist a little. He *knew* the kind of guy she needed. Someone who would treat her with care—not that she wasn't tough as nails—but she deserved someone who would look out for her feelings, respect her, love her. She'd been through enough. And he was not in a position to do that.

Oh, he was over getting dumped and heartbroken—at least, he was finding his way out. It didn't pain him so much anymore to look at Sondra and Xander together. He didn't recognize her anymore as being the woman he'd once loved. But there was no way he was ready to plunge into a new relationship.

Especially with a woman like Maggie who had a kid and clear expectations, whether she realized it or not, of something permanent. He needed something light and casual and he knew—he *knew*—that no matter what Maggie would have him believe, she wasn't the light and casual type.

But how would he ever be able to leave that room they were sharing without having her?

"I can't decide between the coffee-flavored beer flight or the chocolate," Maggie said, tapping her fingers on the glossy wooden bar.

"You order one, I'll order the other, and you can try mine too," he suggested.

"Oh, that sounds like fun," she said, her eyes brightening. She closed the menu and gave the bartender their order. He listened to her engage the bartender in a discussion about his favorite beer and the craft beers her family's bar served.

He smiled. It was fun watching her be thrilled at the smallest things. Except he didn't like the way the bartender was looking at her.

The bartender placed a trio of small beer mugs in front of Maggie, and she took a taste, looking quite taken with it.

Drew took the beer from her and sipped, watching her closely. "This is pretty good," he said. Not really. Coffee-flavored beer? That was plain unnatural.

She offered him the chocolate one, but he shook his head, gesturing for her to try it first. "Wow. This is…interesting," she said, an intent expression on her face.

"You need to get out more," he said, laughing. He wondered what her life was really like, working and taking care of her kid and trying to keep it together after her husband had died. He wondered what it was like to love someone that much, what it was like to go on when the life you thought was forever went kaput.

He didn't remember many specifics from that terrible time from his own childhood, thank God. What did stick with him most over time was the hollow pit in his stomach that never seemed to go away and that nothing could fill, not food, not women, not anything. Like a piece of him was missing. He'd grown accustomed to that, long before Sondra had broken up with him. It was his lot in life, he supposed, to always feel a little like an outsider. Not quite belonging anywhere.

"What do you think?" Maggie asked, pushing over the chocolate one. She had beautiful eyes. Clear blue, guileless. No hidden agendas.

He tasted it, debated, then decided to say exactly what he thought. "Just that in my book, beer's supposed to taste like beer. If I want coffee, I'll get a Starbucks."

Maggie laughed. She set down her mini mug and licked the foam off her lip. "I think that's the first real thing you've said to me all weekend," she said. "Maybe the second. You did tell me a little about Anika."

He lifted a brow. Tried not to be distracted by the cute way she'd licked the foam. And she'd missed a spot. He reached out with his thumb and swiped it gently away. "I'm trying to be more honest and open."

Good thing they were interrupted back at their room. The more he thought about it, the more he realized starting something with her would be fraught with complications. She'd want more, she'd pursue him, and seeing her around all the time would make his life torture. He would only hurt her in the end. He liked her a lot, but he was no longer the type to fall hard. He was just a little obsessed with her right now.

"You know, if you ever wanted to talk some more, I'd listen." She tasted the third beer. "And I like just plain old beer too. With pizza. See? I can share too."

His gaze flicked up to her face. There weren't many people he let into his inner circle, especially since he'd left New York City and had been hiding out from the press. He could count the people he trusted on half a hand.

But there was something about her...he wanted to tell her things. Ask her if she liked her beer and pizza accompanied by a good football game. He loved running and reading thrillers on a rainy Saturday afternoon, and he'd always imagined ending up with someone who loved to read too, so they could lie together on both ends of a couch on a lazy Saturday afternoon. But what good was revealing all that? They were in completely different places. Weren't they?

"I want you to know I'm here for you," she continued. "If there's any way I can help you feel better about all this…"

He raised a brow. "I can think of a way that might make me feel better." There she went blushing again, and he swore, it was the prettiest thing he ever saw. She couldn't hide her feelings if she had to.

"Look, Maggie," he said, "I want to be serious for a minute. I'm sorry I wasn't completely truthful with you from the beginning. And just so you know, I appreciate what you've done, coming here like this with me."

"Why, Andreas Poulos, are you being sincere? I don't detect a trace of sarcasm in that statement."

He grinned. "See? I guess people can change for the better."

"It's a good look on you," she said. Their gazes locked, and the low buzz he always felt around her got stronger, and his mind filled with thoughts—kissing her, their bodies flush and wanting. Thoughts that could get them both in big trouble.

"Look, what I said earlier about the fling…just ignore that. I was talking in the heat of the moment. You need someone who's looking for a lot more, and I'm really not ready for anything like that."

"No, I don't."

"You don't what?"

"I'm looking for something light. Something not permanent. I don't want all the pain that goes along with a real relationship. I just want to start…living again. And you'd be the perfect person to help me out with that."

Oh my God. She was dangling herself in front of him like a ripe fruit ready to be picked. He could do the right thing for only so long before he caved, especially since they were together all weekend. What the hell was he supposed to do now?

"I wouldn't expect anything from you after the weekend. We'd go back to Mirror Lake and just…go on with our lives. No strings."

"Trust me, you're the kind of woman where there are always strings. Plenty of them, hanging everywhere."

She laughed. "I never thought you'd be so reluctant. I mean, all those spreads in *People* magazine… The world followed your, um, exploits."

"Those were different. None of those women expected anything more."

"I don't want anything more. I promise, see? I'll even shake on it." She offered her small hand. "We could agree to be friends, no matter what happens. What do you think of that?"

He took it, of course. Because he couldn't seem to stop touching her. Another reason he was in big trouble. He'd meant it to be businesslike, but the feel of her hand in his—small, slender, warm—did something to him that he felt clear down in his gut. "Friends, huh?" he said, trying to read her eyes, her body language. Did she seriously consider him a friend? Ordinarily he'd be thrilled at the offer of a no-strings affair. But somehow this galled.

"Oh, how sweet," Sondra said, approaching with Christina. "Just look at you two." He realized he'd been stroking the inside of Maggie's hand with his thumb…and liking it. A lot.

"You two certainly played an aggressive match today," Sondra said. "You've motivated Xander and me to take more lessons."

"You know," Maggie said, "we never actually care if we win or lose. We're just happy to be together. True love trumps everything else, doesn't it, honey?" She flashed a big smile at Drew.

"Absolutely," he said.

Sondra frowned a little, as if she was truly thinking about that, or maybe she simply couldn't fathom that some things were more important than winning. After a second, she addressed Maggie. "A few of us girls are going to go outside on the patio with our drinks. Want to join us?"

Christina turned to her brother. "I'm sure Maggie could use a little break from you."

Drew mock-scowled at his little sister and waited until they left before he stepped outside himself onto the expansive patio. He wandered over to talk to his mother, say hello to some aunts, then got a seven and seven from the bar and sat down with his brother.

"So tomorrow's the big day," Drew said, squeezing his shoulder.

"Yeah," Xander said. He raised his drink, encouraging Drew to do the same. "Everything's worked out for the best. No hard feelings about Sondra, right? I mean, you and Maggie look like you're really in love."

"Maggie's great. Look, Xander, I'm glad we have an opportunity to talk. I just want to make sure—"

"Sure of what?" Xander surveyed him with wary eyes. Drew wished their relationship could go back to what it was, long ago when they were boys. When they trusted one another.

He'd considered more than once that all this competition between them, for Sondra and for the affection of their father, was his fault. For being a little too good at things, and maybe also a little too confident, a little too cocky. Maybe he'd driven his brother to it in some weird way he wasn't even aware of.

"I—I just want to make sure you're happy," he said. "That Sondra makes you really and truly happy."

"Of course she does. She's everything I'd ever want."

Drew searched his brother's eyes. Xander had always been an open book, his emotions close to the surface for all to see. He loved Sondra. Drew had no idea how to broach the fear he'd had all along—that Sondra was perhaps playing both of them.

Oh, he had no evidence, no proof. Just a raw feeling in his gut.

"I wish you all the best, you know that, don't you? I want you to have a great life with a great partner who you can't imagine living without. Who loves you and would do anything for your happiness."

Xander laughed. "Look, I know it's been a little awkward between us. But I know we can get past this. I'm really glad you brought Maggie." Then his brother hugged him. Drew knew in that moment that he could never hold a grudge against his brother. Whatever had happened no longer mattered. He struggled with what else to say to voice his fears but came up with nothing Xander was likely to believe.

After Xander took off to talk with the other guests, Drew went and stood at the edge of the patio, taking in the blur of the warehouse district lights, the tangle of cars and honking horns in the distance. Suddenly, he heard a familiar voice drifting up from a lower level of the patio. He could just make out his father's profile as he sat in one of the outdoor seating areas a few steps below.

"You seem like an intelligent woman, Maggie," his father was saying. "Smart enough to know that life doesn't always bring opportunity to your door. Sometimes you need to go out and grab it for yourself."

"Being by myself these last few years, I *do* know about seizing opportunity when it's available." *Maggie.* Every muscle in his body froze. He debated intervening before his father could sink his claws into her, but he found himself turning a little so he could hear their conversation better.

"Drew would certainly be a good provider," his father said. "At least, he would have been if he stayed in the family business. Or if he would accept the family money he's entitled to."

"I don't need anyone to provide for me. And as far as your son goes, you might be surprised that his new business with his brothers is getting off the ground quite well."

"The apple cider business."

"It's apple brandy, Mr. Poulos. And I think it's going to be a

136

big success." There was that optimistic tone she always harbored. She sounded sincere too, like she believed it. Believed in what he was doing.

"Why that boy would start from scratch with an apple farm instead of taking the helm in our family's company, I'll never know."

"Maybe he wanted to strike out on his own? Leave to find himself?"

"Making apple juice." His father made a sound of disgust. "He's defied me at every turn."

"You mean by not marrying Anika?"

"His marriage to Anika would have secured our family's success for generations to come."

"Success isn't all about money. Don't you believe everyone's entitled to try and find a loving partner to spend their life with?"

On hearing Maggie's words, an odd sensation of warmth spread through him. Maggie didn't have to take on Maxim, yet she was doing it anyway.

Maxim grunted. "You're young. Christina told me you're a widow. Surely after losing your husband, you must understand that life often doesn't give us what we want. But family—family is always number one. No matter what else happens, family is who stays at your side."

"Not everyone's lucky enough to end up with the love of their life. But marriage is too hard to end up with anyone you're not fully committed to in the first place. Everyone deserves the opportunity to pick a person of their own choosing."

"In my country, matchmaking often makes a better marriage than picking your own spouse."

"Did *you* always do what your parents wanted?"

He snorted. "Maybe if I had, my own marriage wouldn't have ended in divorce."

"Maybe you should talk to him about that."

"He's had a year and a half to talk to me. And what does he do? Sends me emails."

She shrugged. "Your son is stubborn, what can I say? From what I gather, like his father."

Maxim burst out laughing. "I like you, Maggie. I can see why my son is so taken with you." They both stood, and he put an arm around Maggie's shoulders.

"Well," she said, "I'm taken with him too."

"I'm sorry I was a little tough on you before. But I don't want my son hurt again. He deserves better. I think you *are* better."

She didn't answer for a long time. "Thank you, Mr. Poulos," she said in a low voice. Like maybe she was a little choked up.

Drew suddenly seemed to have a bad case of heartburn. It had to be, the way this ache was getting him right smack in the middle of his chest. He tapped hard over his breastbone to relieve it.

Maggie's words from earlier rang in his ears. Stuff about him being hardworking and levelheaded and making her laugh. Of course she was making that shit up for his sake. He *knew* that. He didn't believe in romance.

But just now, she'd stuck up for him again. The fact that she did, of her own free will, touched him inexplicably.

And Maxim seemed to actually listen.

In fact, he seemed like any worried father who wanted his son to be happy.

Maxim could be manipulative and had a history of going to any lengths to get his way. Drew often felt that he'd taken advantage of his devastation over Sondra to get him to agree to the marriage to Anika. But somewhere in the twisted craziness, perhaps his father did love him.

Drew wondered what it would be like to talk to him about these things, to clear the air. He was never the kind of father who'd said much. They'd never had heart-to-heart talks. And

Drew wasn't the type of man to wear his heart on his sleeve. Opening up was about as pleasant as the dentist's drill.

He reminded himself that he was paying Maggie to act a part, and that was all he was witnessing, her in action, doing her job.

Yet part of him wanted to believe that wasn't completely true. Which was dangerous thinking for someone who had agreed to just a fling.

CHAPTER 12

Despite Maggie's underlying rip current of worry, everything in the church the next morning looked perfect. Drew had crashed with the groomsmen last night, to be with his brother, which was fine, but she worried about not being able to talk with him before the ceremony. She wondered how he was holding up, if the impending wedding was upsetting him. She hoped not. She, for one, would be grateful when it was over and Sondra was happily married, and she hoped Drew was coming to feel the same way.

Talking with Maxim last night had given her a window into Drew's complicated relationship with his father. Maxim wasn't so bad. And Drew…well, the more she learned about him, the more she liked and respected him. She tried to place that safely in the context of friendship. Because friendship was all she could handle, and she knew that all too well about herself. Loving anyone again came with risks she did not want to deal with.

From Maggie's vantage point at the back of the church, she could see the white roses gracing the ends of the pews and delicate white petals scattered along the white rolled-out runner. Big gorgeous bouquets sat on pedestals near the altar. A singer was singing classical love songs accompanied by a guitar and a violin. A celebration was about to take place, regardless of how unsettled Maggie felt.

As she joined the short line of people waiting to be seated, one of the groomsmen smiled at her and offered his elbow.

"I'd love to walk a pretty girl down the aisle," he said.

"She's with me," Drew said, suddenly *there*, taking her by the elbow. But instead of leading her down the aisle, he pulled her away into the vestibule of the church.

He wore a navy tux, a peach-colored rose fastened to his lapel. Oh, he was a handsome, handsome man, lean and broad shouldered, and with all that facial hair gone, she could see his strong square jaw. But no dimples. Today he was not smiling.

"How—how's your brother doing?" she asked.

"He's going through with it."

She didn't know what to say to that, so she said, "I—waited up for you."

Between that whiny dog pining for him all night and all the tossing and turning she did, it had been a terrible night. "I was worried about you. I didn't…sleep well."

"I didn't sleep so well myself."

"Are you okay about…this?"

Suddenly a cloud of violet tulle ran down the aisle toward them—it was Jade, Sondra's sister and maid of honor. She clutched Maggie by the arm. "Sondra wants to speak with you," she said.

"What's going on?" Maggie asked.

"She's freaking out," Jade said. "We thought maybe you could help calm her down."

Great. And Maggie happened to be fresh out of Haldol today.

Maggie gazed at Drew. "Help her to do the right thing," he whispered.

What, exactly, was the right thing here? Not marrying Xander?

Jade pushed a path through the crowd in the vestibule of the church, Maggie following in her wake. When she reached the bride room, she tugged Maggie inside and closed the door behind them.

Oh, bollocks. Maggie found herself in a stucco-walled room with a cheval mirror and an old but decent plaid couch and a few padded chairs. Sondra sat in front of an antique dressing table, a travel bag of makeup spilled out before her.

"Sondra, honey, here she is," Jade said.

Sondra's face was tear streaked, her makeup ruined. Even so, she still looked extraordinary, her long, lovely neck stretching over an off-the-shoulder beaded couture gown that showed off her shapely curves and impossibly tiny waist. "Thanks, Jade," she said to her sister. "Will you leave us alone for a minute?"

Maggie's heart softened a little. If only because no bride should suffer this degree of distress on her wedding day, which should be happy and perfect.

"I can't do it," Sondra said, pulling out three Kleenex from a box atop the dressing table and blowing her nose loudly. "I can't marry Xander."

"Honey, why not?" Maggie said, pulling up a wooden chair and grabbing Sondra's hand.

"I realized something. Something big and important. I've been thinking about what you said last night about our tennis match. That true love always trumps everything else. True love's always the most important thing, right?"

"Yes, true love is always important," Maggie said, even as she was deluged with a flood of worry. Part of her felt she should be encouraging her to break it off with Xander, saving him from a certain life of torture. "What—what are you thinking, Sondra? What's this all about?"

Sondra patted her hand. "I'm so, so sorry, Maggie, but I have to tell you something you may not like." She took a big breath and blew it out. "I'm just going to say it, okay? I still love Drew. I'm crazy about him, actually. And if he still loves me, I'm going to marry him." She sat up taller. She looked resolute.

Something dropped into Maggie's guts. Her heart. Her stomach lurched sickly.

She loved Drew? After all she'd done to him, including dump him for his own brother?

But then, that appeared to be the way she'd lived her entire life. Why should her damn wedding day be any different?

It was Maggie's turn to try to breathe. She struggled to get a grip. Reminded herself of her purpose here. To help Drew's family. To get them through this weekend. This wasn't about her and what *she* thought was best for Drew.

Except it was. Because she wanted him. And her gut wrenched violently with the feeling that she absolutely did not want Sondra to have him. Sondra did not deserve him. Did Drew know that? She hoped so.

"I was very hurt when Drew left, did you know that?" Sondra said. "When he went off to Harvard to get that MBA." She waved her hand dismissively. "He could've stayed here and learned what he needed working under his father. I never understood his need to go off and start from nothing. He left me—he left our dream."

"What about Xander?" Maggie asked. "Don't you love him?"

"Xander wanted the CEO job. He wanted the same dream I did." She nervously fingered her brush, a hand mirror. "I had to do it, Maggie. I had to make sure my own future was secure. There was only one way to make that happen."

Sondra's pretty blue eyes ran over with tears. Slowly, she lifted her gaze to Maggie's.

Suddenly, Maggie put all the pieces together. And the picture the puzzle made was horrifying. Maggie barely forced the words out. "You—you dumped Drew for his brother because Xander took the CEO position?"

"I was angry, Maggie! Drew and I—we could've had everything! He abandoned his family—he abandoned *me*—to chase a dream. His dream—he didn't care about mine! Or about financial security. After my father's company went bankrupt, I swore I'd never put myself in a position like that again. I didn't want Drew to create a new company. I-I'm not a rebel like that. I'd always had a plan. Drew spoiled everything."

Big tears slowly wound their way through her mascara like raindrops down a window. "I tried to love Xander, I really did. But it's not the same. He's just not…Drew."

Maggie pulled another Kleenex out of the box and handed it to Sondra, who blew her nose loudly. "I tried to forget him, honestly I did. But seeing him again these past few days, being with him…oh, I just don't know what to do!"

Maggie did a mental eye roll. She didn't think Sondra was really capable of loving anyone.

"I have to tell you something," Maggie said.

Sondra looked at her with big, mascara-streaked eyes. Dammit, she was still beautiful in a Helena Bonham Carter sort of way. "Wh-what is it?" Sondra asked, blowing her nose.

Maggie opened her mouth to speak. She was not going to let Sondra get Drew. She opened her mouth to tell Sondra what a self-centered bitch she was and how she'd get a chance with Drew—over her dead body.

Oh hell. Maggie unballed her fists. Stepped back a little. Unfortunately, all those years of Catholic school had given her a conscience, and it was rearing its ugly head.

She formed her words carefully. "You need to tell Xander how you feel, and you need to talk to Drew," Maggie said. "You can't get married feeling like this. Your wedding day should be one of the happiest days of your life, not the saddest."

And Drew needed to be the one to decide whom he wanted. Maggie couldn't take that decision away from him. It wasn't hers to make.

God, she sounded like a psychologist. Oh, she was one. Well, at least her skills hadn't failed her when she needed them most.

"And I deserve to be happy, right?"

Maggie swallowed hard and forced a smile onto her face. "Yes, Sondra, everyone deserves to be happy. But don't start your marriage not loving the guy you marry with all your heart. It's not fair to either one of you."

And that was it. Maggie needed a drink, and a cigarette, for that matter, even though the last time she smoked was after Corey died, when she was on a self-destructive penchant and she couldn't afford the luxury of getting drunk with an infant to care for. So she'd leave Griffin with her mom and dad for a little while and go out for a drive along the scenic view of the lake and smoke cigarette after cigarette.

But she was a bad smoker too, because she couldn't stand the smell in her car and on her clothes. Self-pity was never much her style anyway.

"Wh-what should I do now?" Sondra asked.

"That's your decision. But I'm sure Jade will help you with whatever it is you decide."

Because Maggie had gone as far as she could. She could not bring herself to offer to stand up in front of everyone and call off this wedding. No, Drew would have to come in and have it out with her and his brother and resolve all this.

She only hoped he'd have the sense not to fall for Sondra again.

Maggie left the bride room, but when she got out into the

vestibule, her heart was hammering. She felt hot and cold, and dizzy. Her vision blurred—oh hell, she was crying. Crying! How unprofessional. Instead of returning to the church, she turned left and opened one of the massive wooden doors. Gulped in the lovely blossom-scented spring air, which was a little hot and sticky at this point, but anything was better than going back inside. She sat down on one of the big concrete steps that ran the length of the church and led to the street, and put her head between her knees.

Was she having a panic attack? It had happened to her before, after Corey had died. But she'd had her mom and dad there, and her best friends. Here she had…no one. She'd seemed to convince everyone she was a bastion of strength, a professional. Guess now the joke was on her.

She sure as hell didn't feel professional now. She felt lost and alone.

"Are you all right?" a familiar baritone asked from behind her. She turned to find Drew jogging down the wide church stairs until he stood in front of her, eyeballing her suspiciously. No doubt seeing her runny mascara, her tear-streaked face. She swiped a finger quickly over her eyes.

They both spoke at the same time. "I—I have something in my eye, and I came out here for a second, and I—"

"Jade just told me Sondra's calling off the wedding. She's waiting to talk to me."

She stopped wiping her eyes and looked at him. "I know," she said. "It—it's always so sad when a wedding gets called off, isn't it? All those bills and gifts to return and what to do about the reception—" She was ranting, running at the mouth, but God, she couldn't help it.

"Maggie." He sat down next to her and took her hand, and she swore, that made her eyes leak even worse. "Are you okay? I saw you bolt out the door."

"I'm fine." She managed to look him in the eye. He looked so worried, so concerned, and yet—calm. Surely only beginning to wrap his head around what had just happened, yet—how much did he know about what Sondra was going to say to him?

She wanted to ask him if he knew the depths of Sondra's deception. The lengths she went through to dump him and court his brother, all for—for what? Money? Security? Things she'd never understand.

She had a sudden urge to grab him by his lapels and tell him that Sondra wasn't right for him, not at all. "Drew—" she began.

"Drew! We need you in here, okay?" a groomsman called from the church steps.

He cast a worried eye toward the church. "I'll be right there." He turned to Maggie. "I'll find you later, okay?"

"Of course. Sure," she said. More people were calling him. Bridesmaids were running down the church stairs. Chaos was erupting. He was the best man, and he had a wedding to call off. And she was going to tattletale on Sondra? Declare feelings for a guy she'd barely spent time with? Who she hadn't even been on a decent date with?

No, that wasn't possible.

Then why did she feel so upset?

She couldn't possibly be falling for him. It was way too early for that. She'd been with him a total of two days.

She sat there another second, watching him jog back up the stairs. The big door creaked open. One more step and he'd be gone forever. Right into Sondra's waiting arms.

Maggie jumped to her feet. "Drew!" She ran to him, yelling his name again.

She grabbed him by his neatly pressed lapels and pulled. He might have looked a little worried for her sanity, and a little surprised. He reached up and took hold of her hands, probably to keep her from ripping his tux.

"Drew, I have to tell you something." Her mind ran over all the possibilities, starting with *Sondra is a bitch, don't get sucked in by her,* to *I want you, pick me instead!* In the end, she tugged hard on the lapels and kissed him, hard, plastering herself up against him, pressing her lips to his soft, shocked ones, kissing him like it was her last kiss on earth.

She broke away. "I lied. I don't think of you as a friend. I've actually *never* thought of you as a friend. I *hate* the thought of us being just friends. Okay? I just wanted you to know that. Now go." She tried to push him away, but he was a steel mountain of mass and didn't budge an inch.

His eyes were kind and concerned. His mouth tugged up in a little smile, then he reached over and kissed her on the forehead. Gently, slowly. At odds with all the chaos inside the church and inside her. "Thanks, Maggie," he said, almost at a whisper. "I have to go." Then he was gone.

The big church door closed with a thud of finality. The traffic from the street rolled by, punctuated by the honk of a car horn and the slam of the bridal limo door as the driver got out for a smoke.

She should be thrilled that Sondra had come to her senses. That Xander had barely escaped stepping into the biggest pile of horse shit of his life. But now, apparently, the pile was being directed at Drew. She just hoped he didn't step back into it.

CHAPTER 13

A few hours later, Maggie sat on the red velvet throne chair with her head between her knees. She thought that whoever first sat in this chair was probably kingly—or, better, queenly—and commanding and would never succumb to such a gesture of weakness. But no matter how long she sat, the royal courage wasn't rubbing off on her. Finally, she got up and paced the room for the hundredth time.

Drew had been gone for hours. The wedding had indeed been canceled, the guests dispersed, the elegant reception food donated to charity.

Drew had gone into the bride room and emerged, only to pull Xander in there as well. After a while, Drew strode down the aisle and up to the podium and politely told everyone to please go home.

A little gasp had gone up among the guests. She could only imagine Xander, sad and shocked, maybe crying a little on his brother's shoulder. To which Drew would reassure him that things might seem devastating now, but would definitely look up in the future.

But the scene that kept playing over and over in her head was the one where Sondra finally told Drew she loved him. Would he laugh hysterically? Send her packing, making her promise never to torment his family ever again? (She favored that version.) Or would he take her in his arms, whisper to her that he'd never stopped loving her, and give her a real kiss, not the forehead version he'd given Maggie earlier, which she didn't quite know what to make of.

Being alone with her thoughts was making her crazy. Maggie found herself dying for company, even Genevieve's, which made her pretty desperate, but alas, the infatuated doggie still hadn't returned from wherever she hung out during the day.

The walls were starting to remind her of a medieval prison. One glance at the flail and suddenly, she knew she had to get out of there. She put on her swimsuit—the one-piece, mommy version for when she took Griffin to the Y—and a pair of shorts, and headed outside.

Maggie headed down to the Olympic-sized pool. It was a balmy night, the kind Corey would probably grumble a little about, because he hated to sweat. He used to say seventy degrees was his favorite temperature year round. Not her, who never complained about heat in her life. And she loved to swim. Something about cutting a path in the water, streamlined and kicking, arms and legs all stretched out and pushing through the water, made the world go away, and she was seriously in need of that now.

It was she who'd given Griffin his love of the water. Corey never came in but would always sit there and watch them, making silly faces, taking pictures of Griffin's antics. And he'd always grab her a towel and wrap it around her tightly and kiss her when she got out. Just a little sweet gesture.

She missed that, the comfort of knowing someone had your back.

The pool looked like a calm place to be, its surface a perfect, quiet mirror, the shimmering water reflected bright blue in the pool lights against the black of night. "Corey," she whispered before she jumped in and started a lap. It felt good to say his name out loud. Like he was here, not really gone forever. They used to talk about everything, anything. Imagine talking to him about her attraction to another man!

She was so deep in thought and focusing on her strokes that she nearly jumped out of her skin when something pulled at her leg. She would've screamed if she hadn't been underwater. She stood up immediately and pushed her streaming hair back on her head.

Drew stood next to her in waist-high water, the droplets on his chest glistening in the reflections from the pool lights. She didn't know whether to hug him or harm him for scaring her to death. Actually, that sort of schizophrenic reaction seemed to be her usual one to him. "Hey," he said, one side of his mouth turning up in a half smile. "Didn't mean to scare you."

"You did scare me!" she said, wiping water out of her eyes. "What the hell?" She tried to work up the steam to be angry, but honestly, she wasn't angry at all. She crisscrossed her arms in front of her to avoid doing something she might regret, like jumping in his arms and wrapping herself around him like a pretzel.

"Sorry." His voice sounded smooth and velvety. "You didn't hear me, so I came in after you."

"Drew." Suddenly she gripped his arms, ran her hands up and down them like he'd been lost in the Amazon for a month or two. "Drew, I—I'm sorry you're wet." Well, that was brilliant. She'd have to try again. "I—I'm so glad you're here."

He smiled again, that full smile that always made her stomach flip. She had to do better. Tell him how glad she was to see him. As long as he had no plans to run off with Sondra, which, judging by the fact that he was here and the way he was holding on to her, seemed unlikely.

Oh, she loved that his arms were around her, and he was looking at her like he'd missed her, like he was so happy to be with her now, and all thoughts of Sondra went right out of her head.

"Are you all right?" she asked.

"Yeah," he said. "Thanks for asking."

"What happened?"

He released her and leaned against the pool wall, draping his big arms across the ledge. "Sondra said she loved me. I told her it was over."

It was over. Those precious words echoed over and over in Maggie's head as she let out a long, protracted sigh.

"She apologized to me."

"Did you—forgive her?" She had no doubt he would. He was that kind of guy.

"I thanked her."

"For what?"

"I've come to realize her dumping me was the best thing that ever happened to me. And hopefully my brother will feel like that one day too."

She'd been quietly nodding. But inside, she was doing a jubilation dance. "It's been a long day," Drew said. "I don't want to talk about my brother anymore, if that's all right. I looked all over for you."

His gaze was steely and resolute. He was staring at her the way a man stares at a woman he wants to get naked with. *Now.*

Oh, flutter my heart. Even though it had been a while, she knew that look. And it vibrated clear down to her bones.

No Sondra! Oh joy! And he was looking at her like she was

152

chocolate cake. And there were just the two of them together for the entire evening.

Oh dear. That brought up other worries. Like going to bed with him. Which she wanted to do yet was terrified of at the same time.

He stepped so close, she was at eye level with his nipple. And what a lovely man nipple it was. My God, the man was tall. And gorgeous. She closed her eyes and swallowed, trying to stop herself from flinging herself at him like a flying projectile. Or running back to Mirror Lake. If she left now, she just might be home by Monday.

"Look at me, Maggie."

She opened her eyes. She bit down on her lip, clenched and unclenched her fingers. This was it, one of those Moments of Truth she always told her clients about. *Don't back down from it. Don't be afraid to face it,* she'd say. The-truth-will-set-you-free kind of thing. Or the truth could make you want to curl into a ball, fetal style, and not move for a very long time.

She forced herself to meet his gaze. And she was surprised at what she found there. He was looking at her…*tenderly*. And his eyes held a dark mischief, like he wanted to do certain things to her that she wouldn't object to at all.

Drew touched her hair, of all things, combing a wet strand back with the others.

His touch melted her. She held him by the arms, looked into his fathomless eyes. "I was afraid maybe you'd think about getting back with her."

"I don't want Sondra. I want you." He kissed her then, leaving her wobbly and breathless.

"I want you too, Drew," she managed, and it was her heart talking, which was very full and achy and so relieved. "I'm so glad you're here."

"I want to take you back to our room and make love to you. Are you okay with that?"

Her heart tripped and stuttered. He hadn't picked Sondra. He wanted *her*. And he was letting her make the next move.

All she knew was that he was nuzzling her neck, whispering to her how wonderful she felt in his arms, and it felt so damn good, she wanted to cry. And she was here, in a gorgeous pool under the stars with a big handsome man who wanted her just as much as she wanted him. And maybe that was okay. Maybe it was okay to embrace this and live her life again in a way she hadn't in a long, long time.

She grabbed hold of his forearms for leverage and leapt into his arms, wrapping her arms around his neck and drawing him close, peppering his face with rapid-fire kisses.

As her lips met his, he slid his hands over her ass and hiked her up so their bodies were sealed together.

She wrapped her legs more tightly around him, and she couldn't help noticing some…er…developments. That she couldn't help checking out by running her hands over just to check—oh wow.

But she could tell by the way his eyes narrowed that he liked it. Then he bent his head and kissed her well and good. His lips met hers, wet and soft, at once possessive but measured. Maggie made it clear she was too impatient for a slow seduction. She pressed herself against him and tangled her tongue with his. He responded in kind, kissing her passionately, stroke after stroke, making her breathless and wanting, hot and helpless in his arms.

Adjusting her grip on his wet shoulders, she pulled back a little to look at him, pleased to see he was breathing a little fast too. She touched his cheek, ran her fingers over the scrape of stubble there. He had kind eyes, dark and a little dangerous, but he held all his feelings there. The want in them urged her to speak. "Take me back to our room," she whispered.

"Yes, ma'am," he said, lifting her up and slinging her over his shoulder like she weighed as much as the dolphin floatie he had to push out of the way, and carried her out of the pool.

Drew closed the door to his room behind them and tugged Maggie close, pinning her against the door and caging her with his hands.

"The friends thing isn't working with me," he said, kissing her neck. She arched her neck, giving him better access to her sweet lovely skin.

"Me neither," she said.

"So we agree." He kissed her on the lips, curling a hand around her neck and pulling her against him. They were both wet and a little chilled from climbing out of the pool, but the body heat between them was combustible. He forced himself to draw back, stop kissing her.

"About what?" she murmured.

"That we're not just friends." He looked at her, tried to read her but she was still so guarded about her own emotions. He longed to tell her things. That he'd never felt like this before with anyone. That he wanted more than just sex with her. That he loved being with her, talking with her, holding hands with her. But he knew how gun-shy she was. How reluctant to take these steps. And after this whole thing with Sondra, she probably wouldn't believe him anyway.

But he knew something was different about this, about her. Sondra was his past, and she seemed a million light years away.

"Drew, we're not just friends," she said, wrapping her arms around his neck and pressing herself against him, kissing him deep and hard. "But I still don't want anything serious."

"Whatever you say." He gave up on the talking and kissed her back like he'd been fantasizing all these days and nights, pulling her flush against him and cupping her ass and sliding his tongue against hers until she gave a soft little moan. She gave it all right back to him, raking her hands though his hair, lowering his face to hers and kissing him back with all she had, and it all felt so damn good. Like it was what they'd been meant to do from the start.

Drew was okay with letting his actions speak for him, at least for now. He wasn't ever good at talking anyway.

Maggie felt pleasantly pinned between the door and Drew's big, solid body. She was so relieved to have him here, with her, and have Sondra behind them once and for all. And she'd do anything, anything to have him, right now. She tugged at his shorts, not wanting to waste another minute of not having him.

He made short work of his shorts, tossing them in a wet heap on the bathroom floor. He was all sculpted muscle, flat stomach, and powerful calves. His perfect male beauty stunned her speechless.

In one swift motion, he curled his thumbs under her straps and tugged her suit down to her waist. As he gazed at her breasts, his eyes softened with desire and a tenderness that melted her. She tugged off the suit the rest of the way and kicked it into the bathroom to land on top of his shorts. He tossed his boxers onto the pile and stood before her, his erection tall and proud.

Suddenly, he wrapped his arms around her and pushed them both onto the bed, settling himself beside her. She ran her hands up and down the rippled muscles of his back, over his firm buttocks, delighting in his silky hardness. He growled, and his kisses grew hungry and wet, his body flush against hers, hot and hard. She felt wanted, desired, possessed. Yearning for him filled every thought.

He touched her breasts, rubbing the tips lightly until they grew hard. A whimper escaped her mouth, but he kissed it away with deep, driving kisses that she returned in full, her hands roving over the silky hardness of his muscle, cupping his tight ass, grasping his hard shaft.

Gently, he brushed her hand aside. "I won't last," he murmured, placing his lips over her nipple and playing with it, sucking and nipping. A surge of sensation, a flash of pure heat, flooded her, and she arched uncontrollably against him and cried out. He slid his fingers into her and spread her legs with his while she lay there, open and helpless as he rubbed and caressed her, the torturous pleasure building.

Her body could take it no more. Every muscle tightened to the point of bursting. On and on he continued his sensual assault until at last she bucked and trembled and fell apart in his arms in a climax that left her dazed and spent.

Then he was over her, sheathed, poised atop her, looking down on her with a frightful tenderness. She swept a finger over his brow. Looked into his eyes. And she pulled him to her, pulled him inside her, taking every inch of him until he filled her completely.

"Maggie," he whispered, his face close above hers, his weight on his muscular arms surrounding either side of her head.

She saw something in his gaze—*felt* it—in the way he looked at her, the way he held her, and in the absolute joy of the moment. She had no words for what she was feeling. Didn't want to put them into words because that would make them real.

And so she wrapped her arms around his beautifully sculpted back and kissed him and lifted her hips against his until they created a rhythm together that brought them both to a shattering climax.

He didn't release her, simply lay there, his hand circling her waist, his head buried in her neck. She kissed his forehead, his cheeks as he nibbled on her shoulder, locked tightly in his embrace. She thought of nothing other than the miracle of him, the goodness, the tenderness, and how lucky she was to have found him. For the first time in so many years, she felt alive again. And she didn't dare allow herself to think one single thought beyond this magical moment.

CHAPTER 14

"Where did you ever find chicken fingers?" Maggie asked a little later, after she'd put on one of his T-shirts and a pair of pj shorts. They'd turned on a baseball game and Drew had just returned from raiding the kitchen.

"They're left over from the midnight snack that was supposed to be served at the wedding. They're from a gourmet food truck company."

"They're delicious."

"They're cold."

"Even better." She took a swig from a can of Diet Coke, which he'd also brought for her.

"You sure that stuff isn't going to keep you up?"

"Oh, come on now. You don't actually expect to sleep now, do you?"

He raised a brow.

She pointed to the TV and laughed. "I mean, not when the game's in overtime and the Mets are about to score."

"Where's Genny, by the way?" she asked after taking another

chicken finger and scooting back on the bed next to Drew. She hadn't eaten much all day due to distress. Now she was starving.

"Maybe she found a hot date too."

She looked over at the empty dog bed. "Seriously, is this not cause to worry? I mean, what if she's run off?" Maggie wasn't sure if she should even worry about the obnoxious dog, but still. After what had happened here, she had charity to spare.

"I'm kidding. One of the staff told me she was staying with her tonight. It's fine."

Maggie was a little disappointed. About the dog not being permanently gone. But she didn't share that with him.

"I'm going to take her home with me," Drew said.

Maggie looked at Drew sideways. He was sitting up in bed, the blue light from the TV highlighting his strong jaw and the planes of his muscles. A gorgeous man. If anyone had told her earlier she'd be eating gourmet chicken fingers in his bed and watching a ball game tonight she wouldn't have believed it. "I mean it," he said. "What do you think of that?"

Oh God, what did she think? As long as the dog never set foot in her house, what did it matter? "I think no one should ever separate a man and his dog."

He reached out for her can of Coke, grazing her fingers, and took a swig. Then he set it down on the end table and clicked the Off button for the TV.

"It's in overtime," Maggie fake-protested. "How can you—"

"I don't want to waste a minute of caffeination." Then he kissed her, and they stayed up for quite some time.

Drew woke up sometime in the middle of the night, startled at first that he was a) in an actual bed, not on the cold, hard floor and b) that Maggie's cheek was against his chest, his arm was around her and their legs tangled up. He dragged over a blanket with one hand to cover her. In the moonlight seeping in from the window, he could make out her lovely curves surrounding him, her hand tucked under her face.

An immediate wave of tenderness crashed over him, taking him by surprise.

He could not remember a night like this in his life. She was a firecracker, sometimes a tease, and she was incapable of hiding anything she felt. She was sexy in an honest, vulnerable way that was so appealing. And he wanted more. God help him, he wanted more and more.

With all the emotions of this weekend, surely he was in the same boat as she, reluctant to start something real. Old feelings might stir, doubts could cripple. But he didn't feel that way. He felt free for the first time in a very long time.

For so long, he'd stopped thinking of himself as capable of having a relationship. But after tonight, maybe it was possible. Maggie made him laugh, she was trusting and loving and kind, and he knew deep in his heart that he would die protecting her.

He understood this had been a big step for her to make. That it was only natural to want to hold back after all she'd been through. Once she saw that her fears were unfounded, she'd come around, he felt confident. He'd show her how good it could be between them.

And with those thoughts humming around his head, he rolled over and fell into a deep sleep.

Oh my God, what had she done?

Yeah, she knew exactly what she'd done. Slept with Drew. Had a one-night stand. Had sex in what had been the longest time. And he'd been loving and playful and kind and wonderful. And her entire body was humming. She felt boneless, relaxed, and content.

She felt terrific!

Gray light was just seeping into the room. It wasn't long before dawn. But as the shadows lifted, Maggie could make out the large sleeping form of the man next to her, sprawled on his stomach, one big biceps tucked under the pillow, his dark hair tousled over his forehead. He was the picture of hot sexy man. Next to her! And he'd been wonderful, so loving and gentle, so fun and playful too. Part of her wanted to curl into all that muscle and let the warmth of his body seep into her and his big arms wrap solidly around her.

That wonderful, giddy feeling that she hadn't felt for…well, for years, it was swirling through her whole body like she was a teenager again.

It had been fun to be with him. He'd been so kind, so passionate and playful and loving…

She'd gotten swept away. Done something so out of character, but it felt…good.

He was the perfect man to help her move on, the kind who wouldn't make demands of her or expect anything more. He'd been burned too, and he'd said himself that a relationship wasn't in the cards for him. Good.

Because she couldn't do more. Didn't dare do more.

She didn't want a roller coaster ride with wild, unexpected emotions. With the possibility for powerful, deep love that threw you for a loop and put you in the kind of pain there was no recovery from.

Maggie couldn't think of anything beyond the great time they'd just had. She *wouldn't*.

"Hey there, Genny," Drew said as he petted his dog that he'd just let into his room at the crack of dawn. The other half of his bed was empty, Maggie in the bathroom. "Doing the walk of shame?" he inquired of his dog. "Wonder if your night was as great as mine, huh?" Genny flipped over on her back, letting him know in no uncertain terms there was only one guy for her.

By this time, after a night of female companionship, Drew was usually up and out the door, a quick peck on the cheek to the lady in question and then it was on to Starbucks and a million tasks to accomplish. He never stayed the night. Okay, it was a little different here, at home, but still. He'd been sleeping like the dead with no intention to leave. He'd felt so...content. Confident Maggie had felt the same. Because what they'd had together was...wow. And he was hoping for more. Right now.

Maggie cleared her throat, startling him out of his thoughts. How long had she been standing there? "Did you just ask your dog if she got laid last night?" she asked. *Oh, busted.*

She turned those big blue eyes on him, and he swore his heart flipped over. She looked full-court-press gorgeous, with the sheet wrapped around her and her hair mussed and her lips a little swollen from all that kissing...

"Good morning," he said, greeting her with a kiss and lightly tucking a strand of hair behind her ear.

"Hi to you too," she said with a big smile.

"I brought you some coffee," he said, handing it to her from the bedside table. "Not sure how you take it, though, so I just put a little cream in it."

She accepted the cup and took a sip. "That was sweet of you, Drew. Thanks." Impatient, he took it out of her hands and set it down and gathered up her hands. Looked into her eyes. He still couldn't quite read her. But they'd been honest with each other so far. And the power of their intimacy last night made him bold.

"Last night was...amazing." He was struggling to find words. Elocution...not his strong point. But he was trying.

"It was so fun, Drew," she said. "I loved every minute."

"That was some…connection we had, wasn't it?" Oh, he was blowing this—trying to tell her last night *meant* something, but failing epically. Her posture seemed to tense up a little, and she wasn't really looking at him. And her hands were cold.

"It was great and wild and fun," she said, smiling a little too brightly, in his opinion. "But don't get too ahead of yourself, Big Boy. I was an easy target after all that drought."

He frowned. He was trying to talk about feelings, and she was…putting him off. But Maggie was usually all about feelings… What was different now?

She was probably just adjusting to the strong emotions they'd both experienced. Maybe they were throwing her for a loop. He was more than a little discombobulated himself.

"I really appreciate your…helping me out with my problem," she said. "I can't think of a better guy to help ease me back into dating. And I know you've been through this a lot more than I have. So…I know you won't be angry with me when I tell you that I think we should leave this weekend here. It's nothing personal. You've been—fantastic. Amazing. I had a great time. I want you to know that, really."

Really? She was…blowing him off? Telling him what happened in Greenwich was going to stay in Greenwich? Yes, of course she was, because he'd used those exact same words more than a time or two. Fantastic. Amazing. *Really.*

He tried to right himself from the punch. Maybe she just needed time to process everything, gain some perspective. "We could…see how we feel once we get back to Mirror Lake. See how things develop." He felt like he was begging. One look at her face and he *knew* he was.

"I…don't think that's the best idea. I just think both our lives would be too complicated if we continue this. I hope you're not upset."

"Oh. Okay, yeah. Sure. I mean, no, I'm not upset." He plowed his fingers through his already messed-up hair. Fine. He got the picture. No need to tell him twice. "We agreed neither of us is looking for anything intense," he said. "So there's no reason to feel bad. We had a great time, and we got all those pent-up emotions out of our systems. I mean, it's been a hell of a weekend, hasn't it?" Yes, it had been, but even as he said that bullshit, he didn't believe a damn word of it. He wanted her in his bed now, tonight, and every night. Why was he pretending it didn't matter? Why was *she*?

Maggie looked a bit happier now, even relieved. "Great. Shall we shower and get down to breakfast and join your family? I'm starving." She headed halfway to the bathroom, then halted and turned. "Would you mind if I go first? It takes a while for me to dry my hair."

"No problem." But oh, it was a problem. This wasn't what he'd envisioned. He'd wanted to take her back to bed, hang out with her a little more, cuddle with her, oh my God, did he just think that word? Apparently, they were on completely different pages, and he was…stunned.

Funny, but all his woes about Sondra seemed far away. Like they hadn't even existed. Maggie, this crazy, wacky woman with all her rules and problems and headaches and her silly jokes and her laughter and the ability to work her way into his heart…yeah. It was a big, big problem. And he wasn't sure what to do about it.

"Goodbye, my son," Maxim said later that morning in the driveway as Maggie watched Arthur load their bags into the car. Maxim gave Drew a hearty hug. It seemed to Maggie like a much friendlier greeting than a few days ago.

"Goodbye, Dad," Drew said, hugging him back. "Goodbye, Mom," he said, hugging her too. "And Val," he said, giving her a kiss on the cheek. "'Bye, everybody."

"It was a pleasure to meet you, Maggie," Maxim said, hugging her. "You take care of my son, eh? So he has strength to work the apple orchards."

"Dad, I work in the office now," Drew said.

"Come down to Mirror Lake and have dinner," Maggie said. "Everyone. Drew will give you a tour of the company, and you can meet the Spikonos brothers. Right, Drew?"

Maggie knew she was being a bit pushy. And the look Drew flashed her seconded that. But she wanted to make sure this family had other opportunities to get together, and she wasn't entirely sure Drew would encourage that on his own.

The only thing she'd left out was dinner *with us*. Because there would be no *us*. She had to stay firm on that, even if things were more than a little awkward now.

"Any unattached brothers out there somewhere?" Christina asked. "I might be interested."

"Hey, not with any of those convicts," Drew said, kissing her goodbye.

"Goodbye, Maggie," Cecilia said, giving her a hug. "You're good for my Drew," she said in a low voice. "I can tell by the way he lights up around you."

"It was great meeting you, Mrs. Poulos," Maggie said, hugging her goodbye and trying not to take her words to heart.

Fling. Casual. Nothing serious.

"Here you go, sir," Arthur said, handing Drew Genevieve's leash. With the dog eagerly bouncing on the other end of it, of course.

"Thanks, Arty." Drew hugged the butler too—awkwardly— and took the leash.

"You don't mind riding back with her, do you?" Drew asked

once they'd gotten into the car, the dog bouncing around everywhere and finally settling on her lap and looking out the window. "It's only an hour."

"No, of course not," Maggie said, proud that she'd kept her eye roll to a minimum as Drew started the engine.

"You all are invited to dinner for the Fourth of July, okay?" she said out the window. "Mirror Lake has fabulous fireworks."

"Seriously?" Drew said, raising a suspicious brow.

"Well, you weren't offering. So I did. Besides, I thought you might want to invite them to your wine bar opening, but that's up to you. Just sayin'."

He sighed. Heavily.

"I like your family," she said. "It's much better that they're all talking now. Besides, I'm sure your dad would love to see your business. He has a wealth of experience. He might have a few pointers. And I like Valentina."

"I'm capable of inviting my own family to Mirror Lake, Maggie," he said. His voice had an edge. Of course it did. He was angry.

As the car pulled away, Maggie waved out the window. She knew she wouldn't be seeing any of the Pouloses again. She'd hurt Drew. She could see it in his eyes when he looked at her. And she couldn't see any way not to.

Well, what choice did she have? Sleeping with Drew had proved to her she wasn't ready for a real relationship.

It had to be like that. She'd find someone else she wasn't so afraid to love. Someone who didn't make her heart squeeze tightly every time he looked at her, who wasn't kind to her even when he was hurt and angry, who didn't have a very nice, if disordered, family…and who didn't make her want to love him.

Her original plan was a fling. With a nice, decent, but not wonderful guy. Not someone she could love deeply and heartachingly.

Loving Drew was out of the question. She *couldn't* love him. But, she feared, somewhere deep inside, that maybe she already did.

She fastened her seat belt. Because it was going to be a long hour home.

CHAPTER 15

"Thanks for watching Griffin for a few hours," Maggie said to Bella as she walked with Griffin into the big airy kitchen in Bella's beautiful new house. It was the Friday after the wedding, and Maggie had that date with Greg Pollard that had been set up for weeks. She'd decided to keep it. Why not? It would help her to get Drew out of her mind. Which she seriously needed to do, because practically everything she did reminded her of him, from swimming with Griffin at the Y, to taking him to the park, to eating anything from chicken fingers to cheesecake to yogurt. But she especially thought of him every night, when she slipped into her bed alone.

Bella cranked up a musical toy inside the playpen that was set up between the kitchen and a pretty sitting area with a fireplace and turned to hug Griffin. "Roman's out in the fields trying to fix a tractor, so I could use some help getting Vivienne to bed. Then maybe we can make some s'mores around the fire pit. How's that sound, Griff?"

Maggie was tempted to stay and join them. Bella and Roman's

house was built on the lake, at the edge of the apple orchards Roman had inherited from his foster grandparents. It was built in Victorian style, with a turret and a big wraparound porch to die for.

Griffin, who was holding a Captain America superhero figure, ran over to the baby and knelt down beside the playpen. He curled his fingers around the netting and began talking to her. "Vivi, do you want a bubble bath tonight? And a bottle?" The dog, Gracie, a shaggy brown mutt, galumphed up to Griffin and nudged her nose between his hands, licking his fingers. And Captain America's head, both of which made Maggie want to reach for the Purell, but she refrained. Griffin laughed, and this in turn made the baby laugh.

Maggie looked over at Bella. "You sure it's not too much?" She often thanked her lucky stars that she had such a good friend that she could ask at a moment's notice, like tonight when her sitter had called off at the last minute. Still, going out to dinner wasn't an emergency, and she didn't want to interfere with any of Bella's and Roman's plans.

Bella waved her hand dismissively. "Griffie's a sweetheart and so helpful with the baby, and we're just chillin' tonight." She smiled at Vivienne, who had shoved both her hands inside her mouth, and smoothed Griffin's curls. "We'll have fun, won't we?"

"Sure, Aunt Bella. But can I ride the tractor with Uncle Roman?"

Maggie's heart seized, as it always did when a dangerous activity was suggested. Bella gave her an inquiring look, and Maggie quickly shook her head. Riding on a tractor on Roman's lap... They could hit a rock and Griffin could go flying. The very thought made her shudder.

At the very least he'd need a helmet for such a dangerous activity. Or a suit of armor.

Once Roman had taken Griffin for a ride on the tractor, not

thinking anything about it. Griffin had talked about it for weeks, but Maggie had been secretly appalled.

She knew deep inside it was important for Griffin to have masculine influences and not to be afraid of new experiences, but the thought of having something bad happen to Griffin was unbearable.

Bella gave Maggie a little smile. "Um—I think Uncle Roman's going to be out in the field working for most of the night. But you could help me set the table for dinner, okay?"

She saw Griffin's face fall. Her boy was a daredevil at heart. She didn't know where he got that from, because Corey, being a pediatrician, had all the data on why things like jumping on trampolines, not being buckled into an age-appropriate car seat, riding ATVs, exposure to button batteries, and not wearing a bicycle helmet weren't safe. But no matter what, Maggie couldn't change her son's makeup. Nothing she could do, say, or threaten seemed to beat the love of adventure out of him.

As Griffin knelt down and dumped library books out of his backpack, Vivienne clawed her way up the playpen netting and pounded her palm against his head.

Griffin thought this was hysterical. "I brought books to read you. Now, which one do you want?" He held up two picture books.

Ah, such a sweet boy. In that department, she was a lucky woman indeed. Corey would've been so proud. A thought that made her heart crack a little, as usual.

"You have time for a glass of iced tea?" Bella asked Maggie. Actually, she grabbed a glass and started pouring before Maggie even answered. "So, why a date so soon after…you know?"

Maggie took a sip of tea and shrugged. "I…got carried away. I didn't think it through. I was really grateful for Drew's help with my…problem, but he's just not the kind of guy I want to keep dating."

"Why not?" Bella demanded.

"I don't want someone edgy and exciting. I want steady and calm. Did you know he used to own a motorcycle? And there's just too much attraction there. It's really distracting."

"What did he say when you said you just wanted it to be a weekend thing?"

"He reminded me we'd just agreed to a something casual. He was okay with it." Not really. But he would be. It was all for the best.

"Maggie, did it ever occur to you that you might have hurt the guy's feelings? I mean, after the smoking-hot night you had, it had to be a little bit of a buzz kill to get booted like that."

Maggie straightened a little defensively. "I didn't get into this to hurt anyone's feelings. I was honest from the beginning. I told him I wasn't ready for a relationship, and I was right. I mean, we're back home now, not on a fantasy weekend anymore, and I'm a mother, for God's sake!" She felt like she was a lawyer in court, justifying her behavior. With weak, weak arguments.

"Moms have sex too," Bella said quietly.

"It's just that things got a little awkward, and I sort of implied…that I was dry kindling just waiting for a match. To flame into a forest fire. I never got to tell him I had a really nice time."

Bella raised a brow. "You compared yourself to kindling?"

"No! I'm just telling you that."

"Do you mean *really nice time* in a polite way or an *oh-my-God-the-earth-moved* kind of way?"

Maggie's eyes began blurring. She took a sip of tea.

Bella pointed a finger. "Aha, I knew it! You know, earth-moving sex is hard to come by. You might not want to be so hasty giving that up. And I don't really get what you're saying. You don't want Drew, you want somebody else even though you two had an amazing time together and he's fun and attractive and nice?"

"I don't want earth-moving anything. I don't want to feel like a teenager again. I want stable, predictable, even. Besides—he's got the most obnoxious dog I've ever seen."

"That's a shock, coming from you, who never met a dog you didn't like."

"Yeah, well, this dog is completely in love with him. It can't even stand for me to pet it. I've never seen such a jealous, possessive dog in my life."

"Well, there you have it. Insurmountable problems. May as well just give up and go out on a date with someone else."

"Please don't make fun of me, like I'm just trying to dream up excuses to not make this work." Which was exactly what she was doing and she knew it.

"Well, you kind of are."

"I'm just a little messed up right now." Oh, there went the waterworks again. She swiped at her eyes with the palms of her hands.

Bella got up and hugged her. "It's okay, sweetie." You know I just want you to be happy. But do you think some of this is—fear? This is the first guy in three years who got close enough to touch a nerve. Maybe you're a little…scared. I don't want you to do something you regret because you ran away from something that could be really good."

"I am scared, Bella. In fact, I'm terrified. I can't love someone like that again. Deeply, fully, passionately. Losing Corey almost killed me. I'm not setting myself up for that again. So I'm going out with Greg. I'm playing it safe, and if that makes me a coward, so be it."

"Okay, okay. Just trying to examine all sides, right? That's what best friends are for. Not to agree with everything you say and blow smoke up your butt."

"You've never blown smoke up my butt in my life, but I still love you. Almost as much as I love that sweet little baby of yours."

The thud of the screen door made both women startle.

Maggie looked up just in time to see Roman enter the house. Behind him was Drew, in jeans and a T-shirt and work boots, looking like sin and holding two reusable plastic water bottles.

Memories flooded her senses—him above her, looking at her like he wanted her more than anyone ever; laughing together over that crazy tennis match, and being so thrilled when they'd won; the hurt expression on his face when she'd minimized their night together. Shame made her blush and look away.

Roman walked over to Bella and kissed her on the lips. Maggie didn't miss the look Bella gave her husband, full of love and…peace.

Roman gave Griffin a little toss in the air and a flip back to his feet, which left him giggling, and bent to pick up his daughter. "Well, hello there, young lady," he said to the smiling baby. "How are you today? You missed your daddy, didn't you? Well, we were out there pruning apple trees, how about that?"

The baby listened rapturously, her eyes full of adoration, just as Roman's were for his beautiful daughter, Bella smiling at her husband's antics. It almost made Maggie tear up a little. They'd had a long road to happiness, but they'd made it. It gave her hope for her own future.

"Hey, mind if I come in and grab a refill on some water?" Drew asked Bella, but his gaze rested on Maggie. She was certain her face was tomato red to her roots, but managed to say, "Hi, Drew," like she was saying hi to the mailman or to Gertie at the grocery store. Not to the man who'd done things to her deep into the night that would keep her awake for many more to come.

"Maggie. Hi," he said, sounding genuinely surprised. And maybe there was a defensive edge or a detached tone, but maybe it was just her imagination. "Hi, Griffin," he said to her son, fist-bumping him.

Bella walked over and took the water bottles from Drew. "I'll fill them."

"Thanks," he said, dusting off his hands. "If you don't mind, that would be great, seeing as my shoes are full of dirt." Turning to Maggie, he said, "What are you doing out this way?"

"Oh. I um—have a date tonight." There, she might as well just come right out and say it. There was no point in hedging, as he'd find out one way or another anyway. "My sitter got sick at the last minute, so Bella and Roman are going to keep an eye on Griffin for a few hours."

"Great," he said. But it came out an octave higher than usual. He didn't sound like that was a great thing at all.

Maggie glanced at her watch. "Well, it's getting late." She walked over to Roman and kissed the baby on the head. "Thank you for watching Griffin tonight."

"Our pleasure," he said, smiling as Griffin picked up the toy the baby just dropped.

"Help Aunt Bella with Vivi, okay, Griff? I'll see you soon." She kissed her son and gave a nod to Bella. "I'll see you later."

"Have fun," Bella said.

"Bye, Mommy," Griffin called, but he seemed more interested in the apple slice Bella just handed him.

Drew barely nodded and didn't look her in the eye. But as soon as she left, she heard the screen door swing shut and the crunch of big masculine feet on the gravel behind her. "So who's your date with?" Drew asked, easily catching up. "The fireman?" Oh, the annoying man was walking her out to her car. His hands, balled into fists, were jammed into his jeans pockets.

"Yes, actually." She dug in her purse for her keys, anything not to look at him.

"Sounds fun," he said. But a muscle under his eye was twitching.

"Look," Maggie said, "I'm glad we can be adults about this. I mean, what happened between us happened, but we can get over it and be civil with one another."

"That's me," he said darkly. "I'm one civil guy."

Maggie opened her car door. His jaw looked so tight, it might snap off and rattle away down the driveway. But what else could she say? She'd made it clear where she stood.

"Drew," she said, "I want you to know I feel honored to have met your family. And I'm glad things seemed to have worked out pretty well. I-I had a nice time last weekend." Oh, her stomach was roiling and her palms were sweaty and she felt like she was coming down with the flu. Maggie was professionally a decisive person, she understood what had to be done. But everything about this felt...wrong.

"I'm sorry if I hurt you," she said, her voice practically a whisper. She looked away, struck by the stung expression on his face. "I should've known better than to start things up."

"I'm not sorry," he said, leaning a hand on her car window.

She tried not to meet his gaze, but oh, how could she not when he stood there hovering over her like that? Close enough that she could smell his scent, a combination of soap and outdoors that was so appealing. He had these warm brown eyes that reminded her of fall...leaves on the ground, acorns falling, sitting around a bonfire. Every emotion he felt flickered in there, an open book.

"Look, Maggie—"

"Mommy," Griffin called, running down the driveway. "I forgot the iPad. Can I please have it so I can take pictures of Vivienne?"

Griffin *always* wanted to take pictures, and he found it easy to do so with her iPad. Maggie reached in the backseat for it and handed it to her boy, but as he went to grasp it, she pulled it back a bit. She tapped her cheek. "Kiss first."

Gripping his little hands around her neck, he gave her a big squeeze, then a big wet kiss that might have left a residue of cookie crumbs on her cheek. "Bye, Mommy!" he said.

"Bye, kiddo," she called, brushing off the crumbs. Drew had stepped back, crossing his arms over his chest.

She braced herself for more words, but he was done talking. "Have a nice time on your date," he finally said, and turned away to follow Griffin up the drive, leaving her alone.

CHAPTER 16

An hour later, in a strange twist of fate, Drew found himself sitting across his brother's kitchen island from Griffin Michael McShae. Roman had accidentally sliced his finger with a box cutter and Bella had driven him to the ER, dropping the baby off on the way with her dad next door. Drew had found himself saying, "Griff can stay with me, right, buddy?" to which he'd gotten a less than enthusiastic response from the kid, but Bella's dad was a little scary. Plus taking care of an eight-month-old would keep him plenty busy.

So that left Drew and Griffin. Together, both of them staring at each other a little uncomfortably and wondering when the heck Maggie was coming back.

And Drew wondered for the hundredth time why he hadn't gone after her.

"She wouldn't sleep with someone on the first date, would she?" he found himself asking Bella earlier that evening after Maggie had left.

Bella cleaned drool off the baby's chin with the back of her hand and wiped it on her jeans. "Did she do that with you?" she asked pointedly.

"Actually, I guess we never had a first date." *Shit*. Something else he'd done wrong. He'd employed her instead of dated her. Bad move.

Bella's eyes softened. "I've known Maggie ever since kindergarten when we both discovered we had peanut butter and pickle sandwiches in our lunches every day. I could offer my opinion if you wanted it."

He narrowed his eyes. "Okay."

"But I'd have to kill you if you ever hurt my friend."

"She's the one who dumped me." If he could consider himself dumped, that is, after zero dates.

"Or I could just shut up and mind my own business."

"Okay, okay. Tell me."

"Maggie's afraid to get close to anyone who she could really love again. That might be why she's pushing you away. But don't you dare go after her unless you mean it—unless you want a real relationship. She's been through too much pain already, you know what I mean?"

He made a face at the baby, which made her grin in a way that put her two brand-new bottom teeth on display. His little niece *was* awfully cute, despite the fact that he knew almost nothing about kids. "Got it."

He hadn't thought he ever wanted a relationship again, but Maggie made him want to try. He couldn't read her mind, but deep in his heart, he knew that the night they'd spent together was fabulous. Fantastic. Surely she'd felt it too.

A more sensible man wouldn't even be here, thinking about her. He'd go after her, plucking her away from that date of hers and setting her straight on who she should really want to be with.

Him.

But in the meantime, he wasn't going anywhere. And neither

was Griffin. The blond, curly haired little boy sat across from him staring at some kids' game on his iPad.

"So," Drew said, drumming his fingers on the wood.

"I miss Vivienne," said Griffin in a whiny voice, pulling out his lower lip in that sort of adorable way that young children do. "I promised my mom I'd take care of her. But how can I when Aunt Bella took her away? Why can't I go next door too?"

Ah, yes, why? Drew now asked himself. But in those moments of chaos when Roman's finger was bleeding and Bella was doing her best not to freak out about that in front of Griffin, Drew had volunteered to watch him. Big mistake.

"Tell you what. It's a warm evening. How about we go sit on the dock and fish?"

The kid got excited about that, so Drew gathered up some of his brother's fishing stuff, and they walked down to the dock in the backyard, past the orchards, where they dangled their feet in the water and waited for the fish to bite. Which they weren't. Not surprising after the rest of this shit day.

"Have you ever been fishing?" Drew asked.

Griffin eyeballed him suspiciously. "My grandpa takes me. And Uncle Scott."

"You play ball?"

"Mommy says baseball could give me a black eye. Or break my nose."

"How about swimming?" he asked as he checked the tension on Griffin's line.

"My mom takes me to the Y. She says the lake could be full of pollution. Or sometimes people throw broken bottles in and you could cut your feet."

Was this kid ever allowed to have any fun?

"I'm hungry," Griffin said.

Yeah. Dinner plans had gotten aborted with the emergency. Drew did have the foresight to grab a package of Oreos from the counter and a couple of apple juice boxes and stuff them in his bag. He pulled both out now and handed the kid a juice box and a cookie. Who didn't like Oreos? They were engineered for people to automatically love them. That was a no-brainer.

Except Griffin examined the Oreo like it was potentially poisonous.

"My mom says these have dyes and chemicals in them."

"Have you ever had one?" Drew took a pull on his apple juice. God, he could use a beer. Or two.

Griffin shook his head. "I'm only supposed to eat the organic kind." He broke out in a big smile. Cute kid, with the grin and that blond hair, Drew had to admit.

"What?" Drew asked. "Why are you smiling?"

"Do you promise not to tell my mom?"

"Okay."

"Well, I had them once at school. Three of them. Wallace brought them for Halloween, and I ate them before I got home. They had orange icing. Don't tell my mom."

"I think she'd say it was okay tonight because of Uncle Roman's emergency," Drew said, offering the bag. Griffin reluctantly took another one. "Just to hold us over until we can get some real food." Drew felt a little guilty. Like he was undermining Maggie's parenting. But he had a responsibility to save something far more important than the health effects from a few preservatives. Griffin's manhood.

They ate the Oreos in silence. Drew hadn't had one in a long time. He'd forgotten how good they were.

"It's hot tonight," he said. "Want to go for a little swim?"

"I don't have my swimsuit."

"We can swim in our shorts, and I can put them in the dryer when we get back to the house. They'll be dry by the time your mom comes back."

The idea of a swim appealed, so they stripped off their shirts, and to Drew's surprise, Griffin jumped right in. He used a child-size life vest they kept in a chest near the dock to keep Griffin comfortable in the water, but it was clear the kid knew the basic strokes. He wasn't the cautious, frightened kid Drew feared he'd be.

"I want to try the mud slide," Griffin said.

With the advent of summerlike weather, Roman had covered a decent-sized portion of the gentle slope of the bank with a large sheet of plastic. It was something that his grandfather had done at that exact same spot every summer since he was a kid. A hose nearby functioned to keep it slippery so all anyone had to do was slide down, right into the lake.

Their brother Lukas's kids loved it. If Drew could guess, Maggie probably didn't allow Griffin to try it much if at all.

Not wanting to go against Maggie's wishes, he said, "Maybe that better wait until your mom approves. You'd get pretty muddy doing that."

"But you said we could wash my clothes." The kid looked longingly at the slide. Drew remembered his own childhood, which was pretty darn low on spontaneous moments. Cecilia had always been big for planning, and while many of their afternoons were booked with back-to-back activities, none of them were the get-down-and-dirty-and-just-have-fun kind.

Hell, part of *him* longed to slide down the mud slide too.

Drew was a big believer that kids should experience dirt. Especially this one. He was completely dirt deprived.

Besides, he had to admit, for reasons he wasn't entirely clear on, he was desperate to have this kid like him.

"Okay. Let's do it. But you've got to keep the vest on, okay?"

"I'll do it, I'll do it!" Griffin tore over to the top of the hill. Together they adjusted the hose flow to wet the slide. Drew went first to test it out and waited in the water for Griffin, who pushed off down the hill, slipping and sliding and screaming in delight the whole way down.

An hour later, it was getting dark and they were both pretty exhausted, not to mention muddy. He hosed both of them off the best he could.

He stopped in at his own little place, the house Roman's grandparents used to own, and grabbed some clean clothes and a few towels, then herded Griffin—and his car seat, or Maggie would kill him—into Roman's pickup, making sure to text Bella that he was taking Griffin back to Maggie's place. It made sense—besides Griffin having no clothes, it was getting late. He'd get the kid to sleep in his own bed and save Maggie the trip to pick him up.

When he ran back into the house for his keys, a whimper sounded from the corner of his kitchen. Genevieve had been over the moon to come live with him, but she was still adjusting to her new home. She looked so sad and lonely that he scooped her up and tossed her into the truck too. He'd never formally met Maggie's dog, a big mixed breed named Bear, but he was sure they'd get along. If Bear didn't up and swallow Genny whole.

Turned out Bear was a big baby and actually a little frightened of Genny, who trotted around the place, sniffing every corner and eventually lying down in Bear's big bed.

"Genny, mind your manners," Drew said, but Genny just barked and burrowed farther into the bed. So he scratched Bear behind the ears and gave him a dog biscuit, which he took with a grateful grunt.

"Bear's super friendly," Griffin said, petting Genny. "Mommy said she didn't want a hundred-pound dog because he eats more than we do, but she says he has a good heart."

Drew laughed, because it was easy to imagine Maggie saying that. The dog leaned against Drew's leg and looked up with adoring eyes. He was huge, but it was kind of impossible not to take to him.

While Griffin got into his pj's, Drew threw his clothes into the washing machine and made them each an omelet and toast. Then he made some popcorn, and they settled in for some TV.

Drew flipped the channels, making sure to keep away from blood and gore.

"What would you like to watch until your mom gets home?" he asked. "Oh, look, here's *The Lucy Show*."

"Too violent," Griffin said. "It's too late for PBS. We can watch HGTV. I like *Fixer Upper*. QVC or a Hallmark movie is okay too."

"Now why do you like *Fixer Upper*?" he asked. This kid was a pure target for bullies. He was going to get eaten alive at school.

"Because Joanna and Chip are cool. And Chip uses cool tools."

Well, okay, that sounded a little bit acceptable.

"Okay, here's something." Drew stopped on a cartoon classic.

In the first three minutes, Road Runner bashed Wile E. Coyote on the head with a sledgehammer and fell the length of the Grand Canyon but somehow emerged sort of intact. Griffin laughed hysterically, and Drew found himself chuckling too.

So that wasn't too violent, was it?

His guilt over inappropriate television didn't last too long, because Griffin was out like a light within about ten minutes. Hopefully when he woke up, he wouldn't remember much about the violence.

Drew went and found a blanket for him. Griffin was a good kid. With all the rules and regulations he had to deal with, he might as well have *Bully Me* stamped on his forehead. But he had some pushback in him, which Drew saw as a healthy thing.

He just needed some male influence. Whatever happened with him and Maggie, maybe he could help with that a little. As one guy to another.

His thoughts returned to Maggie and just where the hell was she? It was after nine now. How long did it take to eat dinner? Just the thought of her and that firefighter... He couldn't go there. It was making him crazy.

Griffin smelled kind of lake-y and Drew realized he must too, so he went and took a quick shower. Then he got a beer for himself and drank it while he watched part of a ball game, but he was a little nervous making himself at home in Maggie's place, so he got up and walked around the room.

Maggie's house looked settled in and happy in a way the formal mansion where he grew up never did. There were framed photos on the walls, including some artwork Griffin had painted or colored, a cozy throw on the couch, and Griffin's toys tucked in an area behind the couch but spilling out in a trail along the wooden floor. A book lay open on the end table...the newest Harlan Coben. So...she liked thrillers. Interesting.

As he restlessly scanned the room, a photograph caught his eye. He got up from the couch and walked over to the built-in bookshelf to investigate. There, in a simple black frame, was a photo of Griffin as an infant, laughing, in the arms of a tall, lanky guy with reddish-blond hair and a big, flashy smile.

Corey himself. Not a bad-looking guy. Very different from himself, however. Drew was dark and muscular, while Corey was light and lean.

Suddenly, he was hungry to know more. He saw another photo of the three of them, Maggie kneeling in the sand at the beach, Griffin as a pudgy-cheeked baby sitting in front of her with a shovel in his hand and a white brimmed hat on his head. Corey knelt next to Maggie, his arm around her, smiling, but looking a little wan. Maggie had said he'd fought the cancer for three years and had died when Griffin was only one.

There were various photos of Griffin through the years, some with Maggie and some without. Like a cute one of Griffin as a toddler hugging the dog, who towered above him. He hadn't seen any wedding photos or any of just Maggie with her husband. Maybe she kept those somewhere else, upstairs maybe.

Thank God. He really didn't want to see those anyway.

He began pacing the small family room. At first the dogs trailed after him, but then they settled down, this time Bear in his bed (he was smart enough to get there first this time) and Genevieve curled up nearby on one of the towels from his truck. But after a minute, she left the towel and curled up next to Bear. He didn't seem to mind, because both of them were soon fast asleep.

Good for the dogs, but Drew had other things on his mind. He was beginning to worry, imagining things that he didn't want to imagine with nothing else to distract him.

He'd just sat down on the couch with Maggie's book when the sound of female laughter interrupted his thoughts. A quick glance from behind the front window curtain showed him what he'd dreaded—she was walking up to the door with a good-looking blond guy, six feet tall, built like an athlete. More laughter. Drew's stomach churned sickly. Then he saw the guy lean toward her, and he just lost it.

That was it. He'd had enough. Over his dead body was he going to watch Maggie kiss another guy. He was done pretending that this didn't matter—that *they* didn't matter. Done pretending he didn't want more. And he was going to find out just what the hell was going through her mind after they'd had such a fantastic time together. What had happened between them was pretty damn amazing, and he was pretty certain he didn't imagine it. Whatever was going on, he was going to get to the bottom of it. Right now.

He ran to the door and put his hands on every light switch he could find, ready to flick them all in unison. That would dowse anything. Until he could talk some sense into her.

"Good night, Greg," he heard through the door. "I'll see you around."

"Yeah, I had a great time, Maggie. Thanks for going with me."

The sound of a key in the lock made Drew leap for the couch. Griffin was out, snoring softly, his head resting on a ratty stuffed animal dog with floppy ears. Drew lay down in the opposite direction, one hand behind his head, and closed his eyes, just as he heard her final good night and the *click* of the door closing behind her.

Maggie closed her front door to find the lights in her family room were off. In the blue glow of the TV, she could make out two bodies lying on her couch. "This is unexpected," she said quietly, walking over and bending down close to Drew's face. He had such a nice face, with beautiful olive skin and that almost constant five-o'clock shadow regardless of the time of day. She fought the strong urge to run the back of her hand down that rough sexy cheek. But there was a flicker of his lids, a slight tension in the lines between his eyes that told her he was definitely *not* asleep. "And I know you're awake because I saw you peeking at us from behind the curtains," she said. "Gosh, you're worse than my father."

He cracked open an eye. One look at him made her heart want to burst. His long, elegant body stretched out in faded old jeans and a T-shirt that hugged his chest in all the right ways. Something about seeing him casually stretched out on her couch made her wish for things she had no business wishing for. Things she'd blown by pushing him away.

She surveyed the scene. At the other end of the couch, Griffin snored softly into the neck of his old Patrick the Puppy. A bowl of popcorn, an apple juice box, and an empty beer bottle sat on her coffee table, along with her iPad. A typical night at home. As if anything about Drew being here was typical. But she suddenly longed for it to be.

"Have you talked to Roman?"

Drew sat up slowly. "Seven stitches and a hand surgery consult later, and I'm told he'll be fine."

"I wish you all had called me. I would've come right home. And thank you for watching Griffin."

"There was no need. And you're welcome." He pulled himself up to sitting, flexing his lovely muscles in the process. "Did you…have fun?"

"Tell you what. Let me run Griffin up to bed and I'll tell you all about it."

But he rose before her and without asking, picked up her son. The sight of that big, burly man holding her little boy did something to her…something akin to drinking a good whiskey…the flash of heat, spreading all through her chest, her belly, her legs…

She tried to stop it. Lord, how she tried. But apparently she'd left her good judgment on her date with Greg, whom she'd had no problem telling they were better as friends.

She grabbed Patrick from the couch and guided Drew upstairs and into Griffin's room, where she turned down his blankets. Drew deposited him in the bed, and he instantly curved into a half moon and hugged the puppy close. She kissed his cheek. Half asleep, Griffin said, "Good night, Mommy."

"Good night, sweetie."

"I had fun tonight. We watched *Road Runner*."

Maggie didn't miss the mischievous grin on her son's face as he looked up at her sweetly just before drifting back to sleep. She glanced behind her, but Drew was already out of the room. *Road Runner*, huh? She couldn't wait to find out about the rest of the evening.

In the family room, Drew was tidying up the couch pillows, picking up a few stray popcorn kernels from the rug, another gesture that melted her. Dully, she wondered if she was the only woman in the world who considered cleaning up foreplay. He'd turned off the TV and flicked on one of the end table lights. "Want another beer?" she asked.

"No, thanks," he said a little too evenly.

"Coffee? Tea? Ice water?"

"Nope. I'm fine." His gaze was wary, indicating his anger. She didn't blame him. She just hoped he'd listen to her.

She grabbed his arm and tugged a little until he stopped and looked at her. "Drew, I—please. Can we sit down and talk for a few minutes?"

"I was hoping you'd suggest that," he said as they sat down side by side on the couch. Yet still he didn't talk. He was leaving it up to her.

Silence mounted as she mulled over what to say. Her stomach felt like a Ninja blender. She was sorry; she wanted him so badly; he was all she could think of. All risky places to begin. "So, how was your date?" he asked at the same time she asked "So, what did you do with Griffin?"

"Griffin and I went swimming in the lake," Drew said. "I hope you don't mind—I threw his clothes in the washer."

"Without his water wings?" she asked, trying to stay calm. First *Road Runner*, now near drowning. She bit her lip to stop from saying anything further. He'd done her a big favor. She couldn't forget that.

"He did fine with a life vest, and I was right with him the whole time. He's pretty fearless."

"That's what I'm afraid of."

"Don't be."

She shot him a look.

"What I mean is, you've got to let him have some experiences without sealing him up in a sterile container with all the safety latches on."

"Are you criticizing my parenting?"

He sighed. "You're a good mother, Maggie, and your son is a kind, loving boy. But sometimes I feel you've got this intense need to protect him…"

"He's all I've got," she snapped. This wasn't going well. She moved to get up, but he held her back.

His voice was gentle, further stripping her defenses. "I understand that, but you've got to loosen up the reins a little, or eventually, he'll buck you—hard."

"What happened to Corey was so rare, such a fluke. Sometimes I feel like anything could happen to Griffin, and if only I can try to prevent tragedy…"

"Hell, Maggie, none of us knows what's going to happen to us in the next minute, let alone over a lifetime. We roll the dice, and we get what we get."

"That's why it's better not to get attached to anyone."

"Maybe in that respect, we're a lot alike." He paused, his gaze bearing down on her, giving her chills. "I told you I didn't think I was capable of caring for anyone again. But I was wrong."

His words brought a blur of tears welling up. Something in his eyes stirred her—honesty. She owed him the same. She owed him the truth.

She grasped his hands. His beautiful hands, strong and long fingered. "I want you to know how it was with Corey. At first we thought his exhaustion was from being a resident—the hours, being on call—but then we found out he was sick. Of course he had the best care—we even made a trip to MD Anderson—but nothing worked, all the different kinds of chemo, the radiation. We'd have periods of time when we were sure the next thing would work—only to find that had failed too. I suppose I was foolish to get pregnant, but I think part of me thought a baby would give him the will to live, that he would do anything to live to be able to see his son, that God wouldn't be so cruel to let him die when he had so much to live for. And he tried—he tried so hard, but it wasn't enough. Nothing was enough. Every day I watched him grow weaker and weaker, watch all his vitality drain slowly out of him. Watching my husband die took all my love, all my strength, and much of my optimism about life. Then you came along."

Of course she was crying, but she made herself continue. "I didn't want to fall for someone like you. Someone wonderful, and kind, and so funny—it was too terrifying to think that something like that could happen again—not cancer, necessarily, but the fact that life is so random, that anything can happen. That was why I told myself you weren't important. You were just a fling, someone to pass a weekend with. If I believed that I couldn't fall for you, I wouldn't. But I did. No matter how hard I tried not to."

This was the best she could do. It had taken her three years to climb out of the cesspool of grief, and this was as good as she had.

He gripped her head firmly with both hands and pulled it toward him, then planted a kiss tenderly on her forehead. "Don't be afraid," he said in a low, calming voice that touched her to the core. Still cupping her face with his hands, he looked deeply into her eyes and said, "I want us to try, Maggie. To have a real relationship. To go wherever it is you're willing to go." He smiled. "Besides, I can't resist a girl who reads Harlan Coben."

"I do James Patterson too. And Tess Gerritsen. And John Grisham."

"Now you're really turning me on." He reached out and kissed her firmly, possessively. In a way that stamped her as *his*. Then he pulled back a little and scanned her face, tucking a strand of hair behind her ear.

"Don't go out with the fireman anymore."

"Okay," she whispered.

And he kissed her once more. Slow and gently, his lips barely grazing hers. Angling his face better over hers, he brought their lips flush in a deep, sensual kiss. She didn't realize it, but she'd been waiting for this, missing it since the first time they'd made love. Despite the sudden shakiness she felt down to her bones, despite the fact that she was scared out of her ever-loving mind, nothing had ever felt so damn good.

"Maggie," he said, stroking her cheek and looking into her eyes. "I never felt this way about anyone. But I need us to promise to be honest with each other. No matter how difficult it is."

"Okay," she murmured, barely able to concentrate. "I'll be more honest. Your dog is spoiled. And by the way—what, may I ask, is she doing in my dog's bed?"

"They worked it out. So maybe we can too."

Suddenly he was pushing against her, toppling the both of them to the couch, then the floor, kissing her deep and hard and wet, until her toes curled and every sensible thought flew far away. She had the vague impression of popcorn spilling, but it didn't really register. Because his delicious weight was on top of her, and she couldn't get enough of him, of his good clean smell, of his magical lips, of his hands, roving all over, sliding over the hot skin beneath her shirt.

Somehow they'd gotten his shirt off, and as she was pulling off her sweater, he began kissing her breasts. She felt pleasantly trapped, her arms twisted in her sweater while he pushed down her bra and suckled her breast relentlessly until she gasped from the pure, shocking pleasure of it all.

She was beyond control, beyond sense. He was still suckling her, cupping her other breast, running his fingers lightly over her nipple, then unbuttoning her jeans. Finally, he helped her tug the sweater off. Her hands finally free, she grasped the waistband of his jeans and tunneled her way under.

Her eyes widened with surprise. "No undies?" she asked.

"In your dryer," he said. His kisses became relentless, deep and languid, throwing her into a spin of pure pleasure while she pulled down his jeans and tugged hers off.

In the fevered pitch of the moment, she forgot everything—that they were on her living room floor, that her son was just a staircase away. Because his fingers were in her, stroking her, and his tongue was invading, and she loved all of it, the taste of him, the feel of his hands on her, the hard smoothness of his muscles under her fingertips. Everything in her core was building, the exquisite tightening, until she began trembling and shaking and telling him in a low, hoarse voice she barely recognized that she wanted him inside her, *now*.

Then suddenly he sheathed himself and pushed inside her and she was taking him in, all of him, as he lowered himself slowly over her. His body was elegant and lean, yet powerful, so hard and yet with a brush of soft chest hair, and as they came together and he began to slowly move against her, she met his gaze. It was filled with tenderness, with feelings she was afraid to name, and she felt it, met it with her own, wanted to give back to him everything he was giving her.

Just as he went still and uttered a low, guttural cry, she let go completely, clutching his back, shattering on a wave of release so strong, it left her dazed and speechless, the pleasure violent and numbing.

They lay together like that, tangled on Maggie's floor, a peaceful exhaustion drifting over them. The house was still, the dogs quiet, the only sound the tumultuous pounding of her very full heart.

Drew kissed her temple, her forehead, ran his calloused hand over her cheek. Tears welled up, relief that he was here, in her house, loving her like this despite everything. She kissed his neck, his shoulder, pressed her forehead to his shoulder, reveling in the feel of him, never wanting this moment to end.

He tucked her close until they lay together, her head beneath his chin, her cheek resting against his big chest, as he gently stroked her hair. Around that time, Maggie suddenly became aware of a popcorn kernel digging into her back and realized they'd somehow ended up wedged between the coffee table and the couch. Drew tried to right himself but then gave up and lay still, biting down gently on her shoulder.

He plucked a piece of popcorn out of her hair and chuckled. "I never realized popcorn could be so uncomfortable to lie on. Feels worse than nails."

He said it with a boyish grin and a twinkle in his eye, all of which made Maggie's heart tumble hard. This man…well, he was kinda wonderful. He was the full package—smart, knock-your-socks-off handsome, and kind. Before she could think too much more about that, he kissed her firmly on the mouth and helped her up. He took a fuzzy throw from the couch and wrapped it around her shoulders.

"That was fun," he said, a twinkle in his eye, rubbing his hands up and down her arms.

She stood on tiptoe and impulsively kissed him on the lips. "Can you stay?"

"Um, let's see," he said, tapping his finger on the side of his mouth, pretending to contemplate the decision. "Why, yes, actually. Yes, I can."

She gripped him by the arms and looked at him intently. "I just have to ask you if you'd mind leaving before Griffin wakes up. I don't want him to be—confused."

"Well then, let's not waste another moment of time," he said, suddenly scooping her up over his shoulder and whisking her off toward the stairs. She slapped a hand over her mouth to stifle a whoop of surprise to avoid waking Griffin. Drew's soft laughter rang out and touched a spot deep inside.

And she let herself get carried away.

CHAPTER 17

Drew awakened to a bright beam of warm sunlight passing through the crack in the drapes and settling on his face. It took a few seconds to realize he'd just broken his cardinal rule of never sleeping over with the one woman who'd actually asked him *not* to break it. And by the way the light was flooding in, it was way later than his usual predawn escape time. He let out a silent curse.

One quick glance over at Maggie assured him she was sleeping like the dead; at least judging by her soft little snores, it sure sounded like it. Good, he could still get out before she discovered he was still here. Or worse, before the kid did.

He should've made a quick escape after they'd made love the last time. He'd meant to. He'd even gone back downstairs and collected most of their clothes, including his underwear in the dryer. But Maggie had coaxed him back into bed, then she'd laid her head on his chest, her soft curves melting in next to him, her silky hair smelling so sweet and fragrant, and he'd allowed himself to do a very, very dangerous thing. He'd closed his eyes and inhaled that flowery, wonderful scent of hers and rubbed his hand up and down her arm and pulled her closer until her hand circled his waist. They'd talked for what seemed like forever about silly things like what their favorite TV shows were as kids—*Star Trek*, for both of them—their favorite fast food—Cinnabons for him, McDonald's fries for her—their favorite holidays—hers was Christmas (no surprise there, knowing her enthusiasm for just about anything), his Thanksgiving (less hassle).

Then she'd tilted her pretty face up to him, and without thinking, he kissed her, and she kissed him back, then suddenly he'd pulled her on top of him and they were...yeah.

Well. He hadn't planned on a third time. In fact, she didn't think she could come again, so then all bets were off and he was proving to her she could. Then they'd both dropped off into a sound sleep. The sleep of the *very* well satisfied.

And now it had to be at least 8:00 a.m. Always an early riser, Drew generally got up, put coffee on, and did his morning run, and by this time, he was already tackling paperwork.

A sense of urgency broke through his thoughts, pumping through him. He had to leave like, right now. Because she'd made it clear that if her kid saw him, he'd be scarred for life, and he certainly didn't want *that* on his conscience.

Yet part of him was tempted to stay. Curl his body around hers and bury his nose in her hair, whisper something in her ear that would bring on that pretty blush, and tell her good morning in proper fashion.

He glanced next to him at the tousle of blonde hair, the flash of the creamy skin of her back as she lay sleeping on her stomach with her arm tucked between their pillows. The little snores made him smile, because he knew she'd never admit to something so unladylike. He took the white down-alternative comforter and flipped it over her, kissed her wrist, and readied himself to climb out of the bed.

Except he suddenly felt an insistent tap on his arm. Looking down, he caught a glimpse of Griffin's sweet, smiling face.

The little boy's smile brightened and spread across his little face. "Drew!" His eyes grew wide.

Maggie stirred next to him. "Mommy," Griffin called out. "Did you have a sleepover with Drew? Can he stay for breakfast? I didn't get to show him my Star Wars Legos yesterday."

Drew suddenly felt his shoulder being attacked. Maggie was tapping it furiously from under the covers. When he managed to look around, her hair was completely disheveled, and she wore a panicked expression as she pointed under the sheets. *Naked,* she mouthed.

He couldn't help grinning. He just couldn't resist reaching under the sheets and pinching her ass a little until she stifled a little yelp. Which earned him a smack on the thigh. So he took the hint and sat up. "Tell you what," he said, subtly scooping his boxers off the floor and shimmying them on under the covers while Griffin tried to find a way to climb onto the bed. "Why don't you run and get some— slippers, and we'll go downstairs together and—um, let the dogs out? Then you can show me your Legos while I make breakfast."

Griffin, who gave up trying to climb onto the bed, propped his elbows on the bed, his hands bracing on his plump little boy cheeks. The kid had eyelashes longer than a model in a mascara ad.

Drew put his hand on the boy's shoulder and rotated him a little toward the door. "We'll surprise your mom with some…pancakes." He was completely winging this. "You like pancakes?"

"Waffles," Griffin said adamantly. "I like waffles."

"All righty, then." While Griffin headed downstairs, Drew turned to check on Maggie.

"Thank you," she murmured, still looking horrified.

"No problem," he said, sending her a wink. "I know a way for you to make it up to me later."

Maggie kept herself buried under the covers as Drew left the bed for the bathroom and Griffin went barreling out of the room, allowing Maggie to properly wallow in the fact that she was a terrible mother. Because she was naked! Because she'd spent hours…*doing* things with a guy who had stayed *all night* and whom her tender, innocent young son had just seen in his mother's bed! How could she?

That even beat the fact that she'd made love with Drew on the living room floor, when Griffin could have left his bed and caught them at any moment.

She was a bad, bad mother.

She sat up and watched Drew pull on his jeans. Then he caught her gawking at his gorgeous abs and his flat stomach as he zipped his fly. And he flashed her another grin. A big, wide grin that said *caught ya*.

She scooped up a balled-up shirt from the floor and tossed it at him. Too late, she realized it was hers, not his. He caught it in the middle of his chest. Then he walked to the bed and leaned over, lowering his voice.

"It's okay, Maggie. Everything's going to be okay. You'll see." Then he did that forehead-kiss thing, that simple peck of a kiss that for some reason just slayed her every time.

She smiled—a little, tiny smile, because he sounded so sure. And because he was so sweet. And cute. And because she remembered every single thing he'd done to her last night, and that made her whole body flush.

He tugged playfully on a strand of her hair. "See you downstairs," he said, before he turned and left the room.

198

For just a minute, Maggie stretched out in the bed and stared up at the ceiling. Wondered how the hell this amazing turn of events had happened to her. How the most unlikely man could turn out to be the rightest man of all. And how for the first time in three years she felt…alive.

She got up and walked to the bathroom, catching her reflection in the old medicine cabinet mirror. Despite the I-stuck-my-finger-in-the-electrical-outlet hair and the slightly dazed expression, she had color in her cheeks and a lit-up expression in her eyes. If she hadn't known herself, she'd say that her face was glowing. Glowing!

She banded back her hair in a ponytail and put on a T-shirt and shorts, prepared to take over the waffle making, but when she got downstairs, Griffin was standing on a chair in front of the counter mixing batter while Drew was cracking eggs. They'd even found the waffle iron.

Genny was sitting at Griffin's feet, vigilantly waiting to lick any drops of batter that made their way to the floor.

Maggie was about to say "I can take over," but as she neared, Drew handed her a cup of coffee, giving her a quick wink as he listened to Griff, who was animatedly telling him all about some Poke-whatever.

She took a sip of the delicious coffee, trying to process that there was a gorgeous man in her kitchen cooking breakfast, and just watching him use kitchen utensils was making her way too excited. Just then, her big lug of a dog rose from his bed, wagging his tail, wanting his usual petting fest. As she bent to pet him, Drew's dog nudged in front of Bear and began nipping at Maggie's bare feet until she managed to climb on a barstool to get free of the irritating little animal.

"Genny!" Drew scolded in a strict voice, and the dog backed off but remained near her seat, ready to bite off a toe. Or two.

Being terrorized in her own home by a dog that was a little

bigger than her purse seemed odd, but at the moment, she had too many other things to deal with. So she reached down to give Bear a pet and tried, in all fairness, to offer peace and love to Genevieve, but the dog did a little alligator snap and that was that.

Maggie took another sip of coffee, which was dark and strong, just the way she liked him. Or rather *it!* She guessed she would just go with what was happening. They would all have breakfast together, and then Drew would leave, and once her brain began working properly again, she would make a plan—a plan with strict rules like *no sleepovers* so Griffin wouldn't get too attached. Oh hell, who was she kidding—so *she* wouldn't get too attached. Because dammit, she was getting seriously attached!

The doorbell rang, and Bear and Ms. Yippy started a bark fest. As she went to answer the door, both dogs diverted over to eating spilled popcorn, which was strewn messily over the living room rug. It was a stark reminder of everything that had happened last night. A little wanton, a little messy, her overly cautious existence shot all to hell.

She opened the door to Mrs. Vanderbuckel, her landlady, who lived in the other half of the house. "Oh, hello, dear," she said, peering down her glasses. "I brought a coffee cake." Sure enough, she held out a very delicious-looking Bundt cake with drizzled icing on a pretty white plate with scalloped ceramic loops. But Maggie had to wonder about her kind gesture. Because the woman was scanning her apartment, doing acrobatics with her neck trying to see around her head.

"Is there a problem, Mrs. V?"

"Oh, not at all, dear," she said. Then in a whisper, "Is he here?"

"Is who here?" Maggie asked, playing dumb. Because there was no way she was admitting to having male company.

"I thought you might have—ahem—a visitor. A very hunky male visitor, if you know what I mean."

"Mrs. V, whatever makes you think I—"

"Well, you know, dear, I may have...heard things."

Maggie was *not* vocal! She didn't stomp around or have wild parties or disturb anyone's peace! The worst she might have done...

Oh God, no. There might have been a time last night...or two or three...when she might have done just a little bit of vocalizing. Not screaming or anything, but she distinctly remembered a moan or two. Maybe even the prolonged kind...

Her face suddenly felt like she was having one of those hot flashes her mom was always complaining about. Maggie opened her mouth to answer but...she had no words.

"Oh, are those pancakes I smell?" Now the nosy woman was pushing her way into her messy house, reclaiming her coffee cake on the way, noting with raised brows the popcorn all over the floor, the scattered shoes, her sweater thrown over the couch arm...and then she headed straight for the kitchen, where Maggie heard a distinct "Oh my, there you are!" when she'd obviously found Drew.

Maggie was just about to tackle the popcorn problem, which the dogs were still feasting on, when the doorbell rang again.

A quick peek out the window told her it was her parents. Well, she would just get rid of them quickly. Not let them inside. She'd gotten one hand on the doorknob when she paused and did a double take. Horror of horrors—her dad was wearing a kilt and carrying his bagpipes. Not unusual if it was St. Paddy's Day and he was leading the Irish Brigade at the annual parade. But today...

Maggie smacked herself in the head. They'd come to take Griffin to International Music Day at the community college. She'd forgotten all about it.

"Mom! Dad!" she said, opening the door. Bear stopped chowing down on the popcorn and bolted for her father, who was one of his favorite people. Griffin came tearing out of the kitchen and launched himself at her father's legs, then hugged her mother. "Grandpa! Grandma! Guess what! Mommy's new boyfriend took me fishing, and now he's making us breakfast! Come in!"

Thank you, Griffin, for announcing that to the world.

"Mommy's new boyfriend?" Her mother had picked right up on that, raising a fine brow at Maggie, who could only shrug. Her father pretended not to hear at all, choosing instead to focus on petting the dog.

Boyfriend. Kind of had a nice ring to it. It almost made her forget that said man was standing half-naked in her kitchen, soon to be seen by both her parents. Her mother could hardly contain her excitement, telegraphing Maggie knowing looks and peering excitedly past her into the kitchen to see if she could catch a glimpse of Drew, no doubt.

"Hey, Mags," someone said from the doorway. Her brother Scott had come to join the circus too.

"What are you doing here?" she asked. For just having broken up with his longtime girlfriend, he looked okay, not scruffy or undernourished or anything, which she took as a good sign.

"I thought I'd spend some quality time with my nephew." Scott promptly dangled Griffin by the ankles until he giggled uncontrollably, then put him on his shoulders and paraded him around the living room.

"Scott…" Maggie warned as Griffin balanced precariously on Scott's shoulders.

"Chillax, Sis. Geez, after last night, I thought you might be a little mellowed out."

She arm-punched him as he made another spin around the room, grinding in the spilled popcorn, no doubt.

Both dogs, unable to contain themselves, ran right behind them. This really *was* turning into a circus.

"Waffles are ready, everybody. Come on in and sit down."

Drew showed up at the entranceway between the family room and kitchen, beaming a smile at her that was worth the shocked expression on everyone's faces.

Her mother's mouth dropped open. Her father looked as uncomfortable as he did when Maggie was thirteen and her mother suddenly and inappropriately announced to everyone at the dinner table that Maggie had gotten her period. Wearing nothing on his upper body and holding her red kitchen spatula, Drew stood there looking like a model for a calendar entitled *Hotties in the Kitchen*.

Maggie was certain her entire body was blushing. But Drew smiled and calmly held out his hand to her dad. Her father, never one not to give someone a chance—even someone who happened to have slept with his daughter last night—shook it, thank God.

In the middle of freaking out inside, Maggie reminded herself that she had essentially caused zero problems for her parents since she was a teenager. Okay, there was that one time when she and Corey had fallen asleep one night after making out at his cousin's cabin on the lake and woke up at 3:00 a.m., only to learn they'd scared the crap out of everybody, but besides that…yeah. Nada. She'd dated one man. She'd married one man. She'd gotten a PhD and started a successful psychology practice. Maybe she owed them a few more gray hairs.

"This is Drew Poulos," she managed.

"Andreas Poulos," her mother said, stepping forward, her hands pressed together in glee. He held out his hand to shake, but she forwent that and enveloped him in a hug. "Of course. Yes. The billionaire."

Maggie bit back a smile because the thought of Drew being a billionaire seemed so comical. Inconsistent with the image of the guy with the once-bushy beard who wore flannel shirts and did hard labor on the apple farm.

Even seeing his family in Greenwich didn't really drive home the fact that Drew himself belonged to that life. He seemed so removed from that. He cooked his own meals and drove his brother Roman's pickup and took Griffin fishing…and she loved all those things about him.

"Drew works for his brother's brandy business now," Maggie said.

Drew tossed her a grateful glance. Like maybe he didn't want to be known as a billionaire either.

"Oh, I hope you'll be staying in Mirror Lake for good," her mother continued, steering him into the family room. "Mirror Lake is an excellent place to settle down and raise children."

Maggie steered her mother right back to the kitchen, grabbing Drew's shirt, which was dangling from the couch arm. "I'm sorry, Mom," she said, quickly changing the subject, "the thing at the community college completely slipped my mind."

"Yes, dear. I can see how you were—er—otherwise occupied." Her mother was giving her that conspiratorial, knowing look that a good girlfriend might have been able to pull off but on a mother looked ridiculous.

"Griffie, why don't you run upstairs and get clothes on?" Maggie said.

"But the waffles are almost ready, Mom!" Griffin complained.

"Oh, Maggie, you made homemade waffles?" her mom asked.

"Drew made them," Maggie said quickly.

"And Griffin helped," Drew said. "And he's right—they're all ready. You folks hungry?"

"Yeah," Griffin said. "We made enough for everybody!"

"Well, we are early for the program," her mom said.

"Then I suggest," her dad said, ruffling Griffin's hair, "we eat 'em while they're warm."

"We'll be right in," Maggie said, taking hold of Drew's arm

and leading him into the back hall, where she handed him the wrinkled T-shirt.

He smiled, put his shirt on, and gave her a little wink. Like he was saying, *you see, it's all going to be fine.*

She was a bit sad that he'd covered up that ridiculously gorgeous chest of his. But mostly she was touched—by everything he'd done, his unflappability, his easygoing humor. And that his eyes were smiling. At her.

Was she dreaming? Because she felt so…happy. Thrilled, in fact. Bursting with happiness.

She reached up—on tiptoe, as he was that tall—and kissed his cheek. She wanted to tell him how much she appreciated his cooking skills and his ability to enrapture everyone from her four-year-old to her crotchety landlady—all of which he'd done admirably *and* without a shirt. But all those words caught suddenly in her throat. "Thank you," she managed.

No, that wasn't good enough. They'd promised honesty, and she was going to try to do better.

She tugged him farther down the tiny hallway that led to the back door. "Thank you for last night. And for this morning. And for everything. I didn't expect to have half the town turn up for breakfast, but—you made it turn out okay. I can't thank you enough—"

He stopped her by kissing her very thoroughly on the lips. Then he whispered in her ear, "If your kitchen wasn't full of people, I'd have a few ideas about how you could show your gratitude, but I guess it'll just have to wait. Besides, don't thank me yet. You haven't tasted my waffles. And there's just one thing."

Maggie frowned. "What is it?"

"I wish you had told me we were going to have all these visitors for breakfast."

Oh no. Was he angry after all? "Why's that?" she asked.

He smiled broadly and ran a hand along her cheek, such a

simple gesture, but it almost brought her to tears. "I would've bought more eggs."

Drew was sitting at the bar in MacNamara's the next Friday night, eating a Reuben sandwich and fries. He and Maggie had come here to eat before going to see a movie. They'd been working every evening on preparations for the big cancer benefit that was just a week away, and the wine bar opening was coming up that same weekend. But tonight was a well-deserved night off. Maggie, who was sitting next to him talking to her brother behind the bar, kept reaching over to steal his fries.

He didn't mind it. In fact, every time she leaned over him to dip one in ketchup, he was tempted to kiss her pretty neck. Plus her hair smelled terrific.

"You know there's going to be a penalty if you keep stealing those," Drew said.

She swung around to look at him, shoving a fry in her mouth. "Is the penalty better than the fries?" she asked.

"Definitely," he said, dragging her onto his lap, where she picked up the other half of his sandwich and took a bite.

"Okay, then," she said. "Maybe you can order more fries, and then there'll be a *double* penalty."

"Plus extra for snagging the sandwich," he said, circling her waist. That made her laugh. She turned around and kissed him. The kiss was salty and ketchupy and delicious. Just like her.

"Ugh, you guys are too cute." Scott set a tall glass of beer on the bar. "I hate to interrupt all this affection, but can I ask you a little favor, Mags?"

"Sure," Maggie said. "What is it?"

"I'm a little busy back here. Run this over to Carol Ann, will you?"

Scott smiled and waved to someone behind Maggie. Drew

turned to see a young woman with thick glasses sitting by herself reading a book.

"Is that Carol Ann Wasserman?" Maggie asked. "I haven't seen her in ages."

Drew wondered what kind of bar this was, where people sat and read books like it was a damn coffee shop. "That's an awful big book she's reading," he said.

"It's *A Game of Thrones*," Scott said.

Maggie turned to Drew. "*Game of Thrones* is to my brother what Harry Potter is to the rest of the world." She lifted the drink and looked at her brother. "And what might this be, may I ask?"

"It's Angry Orchard on tap. It's okay, she's twenty-one."

"*Barely* twenty-one," Maggie said. "I haven't seen Carol Ann for a long time. What is she, a junior now?"

"She's studying literature at NYU. Smart girl."

Maggie gave him a look. "Since when do you like them smart?" She paused. "And young."

"I'm not some perv, okay? Just give it to her. From me."

"From you? Scott, what is going on here?"

"I'm just being Uncle Scotty the Bartender, okay? She just broke up with her boyfriend, and she's a little…lost."

"And you just broke up with Marcia, and you're horny."

Drew chuckled, and Scott passed him a dirty look.

Scott frowned. "I know she's too young for me. She's just…a nice kid. That's all. Besides, I have bigger problems."

At that moment, their dad came out from the kitchen, a tray of food in his hands.

"Dad! What are you doing here?" Maggie asked.

"Hi, sweetheart," Mr. MacNamara said, passing through the opening between the bar and the seating area. "Just helping Scott out. Date night tonight?" He nodded in Drew's direction. "Hey, you want another beer, son?"

"No, I'm good, thanks, Mr. M." Drew knew it was a sore

point, Maggie's dad picking up bar shifts when he was supposed to be enjoying retirement.

Maggie went to deliver the drink, and Scott turned to Drew, leaning over the bar near where he was sitting. "I haven't seen my sister this happy in a long time."

Drew smiled. He hadn't been this happy either, but he wasn't the type to say that out loud.

"I can tell you're good for her."

"What makes you say that?"

"Because she told me you check her stove burners for her before she leaves her house."

Drew laughed. What on earth *that* had to do with being good for her, he had no idea. He just did it because it stressed her out so much. Plus it got them out of there quicker.

"You laugh, but that used to be a big thing with Corey. He used to think that making her do it herself would cure her of her OCD, you know what I mean? So he'd give her sort of a lecture, like 'See? They're all off. We can leave now.' I loved the guy, but personally, I always thought that was a little condescending."

"Well, your sister does nice things for me too." Like, she made it a point to pack him a lunch every day so he wouldn't be tempted to eat junk food. And put up with him in general when he was being a pain in the ass.

Which sort of sounded like…a real relationship.

"I like seeing her happy," Scott said. "I hope things work out for you."

"Thanks," Drew said.

Then Maggie was back, taking her seat on the stool. "She said thanks, that's her favorite. And she's almost done with your book, she'll return it tomorrow. Scott—"

"Don't say it, Maggie. I know what I'm doing."

She reached over and grabbed her brother's hand. "Okay, I'm sorry. I know this thing with Marcia's been hard."

"Only because she refuses to believe I'm serious about breaking up."

Maggie stood up and leaned over the bar to kiss her brother on the cheek. "Hang in there. It'll get better."

"Right, right," he said. "Gotta go, see you two lovebirds later." Then he headed away to take someone's order.

"Ready for the movie?" Maggie asked Drew.

"I confess, all that fry stealing has got me thinking about other things."

"My punishments?" she asked, her face lighting up.

He laughed. "Want to go back to my place and fool around? Then we could watch a movie—in bed."

She looked at her watch. "Helen's sitting until midnight. We have time."

"Great. Let's go." He stood up, left a generous bill under his plate, and escorted her to the door, giving a wave to her father and Scott. Her father gave him a friendly slap on the back and kissed his daughter on the way out.

This was starting to feel like family, like home. It was starting to feel like forever. And he had to admit he liked it. A lot.

CHAPTER 18

The next Saturday evening, Maggie entered the high-ceilinged ballroom in the Grand Victorian hotel for the third annual Dr. Corey McShae Memorial Cancer Fund dinner. Tables were set with bright yellow tablecloths, decorations hung, and everyone was dressed in their best to come out and honor the memory of her husband. And she could not wait for it to be over.

She must've been nuts to agree to chair the event. Actually, when she'd conceived this idea, she was. She'd been crazy with grief. And so desperate to fill the void of those gut-wrenching hours during all those long, sleepless nights that she'd decided that Corey's memory would live on forever in an annual benefit the town would never see the likes of again. She'd mobilized sponsors, donors, and chairpeople. She'd rounded up a leadership crew of friends, financial advisors, and go-getter citizens who would leave no stone unturned to ensure that the legacy of the Dr. Corey McShae Cancer Center at Mirror Lake Community Hospital would live on in perpetuity.

Maggie thought at the time she'd been doing something

proactive for her grief—proverbially spitting in its face, so to speak—but every year it seemed harder and harder to attend. The benefit dredged up all her longing for Corey, her sense of loss, her grief. And it was all her fault! She'd insisted on being a part of this, when she should have let it go. Let *him* go. She could have ensured he was honored in some less public way, and left herself out of it.

But she could no more do that than stop her daily jog, as much as she hated it some days. She was determined that everyone remember what a kind, bighearted man Corey was. When he himself got cancer, he used his struggle to encourage the children and their families who were fighting it too. He helped establish the cancer center and got doctors from Yale and UConn to staff clinics so families wouldn't have to travel so much. Mirror Lake was a small community, but he believed everyone should have access to great care.

She was determined to keep his cause alive. To keep *him* alive in some way for Griffin.

Corey would have loved seeing all his friends and neighbors here. He was probably looking down on her, laughing his ass off too—as outgoing as she was introverted, he had to know what a sword in her side giving that damn speech on his behalf every year was. But she did it. For him.

Drew, as the event treasurer, had put in a lot of after-work hours too. He'd written checks, but also hauled boxes, hung decorations, and even helped the florist unload the flower arrangements for the tables. He'd brought her coffee and water, or sometimes just passed by with a wink or a little squeeze on her shoulder.

He'd been concerned for her—and nothing but wonderful. But sometimes Maggie caught him staring at her, a flicker of worry in his eyes. She wondered if he was thinking about how well loved Corey had been by the community, and if that comparison troubled him in some ways.

But as the week went on, Maggie grew increasingly uncomfortable around him, for reasons she couldn't entirely explain. That enormous banner at the front of the room—a photo of Corey, stethoscope around his neck, a little pediatric cancer patient on his lap—had been getting to her. It was almost as if Corey were watching her and Drew. And not approving in the least.

Drew joined her just then, kissing her on the cheek, holding her at arm's length. "You look amazing." He scanned her face, a look of concern in his eyes. "How are you holding up?"

Her heart cracked a little just then for his unselfish concern. This couldn't have been easy on him. She longed for it to be over so they could get back to the carefree fun of their early relationship. This whole thing had cast a pall over it that she couldn't wait to remove. Not knowing how to express this in words, she kissed him and smiled. "Thanks for asking. And for everything you've done."

"I'm worried it's too much on you. But you've done a spectacular job."

Just then, Alyssa Covington waved wildly from the doorway. Dressed in a sexy black dress and killer heels that made her look much more like a movie star than a doctor, she came up to them and kissed Maggie on the cheek. "It's so good to see you, sweetie. How are you holding up?" She patted her arm sympathetically while unabashedly admiring Drew.

It took Maggie a few seconds to realize Alyssa was...a little too happy. She had an outgoing personality, but showing up half-tanked at 6:00 p.m....definitely not her usual style.

"Well, hello, handsome," Alyssa said to Drew, her words slurring a bit. "Maggie, where on earth did you find this guy?" She pushed playfully against Drew's chest. "He's hot."

That Alyssa, always joking around, wasn't she? Drew cleared his throat, and Maggie almost kissed him for not doing what men usually did in front of Alyssa. Salivate and ogle, mostly.

"Alyssa, this is Drew Poulos," Maggie said. "Drew, meet Dr. Alyssa Covington. She trained with Corey at CHOP."

"Nice to meet you," Alyssa said. "Corey was so amazing, and Maggie here is also amazing"—she paused to side-hug Maggie— "and we hung out constantly, and we were pregnant with our firsts at the same time. We've been through a lot together, haven't we?"

Maggie would have answered, except that just then, Alyssa's gaze ran up and down Drew in a very thorough way. A way that made Maggie wonder quite ungraciously exactly where her husband was.

"Is Keith here?" she finally asked.

"Oh, the baby wasn't feeling well, so he stayed home." She shrugged prettily and put on a sad, pouty expression. "I'm all by my lonesome."

Maggie was distracted by the director of the hospital and his wife walking up to speak with her. Alyssa linked her arm with Drew's. "Maggie, honey, you wouldn't mind if I asked Drew to have a drink with me, would you? Since I have no one to sit with?"

Yes, she minded. Once upon a time, Alyssa had made similar overtures with Corey, but he'd always laughed them off as simply part of her outgoing nature. Maggie wasn't sure she could take watching Alyssa hit on Drew.

Drew gave Maggie a knowing look. A look that said he had this covered, that he'd get Alyssa to sober up a little and make sure she was seated among friends.

As grateful as she was for Drew's intervention, a flutter of apprehension made her stomach queasy. Alyssa was yet another reason she couldn't wait for this night to end.

The woman hanging on to Drew's arm was talking his ear off. He didn't want to keep company with her, but she was drunk and a bit obnoxious and he'd had no choice but to get her out of Maggie's way as Maggie greeted all the hospital administrators and staff.

He understood that this was a stressful event for Maggie, and he wanted to do all he could to help her. It was clear her husband was beloved by the town and his tragic death hit everyone hard. Hell, for the past week, he'd heard over and over from just about everyone that the man was a veritable saint. There was no sick child he didn't love, no health-care injustice he didn't strive to right. On top of everything else, the giant vertical banner with his photograph on it hanging in the front was making him uncomfortable, but for an entirely different reason.

That reason was jealousy, plain and simple. Corey seemed so...perfect. Levelheaded, friendly, altruistic. Saving the lives of children on a daily basis. What had Drew done in his life that could equal that? *I could balance a mean spreadsheet* was the best he could come up with. Or prune a snarly apple tree. *And I could love your wife.*

But, he was getting the sense, *not as well as you did it.*

He was haunted by the sickening feeling that whatever he felt for her, it would never be enough. Her marriage to Corey had been pretty damn near perfect. The man had no faults. Before this week, he'd truly felt that Maggie had begun letting the weight of his memory go...that she was beginning to see *him* in a special way. That maybe she was even falling in love with him.

He'd always been a man to know his heart, know what he wanted. Sondra was out of his mind for good. He loved talking with Maggie and spending time with her and just hanging out with her and Griffin. When he wasn't with them, he felt restless, and it was starting to feel more natural to hang out at her place than his. He wanted to wake up next to her and fall asleep with her and take her on dates and just...be with her.

He didn't know if now was a good time to say it, but he'd fallen in love with her.

"Let's get a drink," Alyssa said, tottering a little toward the bar.

"How about a coffee?" Drew offered, but she laughed like that was the funniest thing she'd heard all night. Before he could stop her, she'd ordered two double shots. Then she walked outside onto the terrace, where wrought iron tables were set up with flickering candles and lanterns hung from trees with views of a pretty garden blooming beyond.

"Where'd you do your MBA?" Alyssa asked, handing him a drink.

"Harvard," he said.

"Ooh, you're a smart one. Smart and good-looking. Lucky Maggie."

She walked over to the edge of the terrace and looked out over the streets of the little Mirror Lake downtown. Down a few blocks were the shops and the town square, and behind them was the bleached white steeple of the Congregational Church. Blossoms were bursting everywhere, scenting the air with sweet spring perfume. Drew couldn't help but remember that day he'd ducked into the church to hide from that reporter and had found…Maggie.

"Yep, lucky Maggie," Alyssa said again. "She got the greatest guy. Corey was the best. But I almost got him away from her." She held up her thumb and forefinger in a pinched position. "I was this close."

Drew frowned. He hoped that was the booze talking, but he had to wonder if Maggie knew just what kind of "friend" this woman was. The kind not to take your eyes off, that's what kind.

"Keith—that's my husband. He's not here because we're getting a divorce. Lucky me, right? I thought having another kid would save us, but it didn't." She downed half the whiskey.

"I'm sorry to hear that," Drew said, deciding he was going to get the coffee anyway. Right now.

She barely seemed to hear him. "Yep, she got herself a good one. But she doesn't have a clue how close she came to losing him. Of course, after that, he got sick, and then it became a whole different story."

Drew steered Alyssa to a seat. "How do you like your coffee?"

She pulled on his sleeve. "No coffee. Come sit. I'll tell you the story." She tugged at his jacket, but he resisted. He had no desire to hear any story she had to tell. A large crowd of people milled about in the space between the tables, effectively trapping him for a moment. "Corey and I were both engaged to other people when we started the residency program. But there was always this little thread of...attraction between us. You know how that goes sometimes. A little spark." She took another swallow of her drink. "We were always joking together and laughing, and that helped when things were bad at work. You've got to have a good sense of humor when you work with sick kids. Corey was always good at lightening everyone up."

A voice inside Drew's head warned him to *leave now!* But tendrils of dread seemed to twist around him and anchor him in place.

"One night, we were on call. It had been crazy busy, and just after midnight, a two-year-old came in who had bitten down on a laundry pod. We worked on him—he almost died, but we saved him—and we were both on that kind of unbelievable high when you get to cheat death for once, you know?"

Drew knew he shouldn't listen. But his feet felt as leaden as the wrought iron furniture around him. His heart was pounding so hard, he could barely hear what Alyssa was saying. But his gut knew what was coming.

"As soon as we got to the call room, I kissed him. Hard. He looked so surprised, as if he'd had no clue I'd been wanting to do that for months. I told him what I'd been feeling. I asked him if he felt it too."

She fingered the condensation on her glass. "Of course he said he loved *her*. But he couldn't deny our connection. And I was so desperate for him. I thought I could make him see he'd be better off with me." She looked up at Drew. "We made love, right on the call room floor. Didn't even make it to the bunk."

Drew winced. He'd heard more than enough.

"Of course he felt so guilty afterward. There was no talking to him. I begged him to see how good we were together, but all he could ever talk about was her. How bad he felt, blah blah blah. He made me swear never to tell her."

Drew supposed he should be shocked—he was, a little—but not surprised. The whole Corey package was too perfect. There had to be a fault line somewhere, he just hadn't expected one so spectacular. If anything, he was angry. For the deceit. And because this woman held information that could ruin Maggie's perception of her husband. No one should be allowed to do that when dead men couldn't defend themselves. Not that he was excusing Corey's behavior. He just didn't want it to upset Maggie.

Funny, Drew knew how it had pained Maggie, what this woman had—a husband, two beautiful children—never guessing that all this woman wanted was what *she* had.

"Alyssa, maybe you should go home. I could call you an Uber if you'd like."

She laughed. "Don't worry. I won't tell your precious Maggie. Although it might do her some good to learn her hubby wasn't quite the saint she thinks he was. It's never smart to worship a man, is it? They're just so damn...fallible."

If Maggie knew, it would break her heart. Hopefully, this woman was too drunk to know she was spilling her guts to a complete stranger. He was counting on that.

"Of course, I could be persuaded to keep quiet even more if you'd leave with me." Her fake laugh made him understand it wasn't a joke.

Right. Thanks but no thanks.

Cold, seeping dread permeated his bones like a November chill despite the pleasant June evening. It wasn't until later, after he'd gotten her—and himself—a black coffee and finally extricated himself from her side that he fully realized what a fool he'd been. His curiosity had gotten the better of him. By staying to hear the end of that horrible story, he was now the unwilling conspirator in forever keeping this secret from Maggie.

And keep it he would, because it would devastate her. And she'd had enough pain.

Maggie had no secrets; it was one of the things he loved about her, that she was an open book. He hated secrets, down to his marrow, and he knew as well as anyone the power they had to destroy. Being betrayed by the two people in the world closest to him—his brother and Sondra—had taught him that. The irony was that he now carried one himself, and it was a whopper. But what choice did he have except to keep it?

Maggie was doing great until she had to give that damn speech. She'd greeted all Corey's old friends and colleagues, accepted all the awkward condolences from people who tried hard but just didn't know quite what to say. All that was a piece of cake compared to getting up there in front of everyone and talking about him.

It wasn't that she'd recounted how he never stopped fighting for his little patients, even when he was ill himself, or how hard he fought to bring good cancer care closer to town.

She got through the speech just fine. It was just the fact that that damn banner was hanging there with his super-life-sized, young, handsome face beaming out so beautifully. That banner was messing with her mind. It hit her suddenly that Corey looked so large and alive but he was…gone. All his dreams, all his tremendous, enormous potential, his hopes of watching Griffin grow up to be a man… It was all gone. The pain of his loss came crashing back, and suddenly, she needed some air.

She managed to finish, thanked everyone, and stepped away from the podium. But instead of returning to her seat, she walked straight out the French doors, onto the patio, and even farther— out into the winding paths of the gardens. She pulled off her heels and shoved them in a potted palm, finally able to run free, not stopping until she reached the decorative cement wall at the edge of the gardens, on the side that faced downtown.

Suddenly, she felt a pair of arms around her, and her body knew exactly whose they were before her brain even processed.

"You looked upset," Drew said quietly.

He'd found her. He'd come for her. She wanted to fall into his arms, feel the comfort of his big body around her, breathe in the clean, manly scent of him.

She looked at the man in front of her, kind, funny, gorgeous Drew. She'd done so well lately, the promise of a real life ahead making her hopeful for the first time since Corey's death. She'd felt that finally, she'd be able to make peace with her past and look forward to a bright future.

But tonight kept reminding her how much real love cost. It was exhausting being here, remembering all that pain.

"You did your husband proud tonight, Maggie."

He stood by her, both of them saying nothing. Ahead of them was a view of the town, fairy-tale-ish. Store fronts were lit up, the sun sliding down over the horizon in a trail of fiery salmon and pink.

"You okay?" he finally asked. "If you want to be alone, I'm okay with that."

She teared up. Oh, this man. Always thinking of her. She shouldn't want him to witness her being a complete mess like this, but his presence was too comforting. "I—I'm sorry, Drew. I'm terrible company right now."

Eventually, he spoke. "That friend of yours is a real piece of work. You known her for very long?"

"Alyssa? Corey and she were residents together in Hartford. When we moved back to Mirror Lake, we became quite close."

"Can I ask why? Frankly, she seems—I don't know. Jealous of you."

Maggie waved a dismissive hand. "Alyssa went on to do everything Corey and I might have—she joined the most popular pediatric group in town, she had another child, bought a home. It's me who's jealous, not the other way around."

"Okay, whatever you say. But I'd steer clear of her."

"I'm not worried about it. She may be a little drunk tonight, but that's out of character. Did she hit on you or something?"

"No. It's just a feeling I get." He turned to her and gently squeezed her shoulder, smiling that kind, beautiful man smile of his that always made her heart crack a little. "Hey, you want to get out of here? I saw you didn't eat much. We could pick up a pizza, or I make a mean omelet, at least Griffin thinks so—"

Alyssa was the least of her problems, nothing like the weight on her chest that was getting unbearable, that was making her struggle for air, a creeping dread that was threatening to choke her but that suddenly made it clear what she had to do.

Drew deserved better than what she could give him. A woman who could give her whole heart to him. And tonight had shown her that clearly wasn't her. But she'd promised him honesty—she wouldn't screw him over like Sondra did. Standing next to him, looking out over the town she'd lived in her whole life, her eyes flooded with tears. "I—I can't do this," she said, her voice a whisper.

"I know, sweetheart," he said. "It's too much. All the work and then getting up there in front of everyone and having to talk about Corey..."

She grabbed his arms. Made sure to look him in the eyes. "No, Drew. What I mean is, I can't do this—*us*. A relationship." Through the blur, she could see the hurt in his eyes, and it was horrible, that she could cause that after all he'd been through—but she had to continue. She had to tell him the truth. They'd promised each other. "You're a wonderful guy. An amazing guy. You deserve someone who's there one hundred percent."

"Stop," Drew said quietly. His posture turned rigid, frozen. He stepped back. "Look, it's been a very emotional evening—"

"I don't want to hurt you, but tonight made me realize I—I'm messed up. I thought I was ready to move forward, but I can't."

"Can't or won't?" he asked. His voice was deadly and level, aiming straight for the heart. So even toned it was as if all the emotion had been sucked right out of it, the quiet in the eye of a hurricane. But she knew better, knew from his steel-straight spine, the balls of his fists, the twitch of a tiny muscle under his eye.

Drew turned away, saying nothing, which was awful. Couldn't he rant, show his rage, turn on her so she felt properly chastised? Maggie felt paralyzed, every muscle suspended. She should go to him, put her arms around him, tell him that she needed his understanding and some time, but she could not. Because she didn't know *what* she needed. Tonight had done something to her. It had gutted her, and she had nothing left. She needed space. Maybe she'd always need space, and worse, maybe she was incapable of ever moving on, ever truly living again.

"All right, then," he said.

That was it? He was going to take it on the chin? Not even a malevolent tone in his voice, a cruel remark, a reference that what they had was just a fling anyway, so no loss there? No, he was a goddamn gentleman to the end, up until the time he looked at her, his eyes full of anger, his jaw tight as a screw. He turned, started to walk away. Then he spun back around.

"Your husband was just a man, Maggie." He paused. For a

long, frightening time. "It's safe to cling to your memories because memories don't fight back."

The expression in his eyes was level and deadly. There was something irreparable in that look, something irreversible, and it just killed her, what she'd done to make him look at her like that.

And just then, with that one look, her heart that she'd tried so hard all along to protect broke in half anyway.

CHAPTER 19

Drew was bursting with love for her. He wanted to comfort her, tell her it was all going to be all right.

But he knew it wasn't. Because he would never be able to compete with someone she had so far up on a pedestal he was practically the Burj Khalifa.

He should never have let himself fall in love with her.

No, that wasn't true. It wasn't logical, and it wasn't a decision on his part. He'd crashed headlong into love with Maggie despite all his terror and fears of ever loving someone again. She'd shown him, just by being herself, what an honest, loving, unselfish person was. So different from Sondra. She'd helped him understand, to finally slice the ties that bound him.

And now she was rejecting him too.

"I'm sorry," she said.

Anger welled up inside him. He wanted to shake her! He wanted to tell her, yeah, life was hard and unpredictable, but loving each other was worth it. *They* were worth it.

"I didn't mean for things to get so…out of control," she said.

Out of control? Yeah. Understatement of his life. He'd always been able to handle flings. Sometimes the women he'd dated had a hard time saying good-bye, but never him. He knew getting involved with her was a big risk, yet he'd done it anyway.

"I know we started this up as a casual thing, Maggie, but I'm not ashamed to tell you my feelings have changed. I'm sure this benefit has made you upset and dredged up a lot of painful feelings. I mean, the past few days have been a real roller coaster for you…" He forced his lips together so he would *stop talking*. Because now he was on the verge of begging.

"Tonight's brought too many memories back. Painful ones. It's reminded me how much love can hurt. I can't go that deep again, not with anybody. Even you. It's not fair to let you believe I'm capable of something I'm just not capable of."

Clearly, her feelings for him weren't strong enough to make her want to try. To see all the good, the wonderful things they could have between them…and that was what skewered him right in the heart. Drew winced and bit his lip—hard—to avoid the words spilling out of his mouth that were pushing against his lips. *He cheated on you, Maggie,* he could say. *I'd rethink your position.*

But he said nothing. Who was he to tarnish her husband's memory? He didn't know the guy, even though if he did, the first thing he'd do was punch him for fooling around on her.

Don't judge someone who's not here to defend himself. It was Mrs. Panagakos's voice in his head. He wished it would get out.

"Right."

She had no idea he'd treat her so much better. But then, you couldn't convince someone to love you, could you? He knew from his own experience that the heart wants what it wants. He'd just never realized the tables would turn on him…again. Rejected, but this time for a ghost that he could never, ever compete with. Not a chance.

"The perfect life is a fantasy," he said. He sounded angry,

even to his own ears, but he couldn't help it. "Real love takes hard work. You told me that yourself. I think it's easier for you to hide behind Corey's memory than to take a real leap of faith. But then, it's your life. Best of luck with it."

He gritted his teeth from saying more. Then he forced himself to turn away.

"Drew, wait," she called.

He turned around, but only to reach down behind a nearby bench and hand her the shoes she'd ditched earlier in the potted palm. "I figured, judging by the fancy label, when your feet stopped hurting, you might want these again." He watched her tear up and felt a strange twist of satisfaction in his gut, not because she was in pain, but because he knew he'd affected her. "I'm walking home. See you around, Maggie."

Maggie collapsed onto the bench, the lovely parklike setting lost on her. For the first time, she noticed a garishly ornate three-tiered fountain with a fish on top spouting water. It didn't matter. She could've been in the midst of a bank of fog in the middle of the ocean for all she knew or cared.

She wiped away more mascara-tinted tears. Okay, she was officially a wreck. She tried to tell herself she'd just done the right thing, the noble thing even.

It would be good to take a break from the raw, breathless feelings Drew stirred in her. It had been too chaotic with him, too big and exciting, like a little kid OD'ing on Christmas morning. Backing off now before things got too serious was the right thing to do.

Then why did she feel like she'd done something terribly, terribly wrong?

Maggie heard the confident click-clicking of high heels. Alyssa was suddenly sitting next to her, exclaiming, pulling out scented tissues from a little wrapped package. They smelled like her perfume, intense, expensive, *suffocating*.

"Oh, you poor thing. I was getting ready to head out myself when I saw Drew stalk off. I figured something had gone wrong, so I came to find you."

She seemed much more sober now. Drew's words of caution came back to her, and she shrugged them off. Alyssa was her *friend*. Yeah, they hadn't been as close as they once were, but that was to be expected. The situation was awkward. Anyone in a similar one would act the same way.

She was being silly. So she accepted the Kleenex gratefully and blew her nose. "Thanks for coming after me, but I'm fine, really. Just a little emotional."

"Did you and Drew have a fight?"

Maggie sighed. "I just broke up with him. I—I'm just not ready for a relationship."

Alyssa shook her forearm. "Honey, you've got to get a grip. I mean, come on, it's been three years."

Her words were a verbal slap. One half of Maggie wondered where this woman had learned her bedside manner, because it was downright awful. She would never judge a grieving client that way.

On the other hand, what *was* wrong with her? It *had* been over three years. Guilt and shame stung her. Why couldn't she just get over it?

"Listen, don't let the past ruin your present and your future, Maggie. You're going to have to lower your standards a little, you know what I mean? Besides, with a good-looking guy like Drew, the sex has got to be sensational, right? So live a little. You deserve it. Don't expect too much, and you'll be fine."

Everything she heard prickled the hairs on her neck. The idea that Drew was of lower caliber than Corey. That she was in it for sex—it might have started out that way, but there was so much more to what they had than that. And since when was a pediatrician dishing out advice like Dear Abby?

Yet hadn't she made Drew feel he wasn't worth taking a chance on? And wasn't that just like implying he wasn't as good as Corey?

Alyssa put an arm around Maggie's shoulder. Perhaps Maggie was taking this all wrong. Alyssa had always been blunt; some tough love could be what Maggie needed, someone to tell her like it was. She needed to change. Lord knew that she already knew that about many aspects of herself; Alyssa was clearly trying to help her.

"I'd like to get something off my mind that's been bothering me for quite a while," Alyssa said. "I'm thinking it will be a good opportunity for both of us to put the past to rest."

Maggie wiped her eyes again and looked at Alyssa. She was so beautiful. She had it so together. She and her lovely husband and her two gorgeous, insanely smart children.

She took up Maggie's hands. "Something happened one night when Corey and I were on call. It demonstrates that we're all human, we all make mistakes, and that you shouldn't glorify someone's memory too much. When someone dies, it's easy to forget they were a normal human being like everyone else."

Maggie frowned, ignoring the *everybody's human* advice. "What do you mean...something happened?"

Corey often told her stories of his nights on call, but she remembered a couple of times when something had happened and he could not or would not talk about it. Sometimes he couldn't bring himself to talk about it for weeks or months, how some child had come in so sick, so abused, so unsaveable...or how despite everything he'd done, things sometimes didn't turn out well.

Alyssa began talking, staring straight ahead into the garish fountain. "We'd worked together side by side to save a little toddler who almost died. I can't tell you how touch and go it was, how emotional, and how grateful we were that that child lived. We were thrilled beyond belief, and the parents...well, there aren't words for that experience."

For some odd reason, Maggie's spine started tingling. Maggie had always shrugged Alyssa's big personality off as belonging to a beautiful woman who had a lot of confidence. She'd always had a good heart, hadn't she? She would never say anything bad about Corey.

"Corey was so great during that case. So calm and levelheaded. So understanding with the parents. We'd come through something that bonded us together in an unbelievable way."

Maggie blew out a sigh of relief. Yes, of course. That was how Corey was. He loved being in action, and he was always calm under pressure. She understood that well. Alyssa had talked in this exclusive fashion before, mentioning things that only Corey and she shared, but Maggie had always tried not to let jealousy get the best of her. After all, Corey was married to *her*.

"Afterward, we went up to the call room. It must have been the intensity of the moment, but pretty soon one thing led to another and we, well...we lost control."

Alyssa's lips were moving but the only thing she could hear coming from them was babble. She surely didn't say what Maggie thought she said, did she? That Corey and Alyssa...in a darkened call room...bunk beds, mussed sheets...just like in those doctor shows on TV, where they barely make it past the door before they start ripping the clothes off each other.

Oh God.

Maggie shook her head a little wildly. Fought the urge to stick her fingers in her ear canals like a child who simply doesn't want to hear any more. It wouldn't have been necessary, as the pounding of her heart had obscured all other sound. She couldn't have heard right. A repeat was in order. "Wh—what are you saying to me?"

"I'm saying—"

"You're saying something happened between you and my husband?" Maggie's voice was high-pitched and loud to her own ears. She somehow couldn't bring herself to say *You had sex with my husband.* Or, *You made love with my husband.* No, not that. Never that.

This was a joke, right? Tonight was simply a little overwhelming, and she'd surely misheard. Either that or maybe someone had slipped something into her ice water that was making her hallucinate. That was okay, there were lots of docs here. One of them would have a fix for this.

There went Alyssa's hand on her shoulder again. Her earnest, sparkling eyes beamed out sincere and honest. "It was one time, Maggie, I swear. The reason I'm telling you this is that it's not good to make someone into a complete saint. Then you'll never get over him. He was just a man. A good man, but a flesh-and-blood man."

"Stop it!" Maggie spat, pulling out of her reach, scrambling to her feet. "You don't get to tell me what's right or not right to think about Corey. How dare you? That's my husband you're talking about. My *husband.*" She was beating her chest like some deranged person, and surely she was going to attract attention, but at that moment, she didn't care. "Wh-why would you tell me this?"

"He wasn't your husband at the time. You were only engaged."

Only engaged? Only engaged?

Maggie stood there numbly. She was vaguely aware of the lighthearted splashing of the water in the background. The one thing she'd had left after she lost Corey was the assurance that they'd had a fantastic marriage. The fricking thing was made in heaven. From the day when she was seventeen and first set eyes on him, she'd known he was someone special. And he'd been hers. Hers and no one else's.

What a fool she'd been. To believe that love was some kind of fairy tale and that she'd had her own personal prince.

She heard a voice behind her, speaking sharply to Alyssa. "You're a real piece of work, you know that?"

Drew stepped onto the paved path. Moonlight shone on his white tux shirt, making it look an otherworldly blue, adding to the surrealism of the moment.

Drew. He'd come back—how *could* he have after all that? And to stand up for her during the worst moment of her life.

"I was *trying* to help her," Alyssa said a bit petulantly. "It was like I told you, it just happened. It was meaningless."

Like I told you. The words echoed inside her head. Drew knew? Before she did? The relief Maggie felt on seeing him was replaced by incredulity. She stared at him in disbelief. "You *knew* about this?"

"As of a half hour ago."

Maggie rubbed her temples. She really should have put her shoes back on. She could've used the dignity a pair of good high heels would give right around now. She addressed Alyssa. "My God, how many people did you tell?"

"Just him, I swear," she said.

Drew opened his mouth to say something, perhaps to defend Maggie, but she took on Alyssa herself. "You are the worst friend I've ever had, and I was a fool to ever trust you. You didn't deserve my husband and you don't deserve my friendship."

Maggie didn't think she'd ever cut someone off in her life. She got along with almost everyone. But not today.

"I was just trying to help," Alyssa might have said, but Maggie was already walking away down the garden path.

"Let me take you home," Drew said, suddenly at her side.

He reached out to take her elbow, but she shrugged away.

"You knew," she said quietly and, yes, accusingly. "And you didn't say anything. You weren't going to tell me."

"Of course I wasn't going to tell you! Who am I to ruin how you think of your husband?"

"Corey kept that secret to his death, and now you were going to too. After all your talk about honesty."

"You want honesty? Okay, Maggie, I'll give you honesty. I never planned on having anything much to do with you except a weekend fling. You were too complicated in every way. Everyone in town knew you were grieving your husband and you had a kid who only ate food that gets washed three times. You have OCD, and you're quirky as hell."

"I don't need to hear this now," she said, her voice cracking. His words stung more than she wanted him to know. She started to walk away, but he came after her. Held her firmly by the arm.

"Let me finish. Despite everything, I fell in love with you. Did I want to tell you about Corey? I sure as hell did. Because I want you to see what *we* could have. Who *I* am. Me, Maggie. Not just what you had with him. I'm not a doctor, and I don't even have that great a job, but I'm making it on my own. And I'm not who my father wants me to be, but you know what, that's okay. Because I'm who *I* want to be. I figured out who I am. Now you have to figure out who you are. Until you do that, you can't be with me or anyone else."

Tears welled up, blurring his image. These things he was saying, they hurt far more than what Alyssa had said. Because this wasn't about some old indiscretion that, while hurtful, was part of the distant past. She and Corey had lived a whole lifetime together since then, and she knew in her heart that he'd loved her. What Drew was saying was the raw truth—*her* truth, spot-on and slicing to the bone.

Drew was shaking his head, and apparently he wasn't done talking yet. "You're just playing the game, looking to settle for someone who you won't love too much, who's just okay and mostly tolerable. Someone who won't make you feel things. Well, I tried that once, and it didn't work out so well. Now I know I deserve better." His eyes were full of pain. "Good-bye, Maggie." The he walked away from her, down the stone path, getting smaller and smaller until he wound out of sight. And this time, she knew he wasn't coming back.

CHAPTER 20

Maggie opened her door late the next morning to Helen and her mother but no Griffin. One of them had offered to keep him overnight. She'd forgotten exactly which one, but she'd been very grateful for it. The sun was bright and stinging her swollen eyes and birds were chirping as if they didn't have a care in the world. And the mower next door was *so loud*, and her head was sledgehammer pounding, thanks to the bad-judgment quantity of vodka she'd consumed last night while crying at her kitchen table.

"He's with your father," her mother said without asking, pushing past her into the house. "We only have a few minutes before we have to go stuff goody bags for the homeless. But we wanted to make sure you were still alive."

"You still have your makeup on from last night, dear," Helen said, pointing to Maggie's face as she followed Maureen into the house. "And are those cookie crumbs around your mouth?"

Her hand flew up to brush them off. "I'm fine. You both can leave now. Really."

"Not so fast," her mother said from inside. "This is an intervention."

They were already in the kitchen, her mom putting on coffee and Helen wiping Oreo crumbs off her kitchen table. Her mom inspected the empty vodka bottle, lifting a brow.

"What?" she said a little defensively. "So my night was a little rough." She'd been up for most of it, finally falling asleep just before dawn.

"We saw Drew leave a little after your talk," her mom said.

"We broke up. It's over." There. She'd said it. As if they didn't already know.

"Poor Griffin," her mother said, shaking her head.

"Griffin will be fine, Mom," Maggie snapped. "He'll survive. I'm exhausted from trying to keep his life perfect. It got messy, okay? But you know what, we'll all be okay."

"Maybe it's better this way," Helen said. "Better for Griffin. Maybe one day you'll find someone you can love as much as Corey, but Drew just wasn't the one."

Maggie's stomach churned, probably in violent protest at the bad stuff she'd ingested. Suddenly, she wanted to cry. Again. "I said awful things to him," she said in a whisper. "The benefit made me remember all the agony of losing Corey, and I got…scared. I told Drew I just couldn't bear to love somebody like that again."

And she'd lost him. Made her feelings for him seem inferior to those for Corey. No wonder he was pissed.

"Corey was a special man," Helen said.

"Yes, he was," Maggie said. "But he wasn't perfect. No one is."

"No relationship is perfect," Maureen said. "But that doesn't mean it can't be good."

"You and Corey were blessed with a happy marriage," Helen said. "I always said I've never seen two people more in love."

"I was awful to Drew," Maggie said. "Unforgiveable, really. I never gave him a real chance."

"Aw, that's a shame that things didn't work out," Helen said, not sounding very sad at all. "By the way, I can take Griffin on Tuesday after preschool."

Maggie put her hand over her mother-in-law's, not sure what exactly had gotten into her. For once, her talk about Corey was irritating her. "Helen, you know whatever happens, I'll always love Corey."

"Of course you will. I don't doubt that."

"Okay, well, I just want you to know that."

"Oh, look at the time," Helen said, glancing at the kitchen clock. "We'd better go, Maureen." She patted Maggie on the shoulder. "We'll check on you later."

"Your father took Griffin fishing," Maureen said. "You've got a couple of hours to get it together," her mother said. "By the way," she said, lowering her voice. "That's the thing about real love. It's not perfect at all. But it forgives."

Maggie tried to get moving after her mother and Helen left, but she ended up feeling so queasy, she had to sit down on the couch for what she thought was a few minutes. She ended up falling into a deep sleep for most of the afternoon. She awakened when her father called at six thirty to tell her they were grilling out and was it all right if Griffin stayed for dinner?

God bless her wonderful parents.

Maggie ran upstairs to shower and pop a few Advils for her lingering headache. She still had time to surprise Griffin with a Redbox DVD for tonight. Then she would put on a smile and go through the motions for Griffin's sake, as she'd done many times in the past when she'd felt despairing.

Except Drew had made her want to do more than just go through the motions. He'd made her want it all.

A glance at her phone told her the time was creeping toward seven. The Spikonos brothers' wine bar opening celebration was from seven to nine. She felt terrible missing it. Drew had worked so hard for tonight, and he and his brothers would be serving fun appetizers and light fare like flatbreads and giving out samples of their apple brandy. She wanted to be there to celebrate with him. But how could she show up after everything that had happened? Would he even want her there?

Maggie forced herself to get moving. She didn't want Griffin to see her this way for sure. On the way to the bathroom, her wedding picture on her bedroom mantel caught her eye, as it had so many times when she was lost or confused. As if somehow it could give her answers.

She'd looked so beautiful that day—well, felt so beautiful—so loved and blessed. She and Corey were smiling broadly, one of her hands tightly grasping his, the other holding a tight round bouquet of roses and calla lilies, her lovely white dress billowing around them.

Suddenly, it was too much. Her old life wasn't telling her how to live her new one. In fact, it appeared to be mocking her. "Damn you, Corey," she whispered to his youthful, smiling image. Maggie propped her arm upon the mantel and dropped her head down. Her head knocked into the crook of her arm, causing her elbow to bump her shell box, which slid into her wedding picture. The picture and the shell box toppled, hitting the old wood floor hard. The picture frame cracked and the shell box opened, scattering dust across the floor.

Maggie stared at the mess, frozen in place. Not dust. *Corey.* His ashes. Oh God.

She bent down to sweep them up, try to get them back into the box, but the horror of the moment hit her, that she was picking part of *him* up off her floor, that she'd tried to save some of him for herself, and look what had happened, he'd ended up *there*, and she couldn't get all of him, she couldn't pick all the pieces up. As she was frantically sweeping the bits of dust with her fingers, she cut herself. It was no use, there were pieces of glass mixed in, and now she was bleeding. She ran into the bathroom, pulled off some toilet paper, and wound it around her finger, still shocked at what had happened.

Tears rolled silently down her face, but a dead quiet calm settled over her as she came to understand something for the first time. She had no business trying to hold on to Corey. Thinking he was anything other than who he was—a man. A fallible man who had his struggles like everyone else.

As she returned to her bedroom, she saw it. A tiny flash of yellow sticking out of the back of the broken frame. It was a piece of lined legal pad paper.

She reached down and tugged on it. It was wedged between the cardboard back of the frame and their wedding photograph, and it was folded in fours, a tiny neat rectangle.

She plucked it out with shaking hands. Unfolded the tight, pressed creases.

Her heart thumped wildly. Her throat dried up. She was shaking all over. As she smoothed it out, she saw it. Corey's fluid, masculine handwriting.

June, 2013.

The month they found out his cancer had returned for the last time. That he had months to live. The month that their hourglass had begun to run out. *Oh my God*. He'd left her a note. His familiar script told her it wasn't a receipt for the framing or some scrap paper lodged in to make the photo fit better in the frame.

Hi Maggie, My Dearest Love,

Her vision blurred. She managed to make it to her bed and sit down. Impatiently, she wiped her eyes and blinked to keep reading.

If you're reading this, I assume you're changing our wedding picture out of its frame. I know you like to do that every six months, so I figured this would be a good place to put a note I wanted you to read...after. I'll try to say it— after I'm gone.

Maggie wiped her nose on her sleeve. The idiot! She used to switch around their wedding pictures, but not since he'd died! She'd kept her favorite one in the frame all this time. Oh, what had he done? What had he wanted her to know?

All joking aside, I could never tell you this when I was alive, that's why I saved it. Forgive me, my sweet, for writing to you like this, but I never wanted to look into your beautiful blue eyes and tell you what I'm about to say, because it would break my heart.

You know we always joked about you moving on after I'm, you know— gone. I could never bring myself to tell you sure, go ahead, have a wonderful life without me. That I hope you fall in love again and find someone wonderful to be happy with and raise Griffin.

I could never bring myself to say that because I couldn't let you go, Maggie. I could never give you permission to live your life without me because I was too selfish to say that. You're mine, Maggie, my wife, and no one else could have you. Period.

Ah, but that's so small of me. And somewhere along this journey, I realized that maybe you'd hang on to that, even feel guilty about it, as you do with so many things. And the thought of you suffering because of me is something I think about a lot, believe me. Because I see it now, while I'm still here. And I don't want you to keep doing it after I'm gone.

So I will try to be a man about this and do what I could not do face-to-face.

So, my dearest love, if you're reading this, I am gone and you have many,

many years to go on without me. And my deepest wish is that they be happy, good years, filled with love and happiness. It wasn't in the stars for us, Maggie, who knows why. God knows I wish it was, but I love you with all my heart. I always have, and I always will. I loved every second of our life together and our beautiful son. It breaks my heart over and over to leave you and the life we were building together.

You've shown me in so many ways over this ordeal how strong you are, how faithful, how stubborn. But don't cling to what we had for too long. Don't let it ruin your chance to live life.

Now you must show me that you love and honor me too by leading the most raucous life you can. Squeeze every moment out of it, every tear, every smile, love our son double for me, and know that my heart is with you wherever you go and whatever you do. And the person who wins your heart next had better take damn good care of it, or I will haunt him to the grave.

All my love,
Corey.

Maggie felt sucker punched, like the wind had been knocked out of her. Her fingers were trembling. The paper was blurry, oh hell, everything was blurry, and she was doing a lousy job trying not to cry tears all over the paper.

If she'd had any doubt that Corey loved her, she knew now that regardless of what he'd done in a moment of confusion, he'd married *her*. He'd built a life with her. And it was a good life. A genuine one. She felt it now, down to her bones.

But that life was over now, and it was time to make a new one.

Oh, this life was so messy and imperfect. What was it her mother had just said? *That's the thing about real love. It's not perfect at all. But it forgives.*

She'd initially thought of that in terms of her forgiving Corey for what he'd done with Alyssa. But maybe her mother meant something else entirely.

Maybe it was about her considering the possibility that Drew might be able to forgive *her.*

Maggie had a plan. By the time she showered and used a paintbrush and a dustpan to sweep the—er—remains into a little lunch bag—very carefully, so she didn't end up in the ER with a sliced finger—Griffin had returned. She listened to tales of his day, got him bathed and ready for bed, and sat and read a couple of books with him, but her mind kept wandering. But at least she tried to be a good mother.

Finally, it was eight o'clock. She had just enough time to get over to the wine bar before the event ended. All she was waiting for was Helen, who was perpetually prompt and hadn't minded being called at the last minute.

Except tonight, she was fifteen minutes late.

At last, at eight fifteen, the doorbell rang.

As Maggie hurriedly opened the door, Helen stood there, wringing her hands, looking miserable.

"What's wrong?" Maggie asked, gesturing for her to come in.

"I have a confession," Helen said. "It's about Drew."

Oh God, no time for confessions now! But she said, "I understand if you don't care for him, Helen. Any man after Corey…"

"I have another reason."

"Come in and sit down." She wasn't going to make it to the wine bar. She couldn't leave Helen in crisis. What else could she do?

Maggie guided her to the couch. "I've been so lonely after Shawn left me," Helen said. "That on top of losing Corey… It's been hard. You and I have talked about this before, how you have to force yourself to do things you don't really want to do to try and build a new life."

Yes, they'd talked about that a lot, being that they both had a shared grief. "There is one thing I enjoy doing above all else, and that's being with my grandson. I love that boy. I love you too, Maggie, but Griffin is…well, he's my last connection to my son. You understand that, don't you? I don't know what I would do if I'd lose that."

"Believe me, Helen, I assure you, you'll never lose that," Maggie said. Helen was upset, but it had to be going on eight thirty by now. She was going to miss Drew's big event.

"You don't think of things like I do, because I'm older. So let me explain things to you."

Oh God. How could she reassure her that of course not, she would never be separated from Griffin, she was his grandmother, for God's sake, but she really had to get to the wine bar?

"Your mother and father will always be involved with Griffin because they're your parents, and you're Griffin's mother."

"And you're Corey's mother. I don't understand."

"When you remarry—and I say when, not if—Griffin will get new grandparents. I'll become…displaced."

Maggie reached forward and hugged Helen. "That will never happen! I love you. Griffin loves you! You're family!"

Helen was crying. "I've been afraid of this for a long time. It's why I discouraged you from getting involved with Drew. He's a nice man, Maggie. Although I never did care for his beard. I'm sorry, Maggie. Really sorry. I was being selfish."

"Helen, you're a second mother to me. I never would have survived Corey's death without you."

"I never meant to put doubt in your head."

"Trust me, Helen, I did plenty of that myself. Drew is a really, really nice man, and I was too blind to see that I love him. But I have to go now. His wine bar opening is almost over, and I need to talk to him."

"Well, why didn't you say so?"

Maggie kissed her on the cheek. "I love you, Helen."

"And I love you too, dear. Now go and get your fella."

Maggie knew time was short, but she drove past the McShae Cancer Center, which was actually a shortcut to downtown, so making a quick stop there wouldn't set her too far behind. She hadn't passed the building since Corey died. The parking lot was empty. She pulled around the circular drive, up to the front entrance, and, since it was after hours, parked right in front of the door. Then she got out of the car and walked a short distance over to a pretty garden area with a couple of benches. In the middle of the plantings was a large bronze plaque.

Maggie stood there a minute and admired the shiny silver lettering of Corey's name on the building, noting that she was seeing it for the very first time. Corey would likely feel uncomfortable about the fuss but probably would've admitted it looked very classy. A spotlight shone on the plaque, as it was dark now, and in the distance, she could see some lights reflecting off the lake. It was a beautiful spot for patients and their families to sit and enjoy the view.

The wording on the plaque was difficult to look at because it still hurt to see Corey's name, but this time, Maggie didn't shy away from the pain. She even touched the smooth, raised letters. Cried a few tears and didn't even try to hold them back.

Then she opened the bag. Blew a kiss into it. Let the wind carry the tiny bit of ashes (and very tiny bits of glass she just couldn't separate) toward the lake.

She closed her eyes, and just then, a little breeze kicked up. She felt a little brush on her cheek. It might've been her hair grazing her cheek. Or it might have been a kiss, a blessing. For a moment, she felt Corey's spirit around her, and a strange tranquility settled over her, so different from the desperate yearning, the sadness she'd been so familiar with. "Goodbye, my love," she whispered, and touched her fingers to her lips, blowing a kiss into the wind. Then she got into her car, started it, and kicked it into gear, and didn't look back.

CHAPTER 21

It had been a shitty week any way you looked at it. Drew glanced around the wine bar, which was packed with people, most of them locals but a lot of tourists too. The big-assed mahogany bar was finally anchored into place, the stained-glass Tiffany panels lit, and candles flickering softly atop tables. Which were all full, people spilling out onto the small adjacent street-side patio. Everyone was enjoying brandy samples and the simple but tasty flatbreads and appetizers on the menu—with a Greek twist, thanks to Mrs. Panagakos.

The sanded wood and fresh paint might've held the optimistic smell of new beginnings. But Drew's heart just wasn't in it. He was the number cruncher—he didn't know squat about wine or flatbreads or Greek olives, and he was in no mood to celebrate anything. But he was here to support his brothers no matter what it took. So he tried to leave his troubles behind. One blonde-headed bit of trouble, that is, whom he kept checking the door for every thirty seconds.

She wasn't coming.

Well, what else could he do? She'd dumped him. She'd never

said so, but her actions told him he'd never live up to what she'd had with Corey.

Fine. He'd go find himself someone who could appreciate him for himself.

Only trouble was, he wanted *her*.

And still, he hoped—that she'd figure out what they had didn't come around very often either. But he didn't want to be her second pick. He didn't want weak tea, he wanted good, strong coffee, the whole shebang. He wanted everything, all her love, all of her. He needed her to be all in. And he just wasn't sure she felt the same way about him.

He scowled and went back to waiting tables. That was Roman's idea, that he and his brothers served tonight so that everyone in the community would meet and chat with them. Hell, Lukas had wanted to sing all night, but Roman made him wait tables too because he needed the hands. So Lukas promised the crowd to sing later when the chaos was more controllable, but he had a feeling it wasn't going to let up.

If anything, more people were showing up. For tonight, he and his brothers were offering tons of specials and free glasses of brandy from seven to nine, and at eight forty-five, the place was still jam-packed, inside and out. Plus they'd been selling bottles of their brandy. People were buying them as souvenirs.

So he was very busy working. If he could just stop looking up at the damn door every five minutes.

Lukas came up to him. "There's a tabloid reporter here—Lainey Stevens, does that name ring a bell? She wants to interview you." He pointed to an attractive woman standing about ten feet away, microphone in hand, a cameraman at her side. "We've been holding her off, but Roman says you might as well do the interview. We need the publicity."

Drew groaned. "That woman's been after me for months. She just wants the dirt on my love life."

245

Just then Bella ran up to him, pointing behind her. "You've got company."

His heart jumped into his throat. But when he looked up, the solitary, imposing figure in the doorway wasn't Maggie.

It was his father, who caught his eye and smiled and waved. For a second, Drew was transported back to his youth, when he'd played baseball and would look for his father at his games, so proud of those rare occasions when he left work to show up and watch him play.

"Hello, son," Maxim said, suddenly standing in front of him.

"Dad," he said, trying not to sound emotional. Part of him wanted to roll his eyes at himself, for craving his father's approval, for daring to hope for it. Because he *did* want his father to see what they'd accomplished here, and even though Drew pretended it didn't matter, he wanted his father's blessing. But for all Drew knew, his father had showed up to critique and criticize and tell him to get a real job. Which he just might, since he was, at the moment, wearing a bright red apron that said *Spikonos Brothers and Co.* Nothing against his brothers, but he really wanted to take it off.

"Do you need a table? Is Valentina here? Xander?" Drew looked around, but the place was too packed to make out any family members. He was hoping maybe his brother had showed up too. Someday he'd like to have a heart-to-heart with him. Try to get their relationship back on track.

"Just me. I took a drive down. Do you have a minute?"

Not really, but hey, it was his father. "Let me get you a glass of brandy," Drew said.

He began to move toward the bar, but his father grabbed him by the arm. "Later. I came to tell you something."

His blood drained. Did something happen? Something bad?

"Everyone's fine, no worries. I want to say I'm sorry. I hope you will forgive me."

"You drove all the way down here to say that?"

Maxim shrugged. "Your pretty little girlfriend Maggie got to me."

He pretended not to notice he'd called Maggie a pretty little girlfriend, which she'd absolutely hate. Not to mention she wasn't even his girlfriend anymore.

He wasn't sure what made him feel more floored—the fact that his father was apologizing or the fact that he was here because of Maggie. His father had never said the words *I'm sorry* in his life.

"I had no business trying to marry you off to make a merger. But I didn't do it because I'm heartless. The Brewers are a good family. I'd hoped to make a better match for you than that idiot Sondra."

"Dad—"

"I'm not finished. I'm also sorry for being upset with you for not coming into the family business. But while I'm being honest, I will tell you that broke my heart. I love Xander, but he doesn't have your brilliant business mind. But I respect your decision to do what you want, all right? I'm proud of you. You're my son. And I've been trying to make it up to Xander too. At least he didn't end up with that woman, eh?" He laughed and put his hand on Drew's shoulder.

Maxim looked at Drew, and for the first time in a long time, Drew felt that he was getting his full attention. "Greeks are stubborn and hardheaded," his father said, squeezing Drew's shoulder. "I'm trying to put some of that aside. If I'd been less pushy and more humble and talked about my feelings more, maybe your mother would have been happier and I could have saved our marriage. So learn from me. Don't make the same mistakes."

"Maggie dumped me."

Maxim's brows raised, but otherwise, he didn't seem too affected. "So what are you going to do about it?"

"She loves her dead husband more than me."

"You're letting a dead guy beat you out for a woman's affection? I thought I taught you to compete better than that. A flesh-and-blood male vs. a dead guy. Come on, now." He laughed, loud and sonorous.

Drew wasn't nearly as amused as his father, but his dad's general outrageousness did make him laugh a little. "*Yamas*, Dad," he said, grabbing two brandies off the bar and handing one to his dad.

"*Yamas*, my son." Maxim drained his glass. "Oh, I nearly forgot. There's a problem out there you need to attend to." He pointed to the packed patio. "Hurry up and go."

Nothing looked amiss, but all Drew could see from where they stood was wall-to-wall people. With a sigh, he left his father and threaded his way through the noisy crowd.

Outside, the air was fresher. A full moon beamed down from a clear sky. And there, standing against a post under one of the draped strings of lights that ran along the patio, was Maggie.

She was a sight, in a black dress with big splashy red flowers and red heels. Looking like heaven. As soon as she saw him, she smiled.

Ah, he'd missed that smile. He was afraid he might never be on the receiving end of it again.

She ran and met him halfway, the crowd crushing around them. "Drew," she said. "Drew—"

"You came."

"Of course I came. I wouldn't have missed it for the world."

"Table four needs more Cabernet," Roman called from behind him.

"Send Lukas," he said over his shoulder, and caught the line of his brother's scowl. "I'm a little busy."

Maggie's mouth went dry. Her heart was chugging like a runaway

248

train over the din of the crowd, pure terror driving its rhythm. What if Drew had had enough of her? He himself had catalogued her quirks and listed the reasons why being with her was too much damn trouble.

Something deep within his eyes—an intensity in his gaze, even under the deepest of frowns—made her push on. Gave her hope that maybe it wasn't too late.

She met him halfway in the middle of the crowd and grabbed his hands. They were solid and warm, and she was a little shocked when he gripped hers back with equal strength. At that moment, she wanted to throw herself at him, kiss his fingers and toes, and beg him to take her back, but she could barely move with the Times Square-like crush, so she settled for just plain telling him the truth. "Drew, I'm so sorry—for everything. For pushing you away, for hiding behind Corey's memory...and most of all, for being afraid to love you. And I understand now that you could've told me what you knew about Corey, but you didn't, that you were trying to protect me even when you knew Corey wasn't perfect at all."

He blinked, but otherwise didn't move. Maggie's heart pitched and faltered. Finally, he spoke. "Well, Maggie, you *have* apologized before," he said in a gentle voice. Not critical but...cautious. Wary. And absolutely right.

He didn't believe her. He'd put up with too much of her uncertainty and floundering. She had to make him see this was *different*.

"I had to come tonight," she said, "even if you didn't want me here. I had to come and see you because I'm so proud of you, and I couldn't imagine myself not being with you to celebrate. Because we're so good together. Because it breaks my heart not being with you. I'm ready now, I'm ready to move on and experience all the good life has to offer. Because I love you, Drew. I love you with my whole heart. You made me see the good. Not being able to love you is worse than any bad things life might bring. Please, please give me another chance, and I'll prove it to you every day of my life, I swear. Please forgive me."

Okay, now she was bawling and her nose was running. Sexy and romantic, yes? Not the reunion she'd envisioned. Worse, everyone around them was staring, and that made the people farther away get quiet and stare too. An older lady actually dug into her purse and handed her a packet of Kleenex.

She somehow thanked the woman and blew her nose. Drew had placed both hands on her shoulders and stared at her. And he kept blinking, because his eyes were a little watery too. He seemed a little shaken up, and she wasn't sure if it was for the good or for the bad. So she kept going.

"I love you so much," she whispered, placing her hand over his heart. Staring into his beautiful brown eyes.

Then suddenly, in one swift movement, he closed his big body around her and crushed her against his big chest. She was surprised and shocked, and so relieved that she sank gratefully into him, a huge boneless blob being engulfed into all that muscle and his good spicy scent. Oh, she loved the feel of him, the muscular power, and the absolute tenderness of his caress.

"I love you too," he whispered. "I love your kindness, your sweetness, the way you love your son. There's no one you come in contact with that you hesitate to bring joy to. It just…rubs off."

He stroked her cheek, her hair. Then he lowered his mouth to hers and kissed her. His mouth was warm and soft and magical, and she felt his love in his kiss. And his forgiveness. Around them, the crowd began to whoop and clap and cheer.

"There's just one small problem," she said.

"What's that?"

"I'm not sure that dog of yours is ever going to like me."

"Maggie, I haven't met a person yet who doesn't like you. I'm sure Genevieve will come around. Hey, want some brandy?"

"Um—I've had a recent run-in with Oreos and vodka." She clutched her stomach. "I think I'll pass for tonight."

"Oh, in that case, I brought you something." He ran over to the maître d's lectern which was between the patio and entrance to the bar and reached behind it, pulling out a narrow brown bag that was molded around a bottle shape.

"You brought me wine?"

"Nope."

"Champagne?"

"Guess again."

He handed her the bag. She reached in and pulled out an eighteen-ounce bottle of Diet Coke.

"You knew I'd come?"

"I hoped you would." He kissed her on the forehead. "Besides, your mother told me you were hungover and miserable."

She rolled her eyes. Of course she did. She gave him a kiss of thanks and took a swig. Perfect.

As if on cue, her parents passed by, holding hands. "Congratulations, sweetheart," her dad said, kissing her on the cheek and hugging Drew.

"We're going to have a billionaire in the family," her mother said, clapping a little.

"Mom," Maggie said, "we're not getting married yet. We're just trying to figure out how to date."

"C'mon, Maureen, let's go dance," her dad said, which Maggie wondered if she'd heard right. "Let's leave the kids alone."

"Dad, don't you have to work?" Maggie asked as he led her mother away.

He shrugged. "I'm doing less of that now. And more with your mother. We decided that spending time together during retirement was the way to go. It just took getting to know each other again. And it's pretty…fun." Her mother beamed and gave a little wave as they passed through the crowd.

"Maybe it's never too late for a new beginning," Drew said.

"I want to tell you something," Maggie said. "Today I found a note from Corey. It was tucked into the back of our wedding picture. He gave me his blessing."

"His blessing?"

She nodded. "To move on. I—said goodbye." He scanned her face, and she hoped he'd see that she meant it.

"Well then," he said. "Here's to our new beginning." He clinked his brandy glass to her Diet Coke.

Then he kissed her, slow and easy, under the strings of lights and the moon and the soft lake breeze. And suddenly, she became aware that his brothers were standing there, and Mrs. P, and Bella and Sam, and her brother Scott and her parents, and Mr. Poulos. And Drew kissed her again, deeper and harder this time, a promise of many more kisses to come.

"Hey, this calls for a celebration," his father shouted. "Let's have some Greek music."

"Excuse me, Mr. Poulos." Lainey Stevens was pushing toward them through the crowd, her cameraman trailing behind. Maggie remembered her from the day Drew hid from her in the Congregational Church.

Lainey's cursory gaze flicked over Maggie, dismissing her as an unimportant local as she stuck the mic in Drew's face, clearly unaware of what had just happened between them. "Wow, I like you without the beard," Lainey said to Drew. "Is it true you've come out of hiding, and you're ready to let us in on some juicy secrets about your dating life? Like that you might get back together with Sondra Bower now that she's free?"

"I'm definitely not hiding anymore." He grinned at Maggie. "I found exactly where I want to be. But sorry, I have no secrets."

Maggie tapped the reporter on the shoulder. "I have a scoop for you, Ms. Stevens. He's officially off the market."

Lainey frowned. "How can that be? There are barely any women in this town."

"It only takes one," Drew said, beaming a big smile at Maggie. "And she's the whole package."

Maggie beamed right back. "By the way," she said to Drew, touching his cheek. "I like you without the beard too."

He pulled her close, the noise of the crowd fading into the background around them as she became aware of only him. "And here I was going to grow it back. I thought you liked that rugged mountaineer look."

"I love you any way," she said, enjoying the warm, solid feel of him as he held her. "As long as you're with me."

"Opa!" someone shouted, and sure enough, Lukas's band played.

Maggie melted into Drew's big strong arms, feeling like there was nowhere else in the world she'd rather be. And they danced under the lights, the cheers going up loud and happy and long.

EPILOGUE

It was after five on a Friday afternoon in mid-July. Maggie was in her office working on some of her clients' charts when her phone rang.

"I want to make love to you," the familiar voice on the other end said. It was deep and smooth, with a hint of mischief. And it made her blush, even though she was alone in her office.

"Is this one of those dirty calls?" she asked. "If it is, my boyfriend's not going to like this."

"This is your boyfriend. What are we doing tonight?"

"Well, my parents and Scott are coming over for dinner, and everyone's heading over to the park afterward to watch Griffin's T-ball game. Can we still do the"—she got up to be sure no one was in the hall and lowered her voice—"the making-love part?"

"Well, if you just want sex, I'd leave all that other stuff out of it. Family and T-ball games and all that complicated stuff." She could hear the smile in his voice. "On the other hand, all that sounds kind of perfect to me."

Just then, Griffin barreled into her office and tore around her desk to hug her.

"Griffin, what are you doing here?" Maggie asked, holding her phone against her shoulder. He was supposed to be at a playdate, and they'd planned for Drew to pick him up at five thirty.

"I got a question to ask you," her sweet son asked.

She kissed the top of his head, which was a little sweaty. "Okay," she said, amused as usual at his antics. "What is it?"

"Can I have a sleepover tonight?"

"With who?"

"Drew," he said, grinning widely.

"Drew?"

"Yeah. I want him to sleep over tonight. And every night. Can he?"

"Yes, can I?" a deep baritone asked.

Maggie looked up. A bunch of daisies was drifting midair in her doorway. She soon discovered they were attached to an arm. In another second, all six feet plus of Drew Poulos stepped into her office.

"Ask her, Drew, ask her!" Griffin said.

Drew tousled Griffin's head as he walked into Maggie's office and headed directly behind her desk. He set down the flowers, but something clinked as it hit her desk—a can of Diet Coke.

"That's so sweet. You two brought me flowers and a Coke. Griffin, did you pick those?" She felt a little nervous, because Drew was just standing there, watching her. Griffin too looked like the cat that swallowed the canary. What on earth was going on here?

Drew grinned as he took both of her hands into his big ones and dragged her a little forward, tugging her along in her rolling chair. Then he dropped to one knee. She stared at him, stunned. "Oh my God," she murmured, suddenly realizing what was going on.

Oh. My. God.

Miranda Liasson

He looked into her eyes and spoke. If his broad, beaming smile was the smile of an angel, the look in his eyes was positively devilish. "I never believed in the tingling in the arms and legs, the weakness in your knees, the hot, the cold, the sweating, and the feeling like that person *gets* you like no one else you've ever met. But now I do, because of you. You do all those things to me and more. I love you, Maggie. Will you marry me?"

"Do it, Mommy!" Griffin called.

Other heads suddenly appeared in her doorway. She blinked through her very blurry vision and made out the faces of her mom and dad, Scotty, Mrs. P, Lukas, Roman, Sam and Bella...their families. The people they loved.

"Hurry up, you two," called another voice. "There's a bunch of people waiting to party out here," Xander said, gathered with all the rest.

"Hey, bro," Drew called. "Thanks for coming."

"Thanks for inviting me," Xander said. "That's what brothers are for."

"And to bring the champagne," Lukas said, holding up a bottle.

"You mean the brandy," Roman said, also holding up a bottle.

"And the beer," Scott said. "But hurry up, please, I've got to get to work."

"I could come help you out," his father said, until he made an *oomph* sound, probably from Maggie's mother elbowing him in the ribs. "I mean—not tonight, though. It's movie night at the Palace."

"That's right. Not tonight, or any night," Maureen said. "You're going to learn to love retirement, now that I'm in charge of it."

He threw up his hands. "Okay, okay."

"I know I love it," Scott said, giving Maggie a wink. She gave her brother a special wave. It had been a hard year for him, with

Marcia, and his dad coming in and out of the business. She wished him the same happiness she felt so blessed to have.

"We have chocolate cake, everyone," said Mrs. P.

Drew cocked a brow, keeping his gaze on Maggie. "Hold on, everybody. She hasn't said yes yet."

"Oh! Yes! Of course I'll marry you," Maggie said. Then somehow they were both standing, and she was in his arms, the place where she belonged. She put her mouth near his ear and said softly, "You make my heart sing, and you make me feel fully alive again. I love you. With all my heart."

"I love you too, sweetheart." Drew pulled Griffin into their embrace. "And I love you too, kiddo."

And then Maggie kissed Drew. And it made her weak and wobbly, and sent those same tingles as always shooting all through her.

"Drew, you forgot something," Griffin whispered, tugging on Drew's jeans.

"Oh. I was going to drop it into the Diet Coke." Drew laughed and patted his jeans pockets. "Here you go." He held up a ring, something gorgeous and sparkly and just right. And slipped it on her finger.

"It fits," Maggie said, admiring it. "Perfectly."

"It should," Drew said. "I tied a string around your finger while you were sleeping."

"I always worried you were a little pervy," she said. "Even without the beard." Then she kissed him again.

And then there was chocolate cake and Diet Coke and the promise of many, many more happy occasions to come.

Thank you for reading Maggie and Drew's story! I hope it's made you laugh a little, and maybe cry a little too, and that you enjoyed their hijinks and their crazy path to love. If you did, please consider leaving a brief review online. Reviews are so important to authors and are very much appreciated. Thanks again for spending your valuable time with me and the folks from Mirror Lake!

If you'd like to know when my next book is coming, you can sign up for my book release news www.mirandaliasson.com/email-sign-up/.

I hang out daily at my Facebook Author Page and blog most Saturdays at www.mirandaliasson.com/blog/.

I love to hear from readers! You can contact me via my Facebook Author Page or the contact page on my website.

mirandaliasson.com

ACKNOWLEDGMENTS

Maggie and Drew began calling to me to tell their story from the moment in CAN'T STOP LOVING YOU when she poked fun at his recluse-in-the-woods beard and he snuck a piece of bacon to her organic-food-only son. I knew then that these two were destined to torture—and love each other—for all eternity.

They have amused and tortured me, in equal measure, and I did love spending this time with them. This book, however, was quite a journey in the making. It is my first endeavor into the world of self-publishing, and there were many things to learn. I'd like to thank my dear friends who rallied around me, taught me what I needed to know and answered all my questions—and most importantly, encouraged me to do it. My agent, Jill Marsal, my friends AE Jones and Sandy Owens, and the Sunshine Gals, Vicki, Mary, Chris Anna, Wendy, and Sheri, thank you all for your advice and for sharing your extensive knowledge.

Thanks to my editor, Charlotte Herscher, who edited all the Mirror Lake books, and who always amazes me with her vast knowledge of how to untangle the minds of imaginary people. Thank you as always to my dear husband, who is endlessly supportive, and my kids. Words can't express my love for you all.

Thanks to my readers, who asked for this book, and who send me kind notes and take some of your precious time to stop by and chat with me online. You come from all over the globe, yet we are connected in seconds by the power of technology. And somehow our paths have magically crossed in this wide world through our love of romance. You have enriched my life beyond words, and I'm so grateful. Bless you all.

ABOUT THE AUTHOR

As a girl, Miranda Liasson was a willing courier for the romance novels her mother traded with their next-door neighbor because it gave her a chance to sneak a peek at the contents. Today, Miranda writes award-winning romances herself, creating stories about courageous but imperfect characters who find love despite obstacles and their own personal flaws. In 2013, Miranda won the Romance Writers of America Golden Heart Award for Best Contemporary Series Romance. *Can't Fight This Feeling* is the second book in her Spikonos brothers romance series, and she is also the author of three Mirror Lake romances: *This Thing Called Love, This Love of Mine,* and *This Loving Feeling. This Loving Feeling* introduces Lukas Spikonos, the first Spikonos brother. Along with her husband, three children, and Posey, a rescue cat with attitude, Miranda makes her home in Northeast Ohio. Follow her on Facebook at www.facebook.com/MirandaLiassonAuthor and on Twitter @mirandaliasson.

48269854R00165

Made in the USA
Lexington, KY
15 August 2019